TRAUMA

DYLAN YOUNG

To Ingrid:

Happy Retirement.

Dylan

Print ISBN 978-1-913942-12-0

ALSO BY DYLAN YOUNG

The Appointment

The Operation

To E, who started to read it and then couldn't stop.

1

The bar is half full. Over to his left sits Ivan. He's in a booth with three girls. Ivan is not his actual name, but it'll do. He's Russian, Cameron knows that much. The repeated 'Nyet' when he's offered water is what gives him away. Already he and Cam have discussed a tunnel under the Bering Strait and West Ham's prospects of staying in the Premier League. Ivan's a lounge lizard. His hair is too long and dyed an improbable black. He's dressed in a white shirt over a bronzed belly with buttons open to his navel. Underneath he wears a big gold chain and his shorts are tie-dyed. All the girls are blondes in short dresses and heels. They drink champagne out of coupes and chair dance in time to the steady beat of music.

Cam's not sure what's playing. Could be 'Barbie Girl', could be 'Macarena'. Could be any one of several Europop clichés. Sneaky tunes that crawl into your head like a parasitic nematode.

The night is warm. Cam can't feel the heat directly, but he makes the judgement from the way everyone is dressed. They're up on a rooftop bar with garish lights strung from poles and cocktail waitresses in catsuits. Someone is smoking and a heady mix of tobacco and cannabis drifts over on a breeze with a seaweed hint of the ocean on its breath.

Not England. Not London. The warmth, the smells, the stagey music all give it a definite European flavour. But Cam never knows where this bar is. Not exactly.

The detail doesn't matter.

He clutches a cold beer in his fist. A bottle with a quartered lime in its neck. The dark leather of the booth he sits in squeaks like a squeezed mouse when he moves. Away on the far side of the bar, in a corner, someone else sits with their back towards him. Just a vague shape. Impossible to tell if it's a man or a woman because a deep, thick darkness cloaks all detail in that part of the bar.

Opposite, in the same booth as his, is a girl. Her face is candlelit. Cam doesn't know her name, but he calls her Emma because... well, because something tells him he ought to. She has inky hair, pink lips and a great smile. That's all he can make out. No matter how hard he tries, he can't seem to focus on her other features. But her mouth is wide and her teeth glimmer unnaturally. As does her blue-white dress and her tanned arms in the bar's black light. It's as if she's illuminated from within like some ethereal sea creature from the depths.

'Are you ready?' asks faceless Emma.

'No. I don't see why we should,' Cam replies.

'Because we must. It's already happened, silly.'

'What if we don't? What if we just sit here?'

Emma turns towards the vague shape sitting in the far corner. There's movement. A face turns towards them, feature-less, shifting, as if it can't decide what form to take. And as Cam stares, the shadow surrounding it thickens and deepens like boiling miasma, masking the figure's features except for a vague glint where there should be eyes. The overall impression

Cam gets is that if he did ever see the face, he'll end up wishing he had not. Its presence hints at a wrongness difficult to define. It reminds Cam of abominations from his dreams. Like monkeys with wings or spiders that can swim. It doesn't belong here.

Faceless Emma seems oblivious. She gets up and smiles at Cam over her shoulder as she moves through the tables. They've been there an hour. They've talked about the beach, toadstools, the value of the pound and a dozen other irrelevancies. Sometimes with Ivan included. Sometimes not. Now, there's nothing left to say.

'Wait,' says Cam, but she's gone. He follows her towards the edge of the rooftop bar. The wall there is low, barely knee-high.

The dark figure is watching them.

Emma turns to Cam. 'Ready?'

'No,' he replies, but he doesn't object when she takes his hand.

Over her shoulder, a hundred feet below, light from the moon reflects off a thousand tiny waves. Ships bob further out towards the harbour mouth. Cam's eyes drift back to Emma's smile. Then he senses someone behind him. The shifting figure is approaching. Still the details blur because its shadow comes with it, defying the laws of optics, preceding it, billowing around it like smoke in a jar.

Emma lets go of Cam's hand and touches his face before she steps onto the wall and, still smiling, falls into the void. There's no scream as Emma hits the water. Cam turns towards the dark figure, the shadow man who moves with an odd stuttering stealth towards him. Yet Cam feels no fear. Only sorrow and inevitability as he, too, steps up on the parapet.

A dark shadow-hand reaches for him but it does not connect. It can't because Cam is no longer there. There is no hesitation as he steps off and follows Emma into empty night.

But he doesn't make it to the water. Instead, there's a crack and blackness as his head hits hard metal and stone.

There is no pain.

Not then.

But it will come.

2

I've been living alone for almost four months. Finding my way back into a world of unbelievable complexity. Buses, the Tube, mobile phones, Netflix, contactless payments, Deliveroo. If I wanted to, I could cocoon myself. Not leave the flat. Order everything in. Tesco home deliveries for the essentials, Hello-Fresh or LetusPrep for every single meal. There's online banking for sorting out finances. Hell, even dentists do virtual consults now.

But I don't. Of course I don't. I need to get out. Reacclimatise me to the world. Essential for my rehabilitation.

Lunchtimes I have a sandwich, usually tuna, sometimes marmite and cheese toasted in an English muffin. I've even tried a ciabatta, but it was far too much. Before I eat, I get my drugs ready. I rummage in the cereal cupboard for my pillbox. Mornings and teatime I take modafinil. Lunchtime and before I go to bed, quetiapine. Sometimes I mix them up. Easy to do even though they're for different things.

Stop and go. Or rather go and slow down.

Modafinil is the 'go', developed to treat narcolepsy. It helps me from falling asleep during daylight hours. In my case it's prescribed to counteract the sedative effect of the other stuff I pop. Quetiapine, the 'slow down'. That one's actually a catch-all because some patients with my degree of damage can become manic. Both prescribed because they're 'essential in helping with mood swings and the way you react to your brave new world', according to Dr Adam Spalding.

He should know. He's the boss. The doctor. Well, my doctor. One of them.

The doses are low, I know that much. I fill a glass with hard London tap water and sluice the pill down. Two swallows. That do not make a hummer.

Summer, you fool.

Today's a tuna with mayonnaise and tomato day. Then I make a cup of tea and eat a biscuit. My sister, Rachel, says to make sure only one biscuit, singular, because I am now not far off what she calls my fighting weight and I do not want to become a 'lard-ass'. I had to look that up. I don't think I will become a lard-ass, but she knows about that sort of thing so I listen.

When I finish my sandwich, I return to the living room, to my reminder wall which includes a calendar. Today is a Monday and at 2pm I'm meeting Leon. I throw my kit into a bag, grab car keys, exit the flat and head to the green VW Golf that I inherited from Emma. I start it up and drive out, once around Spa Gardens and then back to the same spot. It takes about four minutes.

I park up, pocket the keys and head off to meet Leon, happy that I have not forgotten how to drive since yesterday.

Leon's gym is on the other side of Bermondsey but still within walking distance. A repurposed canning factory of red brick and pitch-treated wood outside, glass and chrome inside. I do this twice a week. I started working with Leon as soon as I moved back to the flat. The rehab consultant told me it was way too early to start strenuous physical activity. I reasoned that if I was going to get out into the world I should try to be as fit as I possibly could be. So I ignored him.

The first couple of personal fitness 'experts' I approached weren't interested when I emailed them and detailed my medical history. About my limp and the various fractures now all healed up with the help of titanium screws. They replied that they specialised in body forming and that I might be better off seeing a physiotherapist.

Body forming then. Not body fixing. Thanks a million.

But I persisted. I didn't email Leon. I went to see him. Face to face. He says that the first time he saw me I was hanging on to a door frame for support and he almost called an ambulance because he thought I was on the point of collapse. When I told him the healed tracheostomy in my throat had left me with a bit of a cheeze (meaning wheeze), he smiled, bought me a juice and sat and listened to everything that I had to say.

Then he asked me what I wanted.

The answer was to be as fit as I could be and not to become a lard-ass. He laughed hard when I said that. He asked if the physiotherapist at the clinic would object and I explained they probably would but that they were only interested in strengthening certain muscles and had no anti-lard-ass programme. That made Leon laugh even more, though I hadn't meant it as a joke.

There were quite a few fitness posters on the wall of the office we chatted in. Lithe black men and women modelling clothes or equipment. One of them looked a lot like Leon. When I asked him if he thought he could work with me although I was a frail white man that would not turn out anything like the athletes in the posters, he almost fell off his chair.

There are technical terms for the way I say things. One is disinhibition. Another is dysphasia. Happens when your brain gets thrown about like a tennis ball in a tumble dryer.

From that first meeting we never looked back. Leon calls our work together 'Cam's workout à la Leon Samuels'. The 'à la' stands for anti-lard-arse. But only we know that.

The gym is on the top floor of a converted office block. All the running machines line up like upright sardine cans with a view out to the street below so those inside can see what they're not missing. I get changed and join Leon in the fitness room. He's younger than me and trim in a black vest and tight training pants that define his leg muscles even though they're not on show. He used to greet me with a hug. Now, thanks to the virus, there is no physical contact. All that is definitely infra dig, man. That's Leon's term. I had to look that up, too. The online dictionary said it was 'below what you consider being socially acceptable'.

Sodding virus.

'Cam, man, good to see you. You're looking sharp.' Leon is full of vim.

'And you.'

'How's your leg?'

I shake my leaden left leg. The one that feels like it has a sack of water around it. It used to feel like a sack of concrete, so water is a considerable improvement. 'Good,' I reassure him. 'I think it was only cramp.' I limped away from our last session after giving up on some squats.

'Cool. Okay. Warm up.'

Fifty minutes, sixty press-ups, chin-ups, squats and leg presses later, I'm soaking wet and huffing like a broken accordion. The gym clock says 2.55pm but Leon takes me through to a chill-out zone and fills an aluminium bottle with water from a cooler before sitting down at a table with me. Once a week he insists on a debrief. Today is debrief day. In all honesty there's nothing much to talk about given that he is the taskmaster and I do as I am told. Leon's a genuine guy so he's keen to ask me if anything we've done is too much.

I want to say everything, but that was only funny the first ten times or so, Leon tells me. I suspect that there's another reason for these chats. Leon trains all sorts of people in this gym. There are two women actors – I always say actresses, but Rachel told me it isn't woke to say that – and at least one retired footballer in his stable.

I, I suspect, am his lame horse. But one he refuses to give up on. Cameron Seabiscuit, that's me. And I have a sneaking suspicion he enjoys chatting with me because, as he once said, 'You keep it real, Cam, man. You keep it so real.'

I answer his questions truthfully. I didn't enjoy the leg presses on the machine with eighty kilos. I did enjoy the boxing session he did with me last Monday.

He writes it down on a clipboard. 'That's cool. We can do more boxercise. Good for balance and strength. But no head-shots, right?'

I put my fists up and go into a stance in my seat.

Leon grins. It's like a sunrise. 'Woah, there he is. Remember when we first started this? You couldn't lift a ten-kilo kettlebell or even walk in a straight line.'

Leon's right. We started out by doing basic exercises. Co-ordination and function mainly. Balance balls, kettlebell swings. Movement and strength. At first, I wasn't even breathing in the right places so I sounded like I might explode at any moment. Not anymore. Leon's à la training works wonders, but I've still got a way to go.

I've set myself a goal. I can now use the treadmill for twenty minutes at a good pace. And not solely to prove to myself I can do it. I have other irons in the fire.

'I suppose I'm lucky to be alive,' I say. Sometimes clichés do the job perfectly.

Leon lifts his aluminium bottle and tips it towards me. 'True that,' he says. He takes a sip before asking, 'You taking your meds, Cam my man?'

I give him an exaggerated nod.

'How's the driving coming along?'

'Good,' I reply. 'Weird thing is that I could drive as soon as I got into the car. Funny that.'

'Yeah, but driving's like riding a bike. You never forget–'

'I did,' I remind him, grinning. 'I had to take another test, remember?'

'Oh, yeah,' Leon says with mock horror. 'Sorry, man.'

'Plus I've got pictures of me in the park learning to ride a bike again because my balance was shot.' I scroll to the photo app on my phone and find one of me seven months ago wearing a bike helmet with someone holding on to the seat as I try to centre myself. The image wobbles with movement. A 'live' iPhone photo capturing three seconds of action. I wince on seeing it. The helmet is awry. It makes me look like a toddler in grown-up clothes. I remember the panic as I turned out of control and hit a stone. Remember the smell of grass as I slapped face first into the ground. Still hear kids laughing at my ineptitude as they zoomed up and down past me.

But it makes Leon laugh again. 'You're doing so good, man.'

'Am I though? Remembering some things and then knowing nothing at all about others doesn't seem so good. I had an itch in my elbow this morning and I couldn't remember what it was called.'

'Your elbow?'

'Yup. All I could think of was top half knee.'

Leon looks at me. I can see he's fighting laughter. It bursts out of him in a roar.

'Top half knee. That's genius.'

'I'm glad you think it's funny.'

'So do you,' Leon goads me.

I shrug. 'Pretty funny, yeah.'

'It'll come, Cam. You know it will. You don't need to be so hard on yourself, man.'

'It's taking a long time.'

'No rules in this game. Your mind needs to heal, like your body has to heal, right? Nothing is your fault, man. Accept that. You got to learn to be good to yourself.'

'Yeah,' I reply. He's right. The person I have the least patience in the world with is me. But knowing and doing are two different things. 'I'll heal a lot faster if bastards like you would stop trying to kill me, I know that.' The swear word slips out before I can stop it. No maliciousness intended. Merely a verbal tic.

Leon shakes his head. 'Harsh, man. So harsh. But on Friday you will do thirty sit-ups as a warm up.'

'You can go off people,' I say.

'I wish,' replies Leon. The sun rises all over again.

3

I hurry back to the flat along damp streets under a pewter canopy of sodden clouds. The wet winter seems never-ending. Though one of the mildest on record the weather has been dull and miserable for months. Ever since I moved into the flat, in fact. Easy to not want to go out. Easier to hibernate instead. Like a forgetful squirrel, or an amnesiac bear.

I swing by the car to check that it's still there, and that I remembered to lock it.

Owning a car in London these days is expensive. Luckily, the flat comes with a parking space. Not every flat does. Car-free zones are now the best theft deterrent there is.

The indicator light flashes on the answerphone lurking on a counter in the kitchen. I've lost several mobile phones so Rachel insists I keep the landline because it means people can at least leave messages. I'm all for that. Besides, the landline is tied in with my broadband deal; superfast with 55Mbps download speed and 25 upload with unlimited usage. Josh, a friend of mine who knows a lot about these things, says it's a boss deal for the money. Josh is someone I depend upon for deciding things like that. He calls himself my consumer guide. Plus he uses words like 'boss' so who in their right mind would doubt his credentials.

I press the play button on the answerphone and listen.

The first call is from Rachel.

'Hi, Cam, cariad.' That's Rachel's standard greeting. It carries no affectation; she uses the word 'cariad' as naturally as she breathes air. A term of affection from her native tongue, courtesy of our West Walian mum. Weirdly, the first words I muttered after the *incident* were also in Welsh, which both Rachel and I spoke fluently by the time we were four.

My utterings, a request for *dwr* – water in English – threw the doctors looking after me completely. Not much Cymraeg spoken in Antalya where I started off after the *incident* as a ventilated almost-basket-case, nor UCH in London where they nurtured the almost-basket into someone who was at least able to breathe on his own. But Rachel soon educated them vocabulary-wise, though the language thing didn't last. As I improved so did my communication skills. Since my education up to university entry was bilingual in the Cardiff school I attended, before you could say Glasgow Coma Scale, I was asking for water in English.

'Just checking in,' Rachel's voice sings out from the box. 'I'll call you tonight at six as usual but if you need to talk, use your mobile. Remember, it's free. Cadwa'n saff.'

I snort. Rachel now added the 'cadwa'n saff' at the end of all her calls. Stay safe. A reference to the virus. Almost a prayer. When her message ends the machine tells me there's another, received half an hour ago.

'Mr Todd, this is John Stamford. I've left you a couple of messages. I very much want to talk to you about some financial issues relating to the passing of your partner, Emma Roxburgh. You can reach me on 07700900735. Thanks.'

He's polite and business-like. I don't ring back. I suspect he'll ring again. When I told Rachel about him she said to leave everything to her. So I do.

I check the time. Half past four, and that means teatime. When I was in hospital, they always made tea at half four. A ritual I cling to like a rock in a tempestuous sea. I put the kettle on, wait for it to boil and pour it over a bag of English breakfast. Then I sit on the sofa in the living room to drink it while I eat a biscuit. Just the one. Don't want to become a lard-ass.

Another wall – not my reminder wall – is dominated by a large, flat-screen TV. And it is big. Eighty-five inches from one thin corner to the other. It hangs there, tempting me. I could lose myself for an hour watching houses being refurbished or open my laptop and click on shiny things on the screen. Something educational like kittens chasing torch beams, but Adam says best if I concentrate on doing one thing at a time. Right now that means tea and a biscuit (McVitie's Digestive today). So that's what I do. But I'm tired from my session with Leon, so I shut my eyes. I won't sleep, but at least I can relax.

The DJ is playing 'The Ketchup Song'. Over to Cam's left, two of Ivan's girlfriends are doing the moves. Ivan bobs his head in time, his gold medallion jangling.

'Want to dance?' Emma asks.

Cam turns back and sees the smile, the suggestion of dark eyes, but the rest is a blur, pixilated out by neurological fallout.

'The Ketchup Song' ends and the music shifts to something techno with a droning beat. The waitress comes and takes away Cam's half-full bottle and replaces it with a fresh one. When the waitress leaves, the girl he calls Emma leans over to talk to Ivan about the cost of flights. Cam joins in. Ivan thinks one day planes will be solar-powered. Cam quips that they'll never land in London because there'd never be enough sunlight for take-off.

'Then we would need to bring our own sun,' says Ivan. It makes no sense, but Ivan seems pleased. Cam sits with him and listens to the music while Emma dances with two of Ivan's girlfriends. The men don't speak. They just watch and listen as the DJ does his set and the lights go down in the bar.

Over in the corner, the shadow man watches in a pool of liquid night. Cam gets up and walks across to where he sits. But as he approaches, the light shifts, the shadows retreat and by the time he reaches the table, the seat is empty. Cam looks back towards Ivan. Now, in the seat he'd moments before vacated, sits a figure enveloped in deep shadow.

When I open my eyes, I'm stunned to find I'm not in the bar but in my flat. In the kitchen with my gym bag open. I've stacked two cans of Heinz tomato soup next to a packet of tagliatelle in the bag for some inexplicable reason. The clock says a quarter to five. Fifteen minutes only of dozing, yet I can recall a whole evening in the bar with faceless Emma and medallion Ivan.

My mental trips to the bar are termed fugues. I can't explain them. There is no logic. They're one of those Cameron quirks inherited courtesy of a metal stanchion on a stone jetty on Cirali beach. That's near Antalya in Turkey. Where I fell.

I'm aware post-fugue that Emma is dead, perhaps Ivan is too. Perhaps everyone in the bar is a ghost. But they're always glad to see me, keen for me to talk. They're wilful. Determined to engage me, reluctant to let me go. I never feel threatened, though I am often left frustrated because the purpose of my visit is never explained. But as I say, there is no logic. How can there be when they only exist in my head?

Back in the living room, my tea is lukewarm. I flash it in the microwave and watch the mug rotate for thirty seconds. When I take it out the mug is hotter than the tea. I drink tepid Typhoo and pick up a notebook so I can write down what happened in the fugue. I have pages of it in shaky handwriting. As yet, not much of it makes any sense at all. But then, none of my life has made much sense for seventeen months.

Rachel says I was in a coma for ten days and pretty much semi-conscious for six weeks after it happened.

It.

I can't remember *it*. I can't even remember what Emma looks like so that's hardly surprising. But the facts are this:

Emma, my partner, died on a beach in Turkey and I almost died too. Those are the pared-down and brutal facts. But all I can remember is a white hotel in Cirali I recognised when I saw a photograph of it. Oddly, I even remembered the number of the room. But that's all. A report of what happened is posted on my wall. Typed up by Rachel to remind me.

I can recite the summary of facts and witness reports verbatim. Still, I read it every day in case something triggers a memory. Sometimes I think I'm doomed to repeat this same act like a character in a film. Josh calls it a 'looping trope', but then Josh would. He suggested I watch *Groundhog Day*. I did, twice, but I'm still not sure about using all that spare time to learn the piano. Electric guitar, maybe. Or drums. But not the piano.

Instead, in my version of the looping trope, I stand here in front of this corkboard and read about a life, my life, that I have no recollection of. And I keep doing that until I'm stooped and grey. In my *Groundhog Day*, when I finally break out of the loop, the last scene is a pillar of dust around a pair of empty slippers belonging to the man who forgot.

Adam says that I should switch out of these thoughts whenever I get them. But it isn't always that easy.

I go to the sink and fill up my water bottle, let it overflow. The water froths over my hands. Cool, tingling. Underneath the blur of bubbles I'm glad to see that today they're steady. They aren't always. Then I slope back into the living room, to the wall where I look first at Emma's photograph and then at the typed report beneath.

4

POLIS Emniyet Genel Müdürlüğü 26/II/2018

SUMMARY FINDINGS INTO THE DEATH OF EMMA
ROXBURGH – FEMALE.

At 8.30pm on 12th October 2018 the body of Emma Roxburgh, 32,
was found in the sea at the Northern end of Cirali beach on the
south coast of Turkey. Cause of death was noted to be severe
trauma of the head and upper torso. The most likely cause was a
fall from the cliff path onto rocks below. Miss Roxburgh's partner,
Cameron Alun Todd, was also found severely injured in the water
nearby. His injuries were also consistent with a fall. Mr Todd was
taken to hospital in Antalya and remained in a coma for ten days.

Toxicology reports indicated a minimum amount of alcohol
and no opiates nor stimulants in either of the victims' blood.
Mr Todd's Glasgow Coma score at the scene was 8, indicating a
severe brain injury. An MRI showed skull and facial fractures
as well as contusion to both frontal and left temporal lobes.

Because of the severity of the trauma, Mr Todd could not

provide any details of the circumstances leading up to the incident involving him and his partner. Eyewitness reports gathered by local police suggest that both Mr Todd and Dr Roxburgh had been in a beachside bar near the hotel they had been staying in an hour before the scream was heard.

Bar staff reported no altercation between the two but that Dr Roxburgh left the bar before Mr Todd. A short time later Mr Todd also left the bar. Hotel staff report him asking after Dr Roxburgh who was not in their room. Mr Todd then ran out of the hotel.

Some boat owners moored just off the beach heard shouting and alerted authorities. Mr Todd was found in the water near a concrete jetty. Dr Roxburgh's body was recovered some hours later under the cliff face where the tide had washed it in. Local police are continuing their investigation. Current theories are:

1/ That one or the other got into difficulties on the path and fell off the cliff.

2/ That Dr Roxburgh fell and Mr Todd injured himself on the jetty in trying to help her.

3/ That they might have been attacked by person or persons unknown.

Metropolitan police officers are currently liaising with Turkish authorities in the investigation. Liaison officer Detective Sergeant Rhian Keely, Metropolitan Police, Central South Basic Command Unit, Southwark Station, Borough Hill Road, London.

I know DS Keely. Small, dark, intense... I like that description of her because it makes her sound like an espresso. Which isn't far off the mark in the way an espresso will give you a kick. Not in a bad way. Not always.

We've spoken many times since I was well enough for visitors at the hospital and rehab unit. She is one of the people Rachel says it is okay for me to talk to without her – Rachel – being present. But there's one part missing from the report. A different theory. One that I like the least of all. That is that Emma and I had a fight and that I threw her off the clifftop and then somehow fell myself. DS Keely has never accused me of this.

But other people have.

~

At six o'clock, Rachel rings.

'Hey, Cam, it's Rachel.'

'Hi, Rache,' I say. Rachel always introduces herself like this in case I forget what she sounds like. But it doesn't work like that, my axonal fallout. Of course I recognise her voice. I only saw her a week ago. It's the past that is a black hole. BT – Before Turkey.

'So, when are you seeing Adam next?'

'He's got some trainees this week. I'm seeing him Wednesday. I am his official number one patient.'

'You don't need to go. Not as a guinea pig.'

'Okay. But when a consultant psychiatrist begs you to turn up and be a star turn, what are you supposed to say? He keeps telling me that hallucinogenic fugues are rare as hell's teeth.'

'It's hen's teeth.'

'That's what I said.' I know it isn't. But this is my sister I'm talking to. Dangerous to show any signs of weakness.

There's a pause while she considers jousting, but she lets this one go and starts telling me about a friend of a friend who also had an accident but who now owns a series of restaurants. A classic Rachel pep talk. I walk to the reminder wall in the living room, phone in hand, and study her photograph. She's two years older than me. A sculpted, wedge-shaped face with chocolate hair and slender brows arching over light-brown eyes. I go to one of the big albums on the table and open it. Rachel has pasted in snaps from our childhood. A montage of a life I have no recollection of living. Beaches, woods, back gardens, swings, parties. I'm in them all, Rachel in half of them. I can remember only one of them clearly. A beach holiday on the Pembrokeshire coast. We caught crabs and Rachel threw one at me. It landed in my hair. Perhaps that's why I remember it. The giggly-screaming trauma of a crab fight.

Rachel ends the apocryphal story and asks, 'How you feeling?'

'Good. I saw Leon today and tomorrow I'm driving out to Emma's old practice.'

'Of course...' Hesitation. 'I still think it might be a good idea if I come with you.'

'But you can't because you're stuck at home with the kids.'

Rachel sighs. 'You remembered that.'

I reel off the litany. 'Ewan's got the lurgy and who knows if it's the virus. So you're being the responsible parent and self-isolating. Owen stays in a different part of the house so he can go to work. And the kids are driving you insane.'

Owen, Rachel's partner, is also a lawyer.

'No need to rub it in. I think they're going to shut all schools.'

'You do?'

'Yes. Look at what's happening in the rest of Europe. At least I won't be the only one tearing my hair out.'

'That bad?'

'Of course not. The kids are great. I can work from home –

sort of. And the talk is that schools will set online work for the kids. That'll help.' She sounds unconvinced.

'How is Ewan?'

'Fine. Probably just a cold, but who knows. It could only be hay fever, but it's a bit early for that so we're being safe and watching him.'

I visualise the kids. They treat me like I'm the best surprise ever when I visit. Like a pair of friendly hyperactive dogs that want to jump all over me. They're amazing and funny and I love them. 'Say hello from me.'

'I will. And remember, even though I am tied here I carry my phone with me at all times.'

Officially, Rachel has two children. But I am obviously her third. She would never say so out loud. She doesn't need to. We both know it.

'I've got your number and Owen's,' I say with a sprinkling of reassurance.

'Are you being careful, Cam? Washing your hands. Got plenty of sanitiser?'

'Yes, Mum. I bought six toilet rolls and so will not be buying in bulk.'

'No joke, is it.' Rachel pauses. I can visualise the worry etched on her face even though this is not a FaceTime call. Mortgage, husband, kids, job, virus. All that's missing is a plague of locusts. I can see her expression perfectly in my mind's eye because this is not our first parley on this subject. 'How was your day otherwise?'

I tell her about the call from Stamford.

'God, that man is persistent.'

'Should I ring him back?'

'No, you should not. You have nothing to say to him and he knows not to pester you.'

'But what if he–'

'Cam. No. Not without me there. If he has anything new to tell you he should do everything through me. End of.'

'Okay.'

'If he harasses you while I'm stuck here, ring DS Keely,' she adds.

'Will do.'

The rest of the conversation is about my pills and what I had for lunch and about Rosie's recovering ear infection. Rachel says that she'll text me every day or FaceTime me. We both know I'm not very good at remembering to do any of that stuff. Sometimes I think she thinks I use my post-injury forgetfulness as an excuse.

Sometimes she isn't wrong.

5

When she rings off I stay in front of my reminder wall. I study the photograph of John Stamford. By this stage of my recovery everyone on the wall is known to me and I will not forget who they are. But Rachel added little bios, especially of the black hats. There aren't many, but Stamford is one... according to Rachel.

Underneath a jowly headshot of a man in his fifties with a crown of dark hair around a smooth, hairless pate is Rachel's stark reminder written in her neat handwriting. She likes using capitals for effect. In my head I hear her emphasising the words.

John Stamford is a PRIVATE INVESTIGATOR employed by Emma's family to dig into her death. He is an EX-POLICE DETECTIVE. If he contacts you, speak to me before speaking to him. Do NOT be intimidated by him.

I've met him twice.

The first time was in a coffee shop. He edged over to speak to me and gave me his card with a big meaty hand. He said he was glad to see that I was out of hospital and that he would appreciate it if I rang him at some point. I was with Josh, who suggested I should not ring any number on the card until I spoke to Rachel.

The second time was when he came to the flat and I let him in. That time, Rachel came back from a Sainsbury's shopping trip and found him asking me questions in the living room. She went very quiet and though her expression stayed neutral, the glare she gave him should have cut him in half. She made him leave and told him never to come back. I don't think I'd ever seen Rachel so angry. But Stamford did not seem too bothered. Teflon-coated, like he'd seen it all before. But then he is an ex-policeman.

In both instances I did not find him intimidating.

But that was three months ago. A lot has happened since then. The truth is that I'm as keen to talk to John Stamford as he clearly is to talk to me. But I won't tell Rachel that. She says that I need to get a lot better before we 'cross that rickety bridge'.

I think I'm a lot better already even if the occasional board still creaks on that bridge.

I heat up a plate of lasagne that Rachel made. She fills the freezer whenever she visits. I don't ask her to, neither do I object, because she's a great cook and always bats away my feeble resistance of the 'you don't need to do this, Rache' type, with her own set of justifications.

'They're leftovers,' she says. 'If I leave them in the fridge all that'll happen is Owen will eat them. And he definitely does not need extras.'

Total fabrication because the lasagne arrives neatly packaged in foil trays and Owen does 100k bike rides with a group of fellow spandex-wearers three times a week on a two-thousand-quid Cannondale.

I rest my case. But as I say, she is my sister.

I throw down my medication and sit down in front of the TV

with a bottle of water. Aluminium, double-lined with images of dogs all over it. A Christmas present from Rachel's kids. Keeps the contents cold for hours.

I have a load of stuff to binge-watch. Josh says I'm a lucky bastard. No memory means a vast back catalogue of films that I may well have seen before but that I cannot recollect. Josh knows what I was into and curated both a Netflix list and an Amazon list and added some from a few of the more esoteric channels. Mostly thrillers, action movies and a 'shitload of ace sci-fi', to use his own words.

Currently, I'm watching *The Night Of*. Josh said that I would like it. He did not elaborate but hinted at the fact that I would work out why for myself. I'm already into episode four and I think I'm on board with Josh's thinking. Not a difficult equation. Riz Ahmed playing Naz wakes up next to a woman to find that she is dead but remembers nothing of what happened. It's a stylish, intense, riveting watch and the parallels with my situation are obvious.

Naz's lawyer and the detective investigating the case soon find out this simple crime isn't as straightforward as it first seems.

Josh tells me that the series won all sorts of awards. I can see why.

Maybe that's why I want to talk to John Stamford, the PI who keeps gently pestering me. He must know things that I don't. He doesn't look like John Turturro who plays Naz's eccentric lawyer. Not in the slightest. But Stamford, in our brief encounters, like Turturro's character, struck me as someone very determined.

That's what I need if I am ever going to find out what happened to me and Emma on that beach in Turkey. I need a gnarled old detective to fight my corner.

Rachel doesn't want me to. Of course she doesn't. She's convinced that he'll be fighting very much in the other corner and I'd never last a round. My argument is that we should at least start the bout.

But I haven't been brave enough to defy her. Not yet. Rachel's been amazing throughout. In fact, I'd be lost without her. But her approach is to put up the barricades. I should say nothing, talk to no one, except Adam who is my doctor and Josh who's a mate. But if I don't ask questions how am I ever going to find any answers?

On-screen, John Turturro is feeding the victim's cat.

I smile. The writers knew what they were doing by giving him a soft spot for animals. Redeeming features. Give the audience a reason, and a way, of liking the outsider. One who on first glance appears highly unlikeable.

I wonder about that. Wonder what my redeeming features might be.

But my life is not a story. It's real. And reality is a lot messier than an eight-part series on a subscription channel with a beginning, middle and end. I'm tempted to ring Stamford there and then, but Rachel's voice is still ringing in my ears. And just about now my evening quetiapine is kicking in. Now I don't think I can concentrate well enough. So I park the idea.

But I'm aware in my heart that despite Rachel I can't hibernate for much longer.

6

My alarm buzzes me awake at 7.30 and I get up. This is a ponderous process. The physios at the rehab unit told me to stretch everything before I start my day. This I do with patience and perseverance. I'd fractured a humerus and chipped a bone in my pelvis as well as breaking my head in the fall. In bed immobile for almost two months as a consequence. I mobilised in stages for another two after that. It had a profound effect on my muscles and joints.

So I do a bridge, downward dog, alternating cat/cow and lunges.

My spine crackles as I do a last cobra stretch. I feel no pain and that's one thing to be grateful for. I roll my neck, hear the ligaments click. I'm good to go.

Downstairs, I scramble some eggs and throw in chopped peppers and cheese. Gap-filling more than gourmet. I add some toast and catsup from a local deli. Rachel bought me a coffee machine. It takes two espressos to get me going and I've become a bit of an expert in beans. Owen, Rachel's husband, calls me a coffee snob. He even printed off a meme and the kids, on one of their visits to Uncle Cam, stuck it on the fridge. A spear of morning sunlight lances through the window and hits the very fridge magnet that holds this meme in place. I furrow a brow, but it draws my eye and tilts up the corner of my lip in a smile.

OCD – Obsessive Coffee Disorder.
Yeah, well I tried working with my eyes closed, and it is **HARD.**

Owen may be right. My favourite beans come from a little place near Spa Terminus called You Mug. They roast their own and I buy a kilo at a time. My choice is Brazilian, comes in a black bag and is 'nutty and understated'. I drink it with oat milk – another Rachel suggestion. Another opportunity for Owen to make a stupid face behind Rachel's back. I'm making it sound like he and I don't get on. We do. He's just a born cynic, but funny with it. Plus he makes Rachel laugh. And anyone who can do that gets my vote.

When I'm fed, I fire up the laptop and check my messages. Strictly email. No Facebook accounts. No Twitter. No Insta. Rachel says I had them all BT and at one stage, when I was a teen, they considered taking me to a specialist to get my phone surgically removed from my fingers, so addicted was I.

Allegedly.

For now, we agreed that too much social media would be a terrible idea. Someone with my history – the accident, the lurid stories in the press about what went on in Turkey – was troll bait par excellence. Might as well dress in a goat skin, tie myself to a tree and wait for the T-Rex to arrive. Of course, I surf the net but with Rachel and Josh acting as my wing persons, so far I've managed to survive. I click on my Gmail account.

No thanks, JD Sports. I don't need new Nikes. Leon says my black Reeboks are fine. Even if he did so with a rictus smile.

No thanks, Sharon, who has an urgent message for me and

will no doubt be delighted to send me some unnecessarily revealing photographs if I so much as waft a pixel of interest her way.

Another half dozen depressing, unavoidable and unwanted ads go to trash.

But I pick up one message from Josh. He's been helping me with getting back up to speed with my coding. Josh runs a software team at Whoneedspensions.com; a company that merges pensions and provides financial advice and support for millennials. 'Yawnsville Central, right?' in Josh's own words. Not that what the company does has much to do directly with Josh's role. He's in the back office caretaking the software that runs their website and systems.

'Backroom boffin then,' I once said.

'Is that a noun or a verb?'

That's Josh. He happens to be a very old friend from uni – according to him.

He's easing me back in by letting me analyse problems that arise on his team. Purely academic, of course. Totally unpaid. And the weird, the really bizarre thing about all this is that unlike the absent memory of much of my life, the maths side of my brain is still functioning. I can still program. We, or rather I, decided to try three months ago as a natural part of my recovery. When I did, I was surprised to find it was like discovering I could speak another language. I just... could.

'That's maths for you,' Josh said. 'Bit like music. Uses a different part of the brain.'

Who am I to argue?

I'm not ready to go back to work yet though. Josh suggests I should consider going freelance. Maybe a little web development or a small Android app. Stuff I can do at my own pace without the commitment of a nine-to-five. I'm not even sure I could cope with a part-time job in an office environment. That,

Adam says, I am not yet ready for. The reasons are complicated. Something to do with sensory overload and my inability to filter out the world in general. Not at all unexpected after an SBI, of course. Josh loved that when I first used it.

'Don't tell me, Stupid Bloody Idiot,' was his suggestion, delivered with a smug boffola.

When I explained it stood for Severe Brain Injury, he showed no contrition, preferring, still grinning, his version. As I say, Josh keeps me grounded.

So, I'm not in a work environment yet because my SBI-induced disinhibition could get me into non-woke trouble very easily. But I am working on it.

Josh's message reads:

Spot on with that Pull Request, mate. We'll get you in to give a talk on code quality. LOL. Fancy a beer later?

I ponder his offer and make a mental note to text him. He won't be up yet. Whoneedspensions are lenient when it comes to hours. Clocking on and off is becoming a thing of the past.

I let myself out of the flat and step out into a bright but blustery day. By nine I'm in the car and heading east towards Woolwich. The streets are fairly quiet this Tuesday. Good day for an eight-mile drive. According to the satnav I'm avoiding traffic but it still takes half an hour. I can't remember any of the streets so I gaze up and around as I go. Taking it all in. Adam calls this experiential triggering. A much better tool for me than trying to recall things abstractly. The idea is that I visit places I'm supposed to be familiar with, hoping it will pull out a memory. Pull out sounds strange, but I embrace that term because Adam says they are all in there, those memories. Merely a question of dragging them kicking and screaming to the surface.

Thanks to two cups of You Mug's understated Brazilian

blend, by the time I arrive I'm all eyes and ears. Ready for anything.

How wrong can a man be?

7

I drive slowly around the area, eyeballing, waiting to see if anything clicks.

Nothing does.

Not even when I see the sign a second before the satnav's soothing voice tells me I'm 'arriving at your destination on the right'.

Mulgrave Surgery is an ugly grey building that looks more like a detention centre than a surgery given there are three storeys and not many windows. But there is parking nearby down a side street. Must be an omen.

I find a spot, lock the car, cross the road and walk in through the entrance to a reception area. No one takes any notice of me. There's a waiting area with fifty chairs in rows and I walk in and sit. I scan my surroundings, hoping that something might make one of those loose fragments of windblown recall constantly floating through my head snag and fall into place.

No one talks, everyone whispers, like church. Except for some staff in a back room who carry on like normal people, talking and laughing, oblivious to the suffering masses outside. Some people might find it unseemly. I don't. Surgeries can be depressing places. No one's here to plan a party. I'm glad of the distraction even though I keep half an ear tuned for anyone coughing. Ready with my accusatory stare. No one does and so the stare stays holstered.

I look for clues, study the posters on the walls. Dire warnings about handwashing for two choruses of 'Happy Birthday' sit next to details of free flu jabs for the over-sixty-fives and special offers from the nearest pharmacy on incontinence pads and mouthwash.

That's the old and the new world right there.

I sit for a jittery half an hour observing patients come and go, hearing their names called out and appearing on the big TV screens on the walls in a vertical scroll. A growing discomfort tugs at me. The press and TV are full of requests that people do not visit their surgeries unless absolutely necessary, but it's business as usual here, and I feel a fraud.

I don't want to introduce myself. I don't want a fuss. That's not why I came. It's only then I realise that I may not have come here many times to meet Emma or to pick her up. Perhaps no one here would remember me. I never worked here. I may not have ever spent much time in the building at all. What I'm certain of is that I don't recognise anything or anyone in this room.

It comes then, a strange sense of displacement. As if the walls are closing in on me. The whispered conversations are suddenly jarring.

I get up. Too quickly. The receptionist picks up on the awkward way I stand. Or perhaps she's triggered by the look of confusion on my face. She asks, 'Are you all right?'

Her words startle me. I glance up, caught out. 'Yeah,' I say. 'I'm fine.'

But I'm not. I need to be outside in the cool air. I need a quiet spot.

I walk out and start to half jog. I'm heading towards the river. The day has gone to leaden crap again. The sun has scarpered, drizzle threatens. I'm vaguely aware of a church across the road. It seems incongruous here in this part of London. Then I'm crossing roads near a roundabout and I see a big car park and a sign that says Thames Pathway. There's a buzz of traffic and the smell of diesel fumes before a welcome calm descends as I reach the pedestrianised walkway. I stare out over the brown muddy river and the open space reassures me. Calms me. No buildings, just sky above the water and the north shore on the other side.

Then I remember.

The reception desk at the surgery has a hinged entry that lifts to allow access to the inner sanctum. I visualise walking through into the corridor behind and a small, brightly-lit room with a desk and a computer screen. On one wall is a curtain rail with the drapes pulled back in front of a bed with an impervious mattress covered by disposable paper sheets and a lamp on a long thin neck.

I gasp and blink.

I've been there before and why else other than to meet Emma because my own GP's practice is miles away and I know for certain what his room is like. I've been there for too many check-ups in the last few months not to be familiar with the sour-faced receptionist and the smell of chlorhexidine.

But here, within spitting distance of Mulgrave Surgery, still no Dr Roxburgh in my mind's eye. Still no clear picture of Emma.

I search the image in my head for more detail, staring at the brown water below lapping up against the muddy bank. Something juts out of the mud. An upside-down boot that once was a Doc Marten. I can see the tread quite clearly from my vantage point thirty feet above. I wonder if there's a leg still inside that boot, part of a body lying head first in the silted-up Thames.

It's a ridiculous thought and I curse Josh because his TV viewing recommendations are what feed my lurid imagination. While I'm cursing someone calls my name.

I swing around and a response springs unbidden from my lips. 'Emma?'

But it isn't her. Of course it isn't.

'Cameron? It is you, isn't it?'

A woman is walking towards me. She's wearing a pink puffer coat against the blustery weather, unfastened but clutched around her with arms across her chest. As if she's put it on in a hurry. Her blonde hair is windblown into a mask across her face that she brushes away with a finger. I note a lanyard around her neck with an NHS ribbon. An ID of sorts over a plain white shirt. Underneath, she wears tight, black, cropped trousers and patent leather boots. She's breathing hard. Like she's run to catch up with me.

The woman stops, waiting for my response. I try to read her expression and can't quite decide if surprise or terror predominates.

I stare back, desperately trying to decide if I should recognise this person. Eventually I say, 'Yes, I'm Cameron.'

She sucks in air, her hand flying to her mouth. I hear a stifled, 'Oh My God,' before she runs across the space between us, eyes lighting up. 'I thought it was you. I saw you leaving the surgery and I... I had to follow. To see for myself.'

I stare at her, glance down at her ID, but all I see is its white plastic back twisted tight against her blouse. Despite the heels, she's smaller than I am and her age and stature makes me think she's still more girl than woman. She sees my confusion, blinks, gasps, pulls back a little.

'It's me. Nicole.' Her voice fractures with little intakes of breath.

'Nicole. Right.' So unconvincing.

She blinks again before a kind of horrified disappointment dawns. She whispers flatly, 'You don't recognise me, do you?'

I shake my head.

She looks stricken. 'They said you'd lost your memory. They said you almost died. But then I saw you at the surgery and–'

'I'm trying to revisit places I've been to before. Or at least people tell me I visited before. Experiential triggering. To try to recall. It helps sometimes.'

'Oh.' A small word that does little to explain the tears that start streaming down her face.

'Are you okay?'

She half turns away, dabbing at the droplets accumulating on her chin. She turns back, trying to smile. But her bottom lip trembles. 'Does it help?'

'A bit. I'm remembering a room behind the desk. A consulting room.'

'Room ten. That's where Emma saw patients.'

'You knew Emma?'

Nicole lets out an odd sigh that's half a whimper. 'I worked with Emma. At the surgery. Admin mainly. Occasionally on the desk. I enjoy that more. We... Emma and I knew each other well.'

'Did I know you too?'

She laughs. A sound full of unspoken meaning. 'Yes.'

'I'm sorry. My memory's shot.'

'I heard.'

A gust of wind catches Nicole's coat and tents it up behind her. She turns her back to it and pulls the coat about her. 'Chilly here by the river,' she says.

'I wanted some space.'

'How about some coffee instead?' She smiles hopefully with hooded eyes.

'Okay.' Coffee sounds excellent. We don't go back to the

surgery. Nicole says it's 'manic' and the coffee is terrible. She takes me to a little place two hundred yards down the Thames Path and away from the river. Bean There is all shabby chic with mismatched tables and chairs, home-made banana cake, chia seed muffins and a woman with a 1940s headscarf serving.

Nicole strokes shoulder-length caramel hair behind her ears as she orders. I sit and study her neat features that remind me a little of a fox or a cat. But her eyes are more feline. Pale blue like a Birman's. She gives the barista a wry smile when she asks for skinny milk in her cappuccino. I look out the window but catch Nicole turning back to check on me more than once. Each time she smiles, but just before it, as she turns, once again I spot that nervous desperation.

She brings back two cups and sits opposite me. She's taken off the lanyard and now sheds a large handbag and the coat. Her eyes drift to the little notebook I left out on the table.

'Nicole,' I say. 'Surname?'

'Grant.'

I write it down. I write everything new down. *Nicole Grant. Emma's friend* goes under *Room 10.*

Nicole picks up her bowl-shaped, oversized coffee cup. Her knuckles gleam white where her fingers intertwine to stop them from trembling.

'I don't suppose there's much chance of you lot working from home, is there?' A statement more than a question. My clumsy way of continuing the conversation. Because I do want to continue. This is someone from my past who knew Emma. And something about her fascinates me. It can't be attraction. At least I don't think so because I only met her a few moments ago. And yet her manner and her glances suggest I'm at a disadvantage here. A gut feeling that Nicole knows more than she's letting on.

'I'm not sure. We'll be key workers. Although they are talking about online consultations for the GPs. And self-isolation for the vulnerable groups will not help with community nursing.'

'Seat of the ants, stuff.'

Nicole doesn't seem to notice my gaffe. Or, if she does, she's nice enough to ignore it. 'It's chaotic. One of the GPs went on holiday to South Africa on Sunday. Now he's not sure he'll be able to come back.'

We both stare at our coffee.

'I was so, so sorry to hear about what happened to you and Emma,' Nicole says and then locks eyes with me. 'I've been meaning to contact you but...' She stops and looks away. 'That sounds pathetic. I'm not proud of it. But someone at the surgery said recovery from your sort of injury takes time and I thought... I don't know what I thought. I told myself to wait. For the right time. But then seeing you today...' She pauses and the tears come again, flowing over her bottom lids. She dabs at mascara with a fresh napkin.

I'm at a loss so I say, 'I'm sorry if this has upset you.'

Her voice is small and broken. 'I'm not upset at you. It's just so hard to think you don't remember...'

She drops her gaze again. I see a tear plop into her cappuccino.

'It's difficult for everyone I meet. No one knows what to say. I didn't even remember my sister when I came around.' I add a dry laugh to try to make light of it.

'And you don't remember–' Another gasp that's more a sob. Once more Nicole looks down. 'You remember nothing about what happened?'

'I can remember the hotel I stayed in in Turkey. That's it.' I try the coffee. There's a hint of liquorice underneath the leaf the barista's drawn in the froth. I take another sip.

Nicole shakes her head. 'Can you remember Emma?'

A simple question with a simple answer. 'I suffer from

fugues, sort of mental absences if you like, where I'm with a girl that could be Emma. But I can't see her face. I watch videos of us together. Studied countless photographs. But it's as if I'm watching someone else. Weird.'

Nicole's hand goes to her mouth, and she lets out a small involuntary moan. She puts her coffee down and takes a breath. 'There's something I need to tell you, Cam. I should have come to see you, but everyone at the practice said you were so ill and with Emma dying I... it was suddenly so complicated. I convinced myself that it would only make things worse. And then you turn up today and...' Her words tail off. But there are no tears now. Her big cat's eyes are dry as they search my face.

'What?'

She reaches for her phone and her deft thumbs fly over the screen in a blur of movement. She swipes and slides and for a few seconds stares at whatever it is she's found, contemplating it, deciding. She turns the phone's screen towards me. A selfie. Two people outside on a windswept mountain. I recognise myself in a beanie hat with an affected dark stubble. I'm kissing a girl's cheek. She's holding the phone and is smiling towards the camera. She's wearing a woolly hat with a fur bobble and a roll-neck jumper under another two layers. But I recognise the smile and the eyes. So I should, because they belong to the girl who's showing me the photograph.

I look up into Nicole's face. I think I must be frowning. I realise my mouth is ajar.

She nods. 'For a month before you went to Turkey with Emma that October, you and I... we were seeing one another.'

8

————

All I can do is stare back at the screen and then at Nicole, my heart twitching. There's music in Bean There but all I hear is the blood rushing through my arteries. I'm dumb for too many seconds. But then I focus again on the image and manage to dredge up some words. 'I don't remember. I don't recall ever seeing this. I lost my phone in Turkey.'

As excuses go this one is spectacularly vapid but it's all I can come up with.

Her mouth forms a thin, tremulous smile. 'This is the only one we took. We decided against taking any others. Safer, you insisted. I wasn't going to argue with a computing wiz. And I do know loads of people whose photos end up in the wrong places on other people's timelines and...'

I transmit my confusion with a well-practised raised eyebrow.

'Until you sorted things out with Emma...' She drops her gaze. 'Softly, softly, catchee monkey, you said. I remember thinking it wasn't like you to say something like that. It sounded racist.' She offers a rueful smile.

It's not racist. Imperialistic maybe, but not racist. Though these days it seems that's almost as bad. Where I dig that morsel of knowledge up from is anyone's guess. Another pearl from under the cloak of utter mystery that fogs my previous life.

'Well anyway' – Nicole shifts in her chair – 'social media sites always ask for access to your photos and the cloud isn't as safe as we all like to think. At least, that's what you kept telling me and you're the expert.'

I shake my head. 'That makes me sound like a real nerd.'

Nicole shrugs. 'You were. But I took this one. For myself. And promised not to show it to anyone. So I haven't.'

I stare at the image again, buying time to think. 'You and me.' My clumsy words come out rudely sceptical.

'Is it that unlikely?' Her brief laugh turns sour and her lip quivers again. 'Am I that bad?'

'No.' I splutter an apology. 'I didn't mean it that way. You're... you're very pity. I mean pretty.'

Her eyes widen and I plunge on. 'All these months everyone has been telling me how so much together me and Emma were.'

Nicole sighs. 'The perfect couple. Only you weren't. At least she wasn't.'

I swallow loudly.

'Oh, God,' she says. 'See how that sounds? Emma's not here to defend herself so I come across as the perfect bitch. What a mess.' Her head drops. She clutches the coffee cup again in both hands. 'We kept it a secret. A big secret with no photos or texts just in case. You didn't want to hurt her, but she had already hurt you. You were going to confront her and then...'

'What?'

'It happened.'

It.

'The accident. And I wanted to come and see you. But with Emma dead and you so unwell, whenever I ran it through my head it all sounded so sordid. And I was scared you might not want to see me and...' More tears. Big, sorrow-filled dollops of them.

'It's been rough on you,' I say because I feel I ought to say something if only to try and stop my heart thumping.

'It has.' She sweeps a finger around the rim of her cup and whispers, 'Still is.'

We sit there. Nicole and I. Ex-lovers. New strangers. 'A shit-load to take in' as Josh would say. But I am desperate to understand. 'So why would I go on holiday with her if all this was going on?'

'It was messed up. You'd both paid for the holiday. She was looking forward to it. You had been too until a few weeks before. And you were worried about her. We both were. Something wasn't right.'

'So how did we...?'

Nicole shakes her head. 'You came to me for help. To try and understand what was going on with Emma, and what happened... happened. As for the holiday, I think both of us knew that everything depended on Emma. About how she'd react. Make or break I suppose.'

'Make or break,' I mutter. I ponder this. It sounds complicated. A minefield. But then relationships so often are.

'I had hopes, but you and Emma had been together for a long time and so I tried to be realistic. I told myself I had to wait and see. I've sort of been waiting ever since.' Nicole dabs her face with the mascara-blotched napkin, reaches into her bag and takes out a thin folder and hands it to me. 'This was Emma's. She didn't keep much at the surgery, but there were a few bits and pieces she'd left around. The police took it all away but then brought it back once they'd finished. I've kept it on my desk because... I thought perhaps you ought to have it.'

I open the folder. Inside I count a dozen bits of paper: Two letters from Southwark Health about accreditation. A handwritten letter from a patient. The rest, photocopies of receipts. Plus a small notebook, five inches by three with a purple cover and ring-bound with black wiring. I flip it open and see a few pages of handwriting that I recognise as Emma's.

Nicole watches me as I inspect the contents. 'Most of it is rubbish,' she points out. 'She was a jotter. She never used her phone for notes because of data protection.'

'Isn't writing it down just as bad?'

'People don't steal fifty-pence notebooks. They steal 600-quid phones.'

It makes sense. Nicole finishes her coffee and glances at her watch. 'I need to get back.' She stands and puts on her coat. I get up. Usually I'm careful. This time I'm not. I grab onto the chair to steady myself. The old cerebellum took a bit of a knock, so I've been told. As a result my gyroscope's a bit ropey. If I move too quickly it decides to go on a waltzer ride of its own leaving the rest of me to hang on to whatever is at hand.

Nicole waits for me to recover and comes around the table and hugs me. It lasts a good few seconds longer than I expect it to. 'Lovely to see you, Cam,' she whispers in my ear. She smells fresh. Her cheek is soft against mine. A dangling earring presses hard and cold on my skin.

She pulls away without looking at me, heading for the door.

I ask, 'Would it be all right to contact you again?'

She stops with her back to me and then swivels. Her expression is questioning, her breathing fast and shallow. 'I don't want you to take pity on me.'

'I'm not. You're a part of this, obviously. A part of what's happened. So is Emma but she's not here. You are and I'd like to get to nose–' I stop, realise I'm prattling, recalibrate. 'I'd like to get to know you.'

An awkward three seconds of frozen nothing before her eyes

widen and her hand reaches out to squeeze my arm. 'You have no idea how long I've...'

There are only a few other people in Bean There. They're taking no notice of this little drama, but the woman in the headscarf behind the counter is grinning.

Nicole's words dry up. I help her out. 'Let me give you my number.'

I read it out and Nicole punches it into her phone. I hear mine ding a message alert as she sends hers back, eyes shining. 'I'd ask you back to the surgery–'

'No,' I say. 'I'd rather not.'

She gives me one of those million-quid smiles and then turns and walks out of the door, leaving me alone with a thousand thoughts stampeding through my head, and Emma Roxburgh's file on my lap.

9

I order another coffee and sit back down with the folder.

The letter from a patient is heartfelt; a note thanking Emma for treating her son's mastoiditis and for putting him at ease during her examination. Dozens of people have told me that Emma was a superb doctor. I add another fragment of corroboration to the ever-growing pile.

I shuffle the receipts. Two are for fuel, four appear to be meals. Expensive meals at restaurants I don't know.

Then I turn to the notebook. There are only five pages with Emma's handwriting. I peruse the last few entries. My guess is that they're patient references with dates, initials and queries. Most have a line drawn through them. I assume because they're things Emma had dealt with.

5/07/18 MR JW — chase up MRI.
7/07/18 Jane D — biopsy result.
11/07/18 Mrs FT — FUP new drug regimen, eye clinic.
11/09/18 Millie's tonsillectomy — private referral.
02/10/18 Mr GM — Gallstones data sheet.

I riffle through the rest and find nothing. But when I get to the end page there's a final isolated note.

02/10/18. Cam's do with Quantiple.
Pants on fire?

That's it. Just the one entry. But I read it a dozen times. The dates and the names mean nothing to me. But pants on fire does. The tail end of a childish phrase that starts with 'liar, liar'.

I'm told that my background in maths and programming helped me take a very logical approach to relearning. I adopted a structured pathway of my own. When I found out that I had a degree and how qualified I was, I knew that the journey back would be a lengthy one, but I started at the beginning. As if I was back in school.

After four months I was playing sudoku. But that was maths. Language was a different thing. I went back to basics, researching words and sayings, writing them down, testing myself. I used the internet to cleave back knowledge that I once had. Of course, I still get things wrong. Goat for ghost is a glorious example. And I once told my therapist that elephants didn't live in rooms and shouldn't live in zoos, either.

But pants on fire I know and understand from Dana, my speech therapist. It was she who made me recite nursery rhymes and practise sayings to tease out abstract meaning, rhyme, metaphor.

Liar, Liar/ pants on fire/ nose as long as a telephone wire!

I finish my coffee and walk back out into morning light. It's still as blustery as earlier but the rain has held off. In two minutes I'm back on the Thames Path looking out over the water, my mind as restless and full of swirling eddies as the flowing river. I find a sheltered spot and sit, staring. And as I stare, the world around me fades.

Emma stands at the edge of the rooftop bar. The same full moon reflects rippling sparkles off the gentle waves of the sea below.

'I'm sure I've seen someone watching us,' Cam says. 'But I can't make out the detail.'

'That's because you never look in the right place.' Ivan's voice comes to them from a table in the centre of the bar.

Cam glances over. Two girls sit either side of him, both drinking something pink through straws.

'Where the hell should I be looking?'

'Somewhere shadows like to be.' Ivan grins and throws his hands out in a gesture that says he has no idea.

Tonight's music is downbeat. Sounds like a chill-out mix.

Emma lets her gaze drift down to the quayside below. 'You think the answer to all this lies in the shadows?'

'Maybe'

Emma considers his answer and, still smiling, steps aside to reveal a mirror hanging on the edge of the parapet in mid-air. Within it, a coal-black image coils and billows. But it clears, and Cam finds his own reflection staring back at him, grinning.

Ivan snorts. 'See, the mirror has answers. If you want to find them you start with yourself.'

'Liar, liar, pants on fire,' the mirror image says. But it isn't in Cam's voice.

He reaches his hand out but it isn't glass he touches. Instead, his hand goes right through towards faceless Emma. And his touch pushes her over into the empty night.

As she falls, she smiles at him.

When I look up, I'm a quarter of a mile from where I originally sat staring out at the water. I'm still on the path, but I'm on my feet near what appear to be gun emplacements. Two iron canons, remnants of Britain's troubled history, point out over the river, guarding London's waterway. I take a moment to orientate myself. I turn full circle twice and bring up Google Maps on my phone. I need to head back east.

But the fugue is still fresh in my memory. Seeing and hearing myself in the mirror speaking in another man's voice is even more enigmatic than usual. I'm clueless what any of it means.

Then I remember my hand reaching out. Towards the faceless girl.

My hand doing the pushing.

Primed with the fresh information Nicole has furnished, it's an image full of disturbing and dread possibilities.

I squash the idea as I hurry back to the car, get in and clutch the steering wheel with both shaking hands. I've still got the file that Nicole gave me. I open it out on the seat and pick up Emma's tiny notebook. I read 'pants on fire' written on the back but one page again. Only the last few words of that silly phrase, but the implication is clear. And it was aimed at me. A comment about a date and a time.

Liar, liar, pants on fire, Cameron Todd.

Worse, the date on the entry in the notebook was just a week before we went to Turkey.

How it might be important or what it means is anyone's guess. But I can't help remembering Nicole's words:

Softly, softly, catchee monkey.

Liar, liar, pants on fire sounds like Nicole and I might not have been as careful as we thought we had.

10

It's 9am, I'm in a consulting room at the Southwark clinic. Fourth floor. Community Mental Health.

'Mr Todd, when was the last time you had one of these fugues?'

I look at the questioner. She's young, Asian, thick glasses, businesslike clothes. She's the studious type. Rachel would say I shouldn't mention Asian. Not woke. She says that a lot.

I wouldn't say it out loud but I can't help the thought. It's registering the facts. Filing people in the right boxes because I have to. A different kind of identity politics, but the way my brain works now. I need to think it through, process it, check it against a list so I understand. All the automatic stuff has gone. Her partner is Asian too. As clichéd a pair of trained medic nerds as I've ever come across.

'Yesterday,' I answer. 'I was out walking. The Thames Path out near Woolwich.'

The trainee frowns. 'Do they always occur when you're out walking?'

'No.' According to Dr Adam Spalding, my consultant psychiatrist and the chap whose clinic this is, I can be a little blunt. He tells me often I should be more forgiving. Of other people and especially of myself. He's always trying to reassure me. We've talked about survivor guilt a lot, although in my case, because I can't remember Emma, feeling guilty about anything is difficult. In my case, confusion and acceptance are the main contenders in my emotional battles.

'Fate is a cold, uncaring mistress, Cameron. You've done nothing to deserve this.'

That's one of Adam's poetic favourites and I want to believe him but I can't. I have triggers. Maybe the trainees use of the word 'they' presses my buttons. Objectifying my little fugue party pieces. Shouldn't annoy me but it does. I'm here at Adam's request because my 'party pieces' are something these two are unlikely to ever see again. So I'm trotted out periodically. I don't mind. At least I try not to. They're both ST2s, run-through trainees two years into specialising. An aeon away from being able to cope with someone like me alone. Hence Adam's super-vision from a back seat near one wall. He sits, vigilant and amused. Occasionally, he'll sense my irritation and answers for me. His replies are always more fulsome than mine and always worth listening to. As is this one.

'No, they occur not only when out walking. Other oppor-tunistic triggers arise when Cameron is relaxing at home or while asleep, but usually during the early stages towards sleep or on the way back to wakefulness. Hypnagogic or hypnopompic phases in the sleep cycle.'

'So they're not sleepwalking episodes or dreams?' the other trainee asks. He's male, no glasses. Wears contacts from the way he keeps blinking. Spring has not yet sprung in London and the air in Adam's room is crisp from the radiator blasting out heat. Not good contact-lens-wearing conditions.

'No,' Adam answers. 'The distinction is clear. The remark-able thing here is that we have video EEG evidence of Cameron experiencing one of these hallucinatory fugues during his time in rehab. He appeared to get up from stage 1b sleep, dressed, walked four feet from his bed and sat down. Nine minutes later, he got back into bed and, now awake, wrote an account of what he'd experienced in great detail.'

I slide him a look.

Adam tilts his head back towards me. 'Believe me, I realise you think there are gaps, but the detail is rich. The smells and sight of the bar–'

'It's always a bar?' Trainee 2 probes.

'Not a bar. That bar. Always,' I reply.

'And it typifies a hallucinatory fugue,' Adam continues. 'Stereotypical venues, and dialogue or involvement with imagined characters. The patient remembers the experiences as if they were real. However, close observation of Cameron while he is experiencing this fugue shows that he is engaged in activity quite separate and distinct from the hallucination. Automatic activities such as dressing, walking across his bedroom, or walking in the park. All physical activities he has no recollection of doing. What he recollects is the hallucination. There is also an element of time slippage. Cameron's experience is that he is away at the bar far longer than he truly is. Sometimes his appreciation is one of hours when in fact it is no more than a few minutes.'

The trainees blink, lapping it up. But I can see confusion and scepticism etched in their faces.

My irritation flares. 'Before you ask, no, not drug-induced and no, not sleepwalking.'

Adam smiles and explains. 'We know that because drug-induced hallucinations are neither internally coherent nor stereotyped. We also know that somnambulism does not play a part because the EEG results showed waking patterns.'

I watch the trainees' expressions. They've deliberately left one possibility out of the differential. I sit, waiting to see if anyone will be brave enough. Rigorousness overcomes Thick Glasses' reserve. 'What about fabricated confabulation?'

I snort. She's gone for the big words. Perhaps in the hope that I might not understand.

Adam smiles. 'Malingering is unlikely because...' He lets it hang in the air.

The second trainee takes the bait. 'Because there's cooperation with the evaluation. He let himself be EEG'd.'

'Correct,' says Adam. He grins at the trainee like the adept teacher he is. Praise where praise is due. 'He's also happy with the diagnosis. People who make things up want no end point.'

I shake my head. So not true. *All I want for Christmas is a bloody end point.*

'And there's enough supporting pathology to provide an explanation.' Thick Glasses redeems herself.

Adam adds another encouraging smile. 'History of traumatic brain injury is a known risk factor for both hallucinatory and dissociative fugue. Before we discuss that, what's the difference?'

No one answers.

Adam, the good teacher, explains. 'The typical dissociative fugue involves patients in a confused state physically travelling to a strange place, often significant distances, sometimes by car or other transport. They may stay at this new location for some time, suffering reversible amnesia characterised by loss of identity and personality. These states may last days, sometimes even months. When they recover, patients usually remember their previous lives and past. Hallucinatory fugues, as with Cameron, on the other hand, are short-lived, display clear recollection of the occurrence but no real major physical displacement. What links both fugues together is causation. In this instance, severe traumatic brain injury.'

And there it is. My monster in the locked cupboard.

Adam turns to me. 'Cameron, why don't you grab a coffee while I finish up with Meesha and Han. I'll join you in ten minutes, okay?'

I smile graciously at the muttered thank yous of the trainees and exit, my job done. I wonder if models who pose nude for art classes feel like this. I've read up on those. Some, the obvious narcissists, do it because... they're narcissists. Others see it as a challenge to their own self-image issues. A few wrap it up in psychobabble, sharing a connectedness with the artists, being a part of the mindful creative process. That's where the analogy starts and ends for me. After all, I'm not baring my all physically. What I'm exposing is my damaged mind. As with life drawing, the students always find it fascinating.

And possibly, in some convoluted, cathartic way, it helps.

I'm here to bare my all figuratively. But then a scene from one of Josh's recommended films flashes into my head. Hannibal Lecter making District Attorney Krendler eat his own sautéed brain at the dinner table. All politeness and gore. I reach for my head in an automatic gesture. My skull is intact. I smile. If Josh could see me now he'd laugh and say something pithy like 'always good to keep an open mind, right, Cam?'

Josh has a lot to answer for.

11

_____

I sit in the soulless waiting room. Stimulus-free apart from a smattering of magazines scattered over a battered laminated coffee table. I don't pick up the Sept 2017 copy of Nat Geo that's on the top. A thousand people will have thumbed through to look at the ridiculously cute proboscis monkeys it features. That's a thousand layers of someone else's unwashed commensals I could gather up and smear over my unsuspecting mucous membranes the minute I rub my nose or massage my eyes, which on average we do sixteen times an hour. Not a good idea at the best of times. And with Covid-19 roaring across Europe like a virulent tsunami these are not the best of times by a long chalk.

The coffee comes in the form of paper tubes full of freeze-dried granules and a silver flask of tepid water. I mix both in a Styrofoam cup, tear open a capsule of long-life milk, sanitise my hands with a little bottle I carry, and sit. The coffee swirls in the cup, whirlpooling undissolved granules on the surface like survivors from a torpedoed ship. I wait for one of them to yell 'help' before I take two sips and then discard the cup and its contents as undrinkable. Fifteen minutes later Adam comes to the door and beckons me back in.

The clinic is an NHS outreach, and the room reflects that. There's no couch, just a clump of chairs previously occupied by the trainees, and a desk pushed against the drab wall with a drab view of South London housing through a drab, anodised, aluminium-framed window. Bits of paper and a screwed-up tissue lie discarded under Adam's desk. I remember seeing them here that last time I visited. He needs to admonish the cleaners. Wake them up to a better level of hygiene. All well and good to attempt informality, create a relaxed atmosphere for the troubled patients. But this room falls well short and only just achieves tawdry. Still, that's not Adam's fault.

The trainees have gone. Adam waits for me to sit down, and then follows suit.

'Thanks for doing that, Cam.'

'Pleasure,' I reply and do my best to make it sound genuine.

It doesn't, and Adam chuckles. 'After you'd gone, Han asked if there was much difference between a hallucinogenic fugue and a lucid dream.'

'Is there?'

'You know there is. With a lucid dream you're in REM sleep whereas you are wide awake when you fugue.'

This is old ground we've trodden over many times.

'So,' Adam says. 'The last one. Anything new?'

I shrug and think back. My fugue venue never changes. Always the rooftop bar. The people are always the same too. Sometimes others appear, come and go. For instance, there's a chatty bloke that wanders around clearing glasses away. He has an accent. But I can't pinpoint it. Then again, he wasn't there two days ago. 'Just Ivan and Emma,' I say. 'Plus the shadow man.'

Adam purses his lips and throws in, 'I told Han and Meesha that you had concentration problems that we were working on.'

Whoop-dee-doo. For concentration read anger. It surges now and a shopping list of familiar sniping thoughts roll through my head like credits for a terrible film. *Did you tell them I'm ridden with survivor guilt? Mention the fact that I'm still under suspicion by the Turkish authorities? Explain that my dead partner's family have a private investigator hassling me?*

But I bite that back. Adam has taught me how to do that through cognitive therapy. Instead of ranting, I say, 'Did you show them my images?'

'Of course.'

They were always worth looking at, my MRIs and CTs. They had the wow factor in the form of spectacular mid-facial and cranial fractures. No one with that amount of damage would emerge unscathed. Okay, there'd been no intracranial bleed, but lots of bruising with most of the damage in the frontal lobe topped off with a bit of temporal, and limbic dysfunction from the axonal torsion that comes from falling fifteen feet and meeting the immovable hard edge of a metal stanchion supporting a concrete ramp face-on.

I'm au fait with all the technical words by now, though I am not medical. The vocabulary comes with the SBI territory along with a host of other things, like learning how to walk and swallow again, and, eventually, how to ride a bike and even drive. All of which has taken an age. Seventeen months, in fact. Adam says I'm lucky and uses words like 'remarkable' when he describes my recovery.

It may be so but doesn't feel like that to me. I can't see much other than light and dark through one eye, I'm still a little slow to start movements from standing and my right foot sometimes feels like it doesn't belong to me. I'm often irritable and I'm intolerant of too much of anything. Add to that a touch of confusion with words and I truly am a prize specimen. But the icing on the cake is the fugues. All thanks to what happened to me that night in Cirali.

Adam sits, placidly waiting for me to change direction or complain. I do neither. I'm glad when he doesn't say 'Emma?' and raise his eyebrows. He can probably tell that I still can't see her face during my fugue. Not clearly enough to recognise her, though since it happened, I've looked at her photograph a thousand times. But I still don't know her. She's a stranger to me even though we'd been together for five years by the time she died.

That, perhaps, is one of the hardest things to accept.

Adam knows that if I'd seen her face during the fugue, I'd let him know right away.

'I got my licence back a week ago,' I say.

Adam punches the air. 'Yes! I told you we'd get there.'

'You did. Already been out for a spin.'

Adam frowns. 'Good. But don't overdo it. You haven't driven in what, a year and a half?'

'I've taken some refresher lessons. All good.'

'Very sensible. But remember that excessive psychosocial stimulation can make things worse from the fugue point of view.'

At least he doesn't wag a finger. 'Come on. Give me a break. I've been a hermit for fifteen months. I don't count the two before that when I was in a comb in that Turkish hospital.'

Adam doesn't correct my vocabulary. He knows I mean coma. He corrects my exaggeration instead. 'Ten days.'

'Whatever. I need to get out. Lay a few goats.' It should be ghosts, of course, and this time Adam laughs. My intermittent aphasia can sometimes be hysterical. 'Only kidding,' I add by way of deflection and Adam laughs again. I don't tell him about visiting Emma's practice. I don't tell him about Nicole. Not yet.

'Not the best of timing though, Cam.'

'Why?'

'Rumour has it we're following Italy on the Covid curve. They've been locked down for a week. Driving may not be so easy in a few days' time.'

'You really think things will get that bad?'

Adam's mouth turns down. 'My brother is an epidemiologist. He says some kind of enforced social distancing is inevitable.'

'Shut down the cities like in China?'

'They have in Northern Italy. And even though as a country we don't do Mediterranean Sundays with Mass followed by all the generations sharing a bowl of rigatoni at grandma's house, we will need to make sacrifices.'

'I'd better get on with things then.'

Adam appraises me. 'This is good, Cam. I can see the thought of driving has cheered you up.'

'Yeah.' I raise my hand and mime twirling a football rattle. He's right, but I can't let him see that he is. It's a game we play. But this time, in response to my sardonic celebration, all Adam does is look a little sad.

Because that's the way the world is at the moment.

12

I walk back to my flat from the clinic. The East London pavements are slick with drizzle and teeming with people; almost nine million in this city all told. London has a population density of 8,000 per square mile. I know this because every virus news bulletin and every newspaper editorial churns out these numbers. Some wag called them petri dish statistics.

I cross Tower Bridge Road; an artery into the city that pulses with traffic but keeps a Victorian vibe. People still queue outside Manze's for pie and mash like they have done for a century. A hundred years before that there was even an eighteenth-century spa near here. But then came the Blitz and the docks died. Regeneration shoehorned sixties towers and eighties style cul-de-sacs between magnificent Georgian terraces and thirties council flat blocks that are almost ornate.

The word is hotchpotch. Easy to get lost if you're unfamiliar with the layout. Easier to be pleasantly surprised by whatever gem is around the next corner. But the people who know flock here, looking for a bit of the real London. The grit in the all-too-often perfumed ointment that regeneration brings. Yet the inevitable gentrification of London's boroughs can't quite rid Bermondsey of its industrial roots. And many of its *new* homes come from repurposed factories and warehouses.

My flat's in a converted warehouse within walking distance of Maltby Street, where nestles a foodie's mecca under the Victorian railway arches. Street food and enthusiastic start-ups abound. Apparently, Emma and I visited every weekend for a wander and Saturday brunch, so I've been told.

The flat is the one we shared; a two bed, two baths with a tiny balcony. We bought it because Emma liked London. She also worked here, so it was logical. A clinical assistant in sexual health at Guy's Hospital, two sessions a week, and a GP for an out-of-hours service one regular Tuesday night. And in between she'd do the odd locum at the practice in Woolwich. Emma must have been very bright.

I wouldn't know.

But other people do and constantly list 'how good things used to be'. I try not to be resentful and succeed on the whole. But sometimes it can be wearing when people keep telling me what a wonderful life I had.

For example, I ran a team of developers for a company in Shoreditch providing business software solutions. Software as a service, SAAS for short, integrating micro services into an existing platform around call-tracking software. The smoke and mirrors that no one sees when they casually surf to that sofa company site and see the call direct number. What the unsuspecting punter doesn't realise is that a minor piece of Java software makes that number unique to each customer, so that when they ring it *everything* they've just been looking at on that site is there for the sales person on the other end of the phone to see. As well as the number of times they've visited, their route to contact – whether directly or via a search engine – and a whole slew of other details. All designed to help secure the sale through advertising voodoo.

People think online shopping is personal and completely private. Yes, well, only to an extent. A lot goes on behind that green curtain, Dorothy.

I've been back to see my old colleagues. Only a dozen people worked at the office and they all knew me. A few people even cried.

I didn't.

Of course, I tried to make the right noises but I've never been back since. There is no job for me there and at this stage, a year and a half on, why should there be? I'm not the same person I was. I have nothing like the knowledge base, though I'm doing my best to catch up. My degree is in Computer Science and Maths. A 2:1 after four years in Edinburgh University. According to Josh we had a 'total blast' even though the sun only ever shone in April and May. It may have done in the summer, but we were never there for that. I'd be at home stacking shelves. Josh would be picking fruit.

Six months after I came out of hospital, Rachel, my sister, announced that the life insurance on Emma's policy had paid out. I used it to get rid of the mortgage with a sizeable chunk left over. Rachel is a solicitor and knows all about this stuff. She did all the legal heavy lifting and it meant that I could stay in London. Why not? I had nowhere else to go. My life was here even if I couldn't remember any of it.

The flat is now mine and so is Bermondsey. I'm at home here in its fragmented, disjointed, chaotic streets. Streets that echo my fragmented, disjointed, chaotic brain pretty well.

∿

I wave the key fob to open the entrance door and tilt my chin up at Don, the concierge. He gives me his usual perfunctory smile. The one that pops up when people notice my limp. The one tinged with pity. My flat is on the first floor. White walls and white-tiled bathrooms that remind me a lot of being in hospital. Strangely, that helps. At least it did to start with. When you've depended on a place and the people that work there for months to do literally everything for you, it can be very disorientating when you're left on your own.

As Rachel said, I was coming back to the flat because Emma and I had lived here for three years. But when I discharged myself from hospital and moved in, it felt like I was walking through the door for the first time. I remembered nothing.

But I am working on that.

I walk straight into the living room. On the reminder wall is a line of three corkboards. Stuck to these boards are my aides-memoires. Photographs of the people in my life that I need to know now, and a different list of people I should know from my previous existence, but who I've forgotten.

Top of that second pile is a photograph of Emma. She's dead, but I study her photograph every day because she's a part of this flat and my life as was. When I do stare at her, I don't appreciate any sorrow or regret because I can't remember knowing her. When I told Rachel that she burst into tears. Everyone that visited me kept talking about her in hushed tones, expecting me to be heartbroken. But I wasn't because where cognisance of my previous life should be sits a huge black hole. An empty chest. No matter how hard I try, when I'm on the rooftop bar in the fugue I still can't see Emma's features on the girl's face. Until I do, I will keep looking at her picture.

A candid shot. Outdoors. From the greenery, it looks like spring or summer. Her blue eyes are wide and she's smiling with an amused, slightly shocked expression at something the photographer has said or done. That photographer is me, apparently. Emma was a head-turner. A heart-shaped face pale against her dark hair. And smiling eyes that make her look so much younger than she truly was. So vibrant and full of fun. I wish I could remember where it was taken.

One day, maybe.

Next to Emma is a photo of my mother. She's dead too. Bowel cancer. When I was eighteen and Rachel was twenty. We were both at university. Rachel says it's a miracle we got through it. We did because we were there for each other. Apparently, I was a rock. And not, like now, a crumbly one. The photo of Janet Todd is from a time before she was unwell. When she was superwoman, working, entertaining us, putting food on the table. She has kind eyes. I know I would have loved her because I see Rachel in her face and my sister is a pearl.

Beneath my mother is a photo of my father and his new family. No single candid shot here. Colin Todd lives in Thailand. Work took him there, marriage to a local woman has kept him. Of course he's been over a few times to see me, but his life is elsewhere. Besides, Rachel says he's completely bloody useless. She feels he abandoned us once we were old enough to fend for ourselves. And who am I to argue. He seemed nice enough the last time he came home. But he also seemed pretty keen to go back to Thailand. I have his eyes. Rachel says they're dangerous because they always look like they're laughing. As if there's a lot going on behind them.

On the middle corkboard are my daily aids. First, a big calendar with the day of the week in red. I can't remember dates, so this is an essential. Plus there are phone numbers and appointments I must keep. Same thing as a lot of people have, except that mine are up there in giant writing so I can't forget.

On the left corkboard is a list, with photos, of the people important to me right now.

Heading that list is Rachel. She was the one at my bedside when I opened my eyes in the hospital in Turkey. I didn't know who she was, and it felt odd to learn that she was my big sister. But she looks a little like me – mainly in colouring and the slightly gap-toothed smile – and she's been there all the way through. I don't know what or where I'd be without her.

Rachel is thirty-seven but wears it well. The photograph is recent, copied from her office website (Meechum Rickards – for all your legal needs). She's attractive and accomplished and professional. The image captures all that perfectly, though she says it makes her look like a hard-faced old trout. Rachel is my anchor to the world of the past, present and future. The Grif-fithses – her married name – live in a Victorian pile in Penarth on the coast near Cardiff. In the photograph her dark-brown hair is highlighted and she wears more makeup than is usual. Much as you'd expect for a corporate website image. But still a light touch. She doesn't like too much of that stuff, she tells me.

Adam is also on that side of my wall and so is Josh and Leon and several more people and names that are vital to me; the Cameron Todd who lives and breathes now and who should, by right, be dead. At least that's what several of the doctors and nurses and physios and rehabilitation experts repeated over the slow months of recuperation. Not nastily, more by way of encouragement at my progress. Which was very different from Emma's sister's reaction when I bumped into her alone on a visit to the cemetery where they'd buried Emma.

While the healers expressed good-natured surprise – 'You're lucky to be alive, Cameron', Emma's sister bristled with hate – 'You're the one that should have died.' Perhaps both sentiments are correct.

Two sides of the same doubloon, as Josh would say.

Sometimes I wonder if I really am dead and that this is all some kind of limbo that I'm in. But then Adam tells me not to be maudlin while muttering something about me definitely *not* having Cotard's syndrome – when people really do believe they are dead. And Rachel... Rachel tells me not to be so bloody stupid, but with even better swear words and in far more inventive ways.

I wonder what she'd say if I told her about Nicole.

13

Hers is the one photo that's missing from my wall. She's also the person I've been thinking about all morning.

I sit, staring at the pasted-up images of my past, unremembered life. Then I fish out my phone and put it on the table, call up my contacts list and search in the N's. I find it easily, exactly where I put it a day ago.

Nicole.

Not made up. Nicole is real. But if she is, it leaves a lot to think about. I sit for five, ten, twenty minutes, thinking. And then, instead of making a sandwich – today would be cheese and marmite – I pick up my mobile again and text Josh.

Thirty minutes later I'm sitting in reception at Whoneedspensions.com's building off The City Road. The whole of the ground floor is taken up with small tables and comfy chairs. There's water and juice and coffee on tap. Fruit in bowls and nuts and granola in hygienic hoppers for anyone to help themselves. WNP believe in looking after their employees. We're eating bowls of ramen brought in by a local restaurant served from a pop-up table on one side of the room.

'Good to see you out and about, mate,' says Josh. He's small and wiry, jet-black hair in unruly curls and a little too much in the eyebrow area. When we were at Edinburgh we shared a scruffy top-floor tenement flat and had – according to Josh – a banging time. Now he lives in Wandsworth with his events organiser girlfriend. She gets lots of comps and so I, gooseberry (fool) Cameron, get to see bands I'm supposed to have liked. Some I do. Others I'm not so sure about. Mainly the electro minimalist stuff Josh loves. I sometimes wonder if he is pushing the envelope of credulity when he reassures me I was a fan.

Josh slurps some noodles, chews appreciatively and asks, 'How was your hospital appointment.'

'Wasn't really an appointment. I sometimes do this thing for Adam. More students.'

'You're their star patient.'

'That's why they pay me the big bucks.'

He squints. 'They pay you?'

'The Tube fair.'

Josh lets out a snort. He has his nose down ready for another spoonful. He sees the expression on my face and says, 'You're supposed to slurp. Something to do with adding air to augment the flavours. Like frothing wine when you taste it.'

'Yeah, but then you spit wine out,' I say in response to this little nugget.

'Don't be a smart-arse. Besides, it was you who told me that after a trip to Japan.'

'I've been to Japan?'

'2015. I'm still jealous.'

Josh slurps. I follow suit. When we've swallowed that mouthful, Josh remembers. 'Hey, did you drive yesterday?'

'I did.'

'And?'

'Didn't run anyone over.'

'No, I mean the visit. To Emma's practice.'

Everyone who's a part of my support circle knows just about everything that I do. Apparently because I'm vulnerable. I know that Rachel has Josh in a WhatsApp group. Called Cam's Carers, I bet.

I wave a hand in a so-so gesture. 'I remembered bits but nothing significant.'

'That's a shame.'

'I met a very nice admin person though. Name of Nicole. Ring any bells?'

Josh begins a Quasimodo impression, but remembers where he is and thinks better of it. Instead, he does an exaggeratedly-slow shake of his head, which is his trademark not-a-clue move. 'Should it?'

'I think you'd remember her if you'd met. She's pity.'

Josh's thick eyebrows go up. One movement.

I sigh and do the correction. 'Pretty.'

Josh smirks. 'Ooh. You getting back on the horse, Cam?'

'I don't think I could even find the stirrups.'

'I don't believe that for one minute.'

I change the subject. 'Do you eat like this every day?'

'No.' Josh is defensive. 'Sometimes we use chopsticks or even knives and forks. Depends on the food.'

I send him a withering glance.

Pleased at his own biting repartee he says, 'On Tuesdays and Thursdays we bring in our own.'

'That must be tough.'

'A full programmer is a happy programmer. Lucky you came today. This might be the last time we'll do this for a while.'

I raise one eyebrow. The other one doesn't move as well post-surgery.

'Social distancing and all that palaver,' Josh explains. 'We've moved the tables further apart.'

'You think it'll get that bad?'

'Our CEO has a place in Spain. They're rapidly catching up with Italy and it is not pleasant. He reckons Spain will lock down by the end of this week. He's already got us planning for the zombie apocalypse.'

'Rachel says it will get worse too.'

'It will. There may even be furloughs. We're considering moving at least half the staff to a home-working schedule. And speaking of that, the last bug fix ticket you did was spot on.'

'Thanks.' I slit my eyes. 'You're not just saying that?'

'Definitely not. I'm pretty sure you'd smash the technical side of any interview for a senior dev job.'

I'm delighted because the money I'm living on, savings and what's left over from Emma's insurance, will not last for ever. I need to get back to work. If anyone will have me, that is. And that's the point. Cam the technical developer is fine. But Cam, the man who may not cope so well in a room full of people has a way to go.

'Any time you want me to put in a word, give me the nod.'

'I will do that.'

Josh sighs. 'Fancy a beer later?'

I make apologetic noises and look doubtful. 'I've got some stuff to sort out.'

'What, things you can't sort out during daylight hours any day of the week? Is it something nocturnal? You shooting a wildlife documentary on lemurs?'

'No. I'm doing something for Rachel.' The lie comes easily because I often am doing things for Rachel. Usually computer-related. Since I am their go-to family-tech guy, even the simplest of tasks requires my input. Rachel couches it in terms of doing her bit for rehab.

'Okay,' says Josh. 'But you are still on for beers on Friday night?'

I incline my head. 'I'll check with my social secretary and get back to you.'

Josh grins. 'Five thirty at the Grey Goose it is.'

'That'll do it.'

'We must preserve these ancient cultural traditions for as long as possible. Who knows, after-work drinks may become a thing of the past.'

'Should I be worried?'

Josh waves away my concerns with a spoon. 'Hell no. I have a nuclear bunker at the back of my fridge and at least three weeks' worth of Quavers still in their boxes. Your task for the next few nights is to watch *World War Z*. Brad Pitt as the badass UN troubleshooter tracking down the source of the end of the world as we know it. Ironic or what? There will be an exam in the Grey Goose. Guaranteed to ease any worries you may harbour about the pandemic.' His grin is manic.

We sit and chat over a half-decent coffee for fifteen more minutes. Then I leave and go home again. If anyone knows about Nicole and me, anyone I think I might have confided in, Josh sits at the top of the list. Him not knowing her means that we must have kept things very close to our chests.

Just like she said we did.

I wander back and call in to a Sainsbury's for some essentials. And two bottles of wine. By the time I'm home it's almost five. I've decided what I will do. I send a text to Rachel, reassure her that all is well and repeat, more or less, what I said to Josh, but without mentioning Nicole. I sense that somehow I would not have told my sister about an affair. I also suspect that if I had, she would have broached the subject by now. Reconnecting with Nicole might have helped with my recovery. Another face as a trigger. Rachel would not have been shy about bringing her to my attention.

I get a text back telling me that home-schooling is in-sodding-sane, Ewan is fine but that Rosie seems to be coming down with another fever and that the dog has learned to chew slippers.

It sounds like she's having fun. My mobile rings. It's Rosie. She wants to tell me to remember to wash my hands for twenty seconds and sings Happy Birthday twice so I know how long twenty seconds is. I can hear her hacking cough. I tell her and then a slightly frantic-sounding Rachel to look after themselves and that I will be fine. I use the landline to phone a different number. No one answers, so I leave a message. I find some decent clothes to put on, lay them out and have a shower.

I'd better make an effort because I've just asked Nicole over for a drink.

14

Nicole arrives at 7pm on the dot. I'm on the first floor so I buzz her in and then wait with the flat door open for the lift to arrive. She's smiling as she steps out and stands in the hallway. There's an awkward moment as we regard one another and then I invite her in and close the door. She looks around, her body language tense.

'This is nice,' she says.

'You've never been here before?'

Her smile is tight-lipped. 'No. This was Emma territory.' She slips off her coat. She's changed out of her workday clothes into tight jeans and something strappy and sleeveless. I think Rachel would call it a camisole. But I don't attempt that. Given my aphasic luck, it could come out very wrong.

'Come through,' I say, and Nicole follows me into the living room. The only room with decent chairs. Her bare shoulders and arms look toned and she moves with a fluid grace. But when she crosses the threshold, she stops and stares at my wall. After a few seconds she approaches and her eyes dart from one photograph to the next, tracing the lines I've drawn to connect them.

I feel the urge to explain.

'This is to help me remember who everyone is. Or was.' I point to my mother's image labelled by Rachel.

Nicole's eyes open wide as she reads the label beneath. 'You don't remember your mother?'

I shake my head. 'Or Emma, or my father, though he lives abroad anyway. I didn't recognise Rachel when I woke up in the hospital in Turkey. Everyone here' – I sweep a finger to indicate the wall – 'had to be reintroduced to me. Like you. Some bits have come back but they're random.' I tap the side of my head. 'Last week I had a vivid image of a seaside town and me and Rachel playing on a beach. She said it was more than likely Tenby, where we always went on holiday. When I googled it, there it was.'

I'm standing close to Nicole. She's wonderfully fragrant. Her eyes never leave the wall. 'They said at the practice that it was a severe injury. That you'd suffered some brain damage. But I didn't appreciate how bad.'

'You're not going to cry again, are you?'

She sniffs and it turns into a laugh. 'No. I promise.'

'My neurosurgeon says that I had massive bruising of both frontal lobes and my parietal lobe on one side. They had to give me drugs to reduce the swelling. Those bits are responsible for memories, comprehending language and interpreting meaning and emotion. And then there's the diffuse axonal injury.'

She turns towards me, eyes wide open.

I stand behind her, inhaling. 'There was a concrete jetty where a tourist ship tied up; a kind of sailing ship. Cheap boobs and... I mean booze and loud music. They'd sail around the bay and party for a while, then go off somewhere else. They think I might have fallen off this jetty in the dark and hit my head on a metal truncheon. I mean stanchion. Either way I suffered what's known as a blunt deceleration injury. It causes a shearing force in the white matter.'

Nicole turns from the wall to look at me, horrified.

'Sorry. I know this stuff off by heart. I'm telling you because it's the reason I've taken so long to reintegrate. The reason I've only just started getting about.'

She says nothing, so I offer her a drink. It's a sudden swerve. I resist the urge to tell her it's all a part of what's happened to me – technically, they're called rapid flights of thought. Instead, she accepts the offer and we move across to the sofa. When we've both got our glasses half full of the best Riesling I could find in Sainsbury's, I raise one to her. 'Thanks for coming.'

'Thank you for inviting me.' Her fingers play with the stem of her glass. 'As I say, I thought I'd never see you again.'

'Well, here I am. Damaged goods, but still me.' We clink glasses. 'If you want to eat, I can send out.'

Nicole shakes her head. 'I'm not hungry.' She taps a flat stomach. 'Too many butterflies.'

I don't know how old she is. Younger than me, that's for certain. My best guess is late twenties but age-gauging has never been my strongest trait.

'Why did you ask me here, Cam?'

Her question is fair and there is no point in me lying. I struggle with the nuances of that anyway. And Adam says blunt is better than saying nothing. 'What you said to me yesterday gave me quite a shock. I needed time to detest it. I mean digest it.' I shake my head. 'I get words muddled up sometimes. I'm sorry.'

Nicole's brows furrow and she waves a hand in dismissal. 'Don't apologise. Now that you've had time to digest it, what do you think?'

'What I'm wondering is, did Emma know?'

Nicole's head shake is vehement. 'No. No way. I used to see her every day when she was locuming. No way could she have known.'

'Didn't she even suspend... suspect a little?'

'No. I honestly don't think she did.'

I look at the wine in my glass. Swirl it around so that it mimics the thoughts in my head.

'Have I made you feel bad?' Nicole asks.

'It doesn't sound like a particularly honourable thing to have done.'

She sits up then. 'There is nothing for you to be guilty about, Cam. Not after what she was doing to you.'

'Doing to me?'

Nicole lets out a deep exhalation. 'Emma had been playing away with someone at the hospital she did sessions at.'

I want to say something, but suddenly I'm dumb. This is even more startling news. Why is it only now I'm hearing of this? Annoyance flairs but I check it, wondering again who else, if anyone, even knew. Nicole sees my confusion.

'It had been going on for weeks. You suspected something and turned to me. You knew Emma and I were close at work. We, you and I, met in the same cafe we had coffee in yesterday. You asked me outright if I knew. I couldn't lie to you. I couldn't stand to see what it was doing to you. You broke down and... things kind of spiralled from there.'

'So Emma had an affair first?'

'She did.'

'All sounds very complicated.'

'It was. But it isn't anymore.' Nicole puts her glass down and turns towards me. Our knees touch. I shift back.

'Why didn't I confront her?'

'You were going to. You started looking for evidence.'

'Evidence?'

'You found some bills. Credit card receipts that Emma had from restaurants you'd never been to.'

I get up and retrieve the folder Nicole gave me. I show her

the photocopied receipts. Nicole lets out an empty laugh and her gaze slides up to engage mine. 'I saw these, but I never twigged. You made copies but then you said they disappeared from your briefcase.'

We eye the sheets with new suspicion. Nicole adds, 'This was all just before you were about to go away. You said it would be a great opportunity to get everything out in the open. No distractions.'

'Didn't you mind that I was going away?'

'Yes. But it had to be done. Something was up with Emma. The person she was involved with had a terrible reputation.'

'In what way?'

'The rumour was that she might have been pilfering opiates.'

'She?'

'That's what I heard. Some anaesthetist.'

I try to process this, search for something to say. Come up with, 'Is she still around?'

Nicole shakes her head. 'Long gone. The Middle East. Kuwait, or the UAE.'

A longer pause. More processing. 'So Emma stole the copies I made?'

Nicole shrugs. 'Looks like it. All I know is you couldn't find them.'

I get up and walk across the room. Rain drums at the window. I pace a bit. It helps. 'This is all so monkey... I mean murky.'

'I'm sorry if I've upset you.'

'No. I need to know these things...' The sentence trails off because I don't want to say the words aloud.

I need to know these things because of the bearing they might have on what happened in Turkey.

I turn again to the wall and peer at Emma's photograph. 'I can't remember her. I feel nothing when I look at her photo.'

'And what about me, Cam? What do you feel when you look at me?' Nicole gets up and joins me at the wall. This close she smells wonderful.

I let my head drop. 'I don't know what to think.' My default state.

Nicole's hand is on my chin, lifting it back up. 'Maybe I could remind you.'

Her kiss is soft and long and for a moment I'm paralysed. But she doesn't move away and I let go, lose myself in the moment.

Eventually, we break off and Nicole waits with a questioning look. My reply is to lean in and kiss her again. She pulls me back over to the sofa, pulls out her phone.

'We had a playlist,' she says. 'Can I hook this up?'

There's a small, neat Bluetooth speaker on the bookshelf. Nicole walks over, presses a few buttons on the machine and her phone. Seconds later George Ezra is telling us all about Budapest. Nicole comes back to where I'm sitting and starts, slowly, to undress, swaying to the music, until, to my feverish astonishment, all she has on is matching dark underwear. She works out, no doubt about that. Her skin has a glowing tint. What I see is flawless.

'Remember me now?' she asks.

I don't answer. I can't.

'Where's the bedroom?'

I point. She holds out a hand and leads me to it. I want to tell her I haven't slept with anyone since the accident, but somehow it doesn't matter. With Nicole's help I know what to do. And she's very helpful. We do lots of things I don't think I've done before. Or I didn't know I could. Her hands are small, her fingers strong and probing. I think Nicole is adventurous. And I don't argue. No man with a pulse would.

A good hour later I get up and slip on a T-shirt and jeans and make us both an omelette. Nicole pulls one of my old rugby shirts from a drawer and pulls it on. She doesn't bother with anything else. She joins me at the table in bare feet. She seems very relaxed, even laughs at my stupid jokes while we eat. I tell her about my journey from a hospital bed in Turkey to now: my slight limp, my funny foot, the scars around the left side of my face where they put me back together. And not forgetting my duff eye.

I tell her what I truly can and can't do. She tells me about the three weeks we spent together before Turkey. The clandestine meetings in cinemas and cafes. Sneaking into her bed when her flatmate was out. About how we were both upset about the change in Emma. How we were guilty about the duplicitousness but sought refuge in each other. How I was planning on confronting it once and for all.

At one point she looks up and scopes my countertop. 'Why are there two coffee machines?'

'My sister bought me one. I liked it so much I bought another. In case the one she bought broke down.'

She looks at me as if waiting for a punchline. There isn't one.

'Okay.' She tries to keep a straight face but fails.

'Rachel says I'm impulsive. But I don't think it makes me a terrible person.'

Nicole gives it up and throws her head back in a full-throated laugh. 'There are worse things to be.'

When we've finished, she asks for the bathroom. While I'm stacking the dishes, she comes back out into the kitchen again, naked. We go back to the bedroom. Another hour flies deliciously by.

At around ten, Nicole gets up and dresses and sits on the edge of my bed. 'I better go. I brought nothing to change into and I have work tomorrow. I wasn't sure how this would go.'

'I think it went well.' I know I'm grinning.

'Feel better?'

I nod.

'Thank you,' she says.

'For what?'

'For letting me have this. I've waited two years for you to turn up at my door. Hoping you'd be a white knight.'

I start. 'I'm no hero. But I'm glad I went to Emma's old practice. I'm glad you saw me.'

She grins a delectably mischievous grin. 'We can do this again. Any time. Softly, softly still if you like.'

'I can't believe you don't have a boyfriend.'

'Who says I don't.' Nicole tags a giggle on the end of her words.

'I... I assumed...'

She puts her hand on my chest. 'That's the other reason for keeping this low-key for the moment. There is someone but it isn't serious. Nothing like what we had. What maybe we could still have.'

I stare into her eyes. They stare back into mine.

'Don't worry,' she says. 'I will sort that out within days. That is if you want me to?'

I blink. Still so much to process. I say, 'Why do you think Emma wrote *pants on fire* in her notebook on the last but one page?'

Nicole tilts her head back. 'Guilt? There were other things too, weren't there? Dates when you'd be away, am I right?'

'I think so.'

'Then maybe she was planning things with her junky lover and felt bad that she was lying to you.'

I wince at her words. Emma's been portrayed as this perfect partner. It's hard for me to hear she might not have been.

'We'll never truly know, though, will we?'

She's right. We will never know. I get up and follow her to my door. Let her out.

'Text me when you're ready,' she says. 'I'll be waiting.' She kisses me once again and then she's gone. I go back to the living room to look at the wall and realise, with a pang of regret, that I have no photograph of Nicole to put up there. Then again, if I did I'd need to explain who she is and I'm not quite sure I'm ready to do that yet.

She said we could do this any time. I'd like that. Very much. But first I have to think. I sit down and stare at the wall aware that in the space of forty-eight hours everything has changed. But in reality, nothing has. When I went to Turkey with Emma, our relationship might not have been in the best of health. But, besides Nicole, I am the only one who has this knowledge.

Or am I?

15

There's still some wine left so I half fill a glass and flip open my laptop. The screen lights up with the last image I'd viewed. A film I was halfway through when I lost concentration. That happens a lot, wonderful film though it was. One of Josh's special recommendations. 'A simple tale of seafaring folk' in his words.

Duuun dun duuun dun...

Yeah. Thanks, Josh. It didn't exactly give me nightmares but it has made me think twice about going to the beach. Now I know why Josh so loves saying, 'We're gonna need a bigger boat' whenever he gets the opportunity. Which seems to arise at least twice a week.

I open up Chrome and navigate to Emma's memorial page on Facebook. There are lots of posts. But none from me. It was Josh who explained that Facebook have a process for deceased people. They will mothball accounts unless told not to do so. The way they avoid that is with legacy accounts. A page like this will have a legacy contact who manages it. In Emma's case it's her sister, Harriet. She decides who can post, which profile pictures can be seen, and what last message from Emma's profile can be read by random visitors like me.

Some people think it's macabre; especially since designating a legacy contact is done by the Facebook page owner while he, or she, is alive. But I can see the sense of it. Of course I can, under the circumstances. Though it has made me wonder what could have made Emma ponder her own mortality enough to act on this and even discuss it. Perhaps it was a pact they made. The sort of thing sisters do. That's sheer conjecture on my part and I should probably ask Harriet. Or I could stick my head in a wasp's nest. It's a toss-up which one would be the more excruciating.

But the memorial page fulfils a function. Emma's friends got no chance to say goodbye. This gives them the opportunity to do so. It lets friends and family post memories and stories. Everyone except me. Josh says Harriet went a 'bit mental' over what happened.

She certainly went more than a bit mental when she verbally accosted me at the cemetery.

I scroll through the messages of condolence. They're called tributes now. It was Emma's birthday last month and that triggered a flurry of posts. Some names I recognise from contacts and photographs Rachel has talked me through, but most are meaningless to me. I would have liked to have posted something, even a simple 'thanks for the memories' birthday thing, but no chance. Sometimes I wish that I could message Emma herself, see if she's still out there somewhere, or her spirit at least. See if she has any answers to the questions my trip to the surgery and meeting Nicole has thrown up.

But that's just wishful thinking.

I fall asleep a little after eleven, my concentration shot to pieces. Partly because of Nicole and the wine, partly because I forgot to take my modafinil that teatime, allowing this evening's quetiapine to work unopposed. A real brain-musher when mixed with too much alcohol.

So I sleep and I dream. The odd thing is, despite my fancy fugues, my dreams are usually boring affairs. Adam has gone through the difference between fugues and lucid dreams many times. The REM thing is the key. I'm awake when I fugue and I've never managed the lucid dreaming thing while I'm asleep, despite Josh's enthusiasm for it. He, of course, has all sorts of theories. Entire subcultures of wannabe lucids live out there with a raft of suggestions of how to achieve it. But none of my dreams, at least the ones I recall, are worthy of me ever wanting to get involved even if it were possible.

Yet, when I wake up the next morning, I sense that something has been processed. My subconscious has had a clear-out and for once things seem more in focus. My *to-do* drawer has acquired a filing system.

But I have questions about Emma that need answering. As of this moment I can only think of one person to ask.

I fix a second Americano, pick up my mobile and scroll to the K's in my contacts. I haven't dialled this number once since my accident, though the person it belongs to has contacted me frequently. Rachel would have a fit. But Rachel is in voluntary self-isolation with her kids.

So I bring up the number and dial it.

16

Detective Sergeant Rhian Keely stares at her computer screen, waiting for the system to download some files. The server has been playing up again and is taking for ever. Another fatal stabbing in Peckham has thrown up gang connections and she is compiling a known associates list so that the Violent Crime Task Force can pull someone in. A shitty case that ends a shitty week. Two other knife crimes have left a thirty-one-year-old mother of three a widow and a second victim on life support at the ITU in Guy's.

This latest case, an apparently random attack on a twenty-year-old student walking home minding his own business, is, she suspects, connected. Tit for tat, only this time the perpetrator, a fifteen-year-old kid called Antoinee Michales, mistook his target and stuck the wrong guy. A completely innocent kid on his way home from the Tube. Somehow it makes the whole shit-show exponentially worse.

Keely is thirty-five, joined the ranks when she was twenty-seven and got her sergeant's exam relatively early. There's been some pressure on her to take her inspector's exam because her superiors know talent when they see it. Keely knows that the money would be nice and is not bothered about the extra responsibility. She knows she can do the job. Indeed, on more than one occasion because of recruitment and promotional freezes, she's acted up and earned a pat on the back for doing so. Her ambivalence has nothing to do with lack of ambition. It has everything to do with when she and Viri, short for Virat, produce the first of the two children they have planned. They'll need a bigger space than the flat they currently share in Norbury. Viri teaches science to high achievers at an all-girls' school where the annual fee is more than his take home pay. They've only been trying for a couple of months and Keely senses it won't be long. She's not hung up on it. Knows it can take a few tries. Viri's all for that. And it'll be a lot easier to fend off those encouraging looks from the super once a bump starts to show.

These thoughts churn around in her head as she watches the maddening little wheel go round and round in the corner of her computer screen.

Her phone vibrating is a welcome distraction. She glances at the name that comes up and for a second it doesn't register. Todd isn't a name she... but then her excellent memory kicks in. She frowns, accepts the call and puts the phone to her ear.

'DS Rhian Keely,' she announces.

'Hi, Sergeant Keely. This is Cameron Todd. I wonder if you remember me?'

Keely almost laughs out loud. Remember Cameron Todd? How could she forget? The Emma Roxburgh case made headlines for months and she, along with a DCI called Thom Larkson, were designated as liaison officers. They caught the case because the only witness, Cameron Todd, was brought back to the UK from Turkey for treatment and rehabilitation and both Todd and the dead woman lived on their patch in Southwark. 'Mr Todd, nice to hear your voice. Are you well?'

'Not bad. I've been out of hospital for a few months. Mudding through.'

Keely knows he means muddling but doesn't correct him. Her conversations with him previously were peppered with these linguistic errors. She remembers Mrs Coren, her English teacher, calling them malapropisms. Used to denote ignorance particularly for comic effect in literature. But here, Todd's horrific injuries are to blame. And unless he laughs, she isn't going to.

'You must be wondering why I'm calling you?'

Keely smiles. Todd is nothing if not direct. 'I'm all ears.'

'Something's happened that's made me think about the accident.'

At this Keely sits up. She knows that Todd's recovery is little short of a miracle given the extent of his injuries. Yet despite reassurances from the doctors and surgeons that his amnesia is a genuine manifestation of this trauma, Keely has harboured a healthy scepticism because that is what she's paid to do. 'What is it you've been thinking about?'

'Emma. I still can't remember her. I've tried talking to her family but it's not easy.'

An understatement if ever there was one. Even though Emma died in Turkey, the Met decided to furnish an FLO; a family liaison officer to help the Roxburghs navigate the choppy waters of being interviewed by Turkish police through a translator, and the media feeding frenzy that accompanied all that. Keely experienced at first-hand the bitter resentment expressed by Harriet Roxburgh who blamed Cameron Todd for her sister's death. And continues to do so in the absence of any shred of evidence that he'd been directly involved in any wrongdoing. Her bitterness stems from a deep and old-fashioned belief that Emma had been Todd's responsibility. And however and whatever had happened he was therefore to blame. It was irrational and visceral and not open to discussion, fuelled as it was by a typhoon of grief.

'How can I help?'

'I want to be sure that there's nothing in our past – or her past – that might have had any bearing on the... on what happened.'

Keely feels her eyebrows knit. Todd's words are clumsy but she can just about decipher the subtext. Guilt. 'What's brought this on?'

'I'm driving now. I went to Emma's old surgery, where she used to do locusts–'

Keely knows it's locums.

'–and it jogged a bit of memory. I need to know if it's important or not. And I thought, if anyone knows Emma's story – her past and all – besides her family, it would be you. And you might actually speak to me about it.'

Keely ponders this. Is it a fair request? As their FLO, she is indeed familiar with Emma Roxburgh's life. And despite what Harriet Roxburgh and, by default, Emma's parents might want in terms of contact with Cameron Todd, she is under no obligation to acquiesce to their bruised wishes. Besides, the Turkish police still have Emma Roxburgh's death as an open file. She can't quite remember the last time she corresponded with them, but it was on the basis that they keep lines of communication open. A year ago she might have rung DCI Larkson for a chat about this, but he has long since left, promoted to Thames Valley as a super. As far as the Roxburgh case is concerned, Keely, and Keely alone, is Southwark's one and only expert.

'You have as much right to know as anyone. Though there isn't much to tell,' Keely says.

'I get the impression that those around me tell me only what they think I should know. That Emma was lovely and a beautiful person and that we were a good batch. Match. But people don't want to upset me. I want to find out what really happened in Turkey, sergeant. I think I'm ready to do that.'

'I'm all for that, Mr Todd–'

'Cameron. Call me Cameron.'

'Okay, Cameron. Why don't you come into the station? I'll make myself available this afternoon, say two-ish? We can go through what's known. Unless you want me to come to you?'

'No, I'll come to the police station. I know where it is. I'll walk. My trainer says that walking is good for me.'

When Todd rings off, Keely turns and calls to a detective sitting a couple of desks away. A straight-out-of-college-with-a-degree newbie called Daniel Messiter. 'Dan, your lucky day. You get to hold hands with the server while she downloads all we have on that charming group of individuals known as the Woolend Crew.'

Messiter looks stricken. 'But I'm supposed to get these reports done–'

'Multitasking. Part of your apprenticeship. Write and watch the screen at the same time. You'll get the hang of it. Sit here while I use a different screen to request some more files because I do not want to log off and lose what we have so far.'

'But how–'

'Do the report on a pad. Use paper and a pen, then type it up. You'll be amazed how much time you'll save having edited it before you punch it in.' Messiter eases his long frame out of the chair and walks over.

He's a foot taller than Keely, but a mile naiver.

17

After I've spoken with Keely, I mooch around, do some chores, and watch the news. Italy is tightening the lockdown, all schools and universities shut, all businesses except those providing essential services shut. The USA has ordered a flight ban from twenty-six European countries. Australia and New Zealand are calling all their residents home. I wonder why I find all this more disturbing than *World War Z* which I've made the mistake of starting to watch. In the film, at least you can tell who your enemy is. At least you can see the zombies coming. Covid-19 is a silent, creeping, stealthy killer. Could be the bloke next to you in Sainsbury's. Could be the handrail on the Tube.

I shut off the TV, go to the kitchen and do some work for Josh, eat a biscuit for breakfast while I do so.

I watch the last half hour of *World War Z* and am amazed to see the finale of the film takes place in a remote WHO research facility on the outskirts of Cardiff of all places. I know Cardiff. They tell me I played a little rugby and had been to the Principality Stadium more than once to watch international matches. When I see images, a vague recollection stirs. Like seeing a photograph underwater; insubstantial but there. The stadium is in the heart of the city. No long march out to the suburbs like Twickenham or Dublin. I'd like to go back one day and soak up the atmosphere.

By half eleven I'm flagging but I don't give in to it. My skin seems greasy and I need a shower. So I haul myself to the bathroom, my brain clogged with the events of the last couple of days vicariously mingling with Brad Pitt's fantasy adventures, slow-cooked in the real-life terror of a world in the grip of a creeping nightmare.

I stand in the shower and let the water hose me down from head to foot. Rachel has given me some shampoo that smells of coconuts. I massage a dollop into my scalp, lather up the rest of me with soap and get my thoughts in order, setting what's real and what isn't in their rightful places. It's astonishing how little difference there appears to be between the two.

Brad Pitt goes into fantasy.

Covid-19 unfortunately doesn't.

Nicole, for a moment, hovers between the two. But then I remember what we did last night, and my flesh responds accordingly. Proof she's real. Oh yes, she is real. And so is DS Keely and Josh and Rachel. But as the water sluices and pummels my skin, I sense too that I am not the same person as I was before I got into Emma's VW and drove to Woolwich.

I've been through a sea change. Something that needed to happen to break me out of the doldrums; still I am not sure what it'll bring.

The shower is as good as a double espresso. I think of Nicole and get an image of plain sailing.

But then Keely swims into focus and I wonder if I'm heading towards rougher seas.

18

At 13.55 Thursday afternoon, Keely gets a call from the desk sergeant. Someone in reception for her. She walks down from her first-floor desk in Southwark Station and sees Cameron Todd sitting on the bench. He's put on a little weight since she saw him last. Not a bad thing given his previous scarecrow appearance. She wonders when it was they last talked. A good six or seven months, she reckons.

He stands when she comes through the security door. Slow movements, careful. His gait is broad-based, his stance rigid, favouring his left leg. She remembers he had balance issues. He looks at her with an intense, serious gaze. She remembers reading in the reports that he has a blunted affect. The report was lengthy, and that little diamond was in the middle of a list of medical problems. She hadn't known what it meant and had to look it up. But she remembers what she read.

```
A person with blunted affect has a
significantly    reduced    intensity    in
emotional expression.
```

He is difficult to read. His emotional tone may or may not be appropriate to the situation he finds himself in. That bothers her because she believes she's become good over the years at sniffing out the petty liars and cheats. Not that Todd was ever one of those. Again, she finds it oddly disconcerting but pushes it away and offers a greeting. 'Mr Todd, good to see you.'

'Likewise, Sergeant Keely. But it's Cameron. Please.'

He doesn't reciprocate when she smiles. Instead, his eyes track hers with unnerving directness. Took her a while to get used to it before, even though she now knows there's no subtext. Merely his way of trying to read expressions. A skill that most people take for granted but which he has had to learn afresh. She notes the scars over the left side of his cheek, the lines and a jagged star whiter than the rest of his skin. A slight depression in the bone signifies where metal has been used to repair some fragments too, but his left eye, the one damaged in the accident, is no longer red and angry-looking.

'Still no vision in that one, I'm afraid. I see vague shadows, light and dark. They got to it too late.'

Keely nods, annoyed with herself at making the tell so obvious. She hadn't meant to stare at his damaged face. But that's the thing with Cameron Todd. There's no outward sign that he's aware of what she is doing. But he's intuited it anyway. He'd make a great poker player.

She's read the reports again prior to his visit so she remembers that his retinal detachment went untreated while they kept him alive, though they pushed it back with a gas bubble eventually. Difficult to blame the doctors; they'd left it so long because they'd had no idea he would survive. Loss of vision in one eye was on the bottom of their list of potentially bad outcomes. It said so in the reports.

His dark hair is short at the sides and back, a little thicker on top, flecked now with a little grey at the temples. He's clean-shaven and when he moves to follow her through the door into the belly of the old building, he does so smoothly. None of the staccato movements she remembered from before, though there is that slight remnant of a limp, she notices.

'You found us all right then?' she calls over her shoulder.

'I did.'

'Another couple of years and I doubt we'll be here. Budget cuts and all.'

'That's a shame. I like this old building.'

'Bugger to heat in the winter.'

She takes him to an interview room and gives him some water in a paper cup while she retrieves her file from her first-floor desk. An informal chat, not an interview. Even so, he deserves a little privacy.

'You're looking well, Cameron,' she says, re-entering the room.

'Thank you. So do you, sergeant.'

Keely cocks an eye. She knows he's being polite and that she needs to get to the gym more than the once a week she's managing now. And she needs to stop going to Viri's mum's for supper every Friday night. Trouble is the food is wonderful and far too convenient even if it is in Harrow. She goes because Viri's their only son and he's dutiful. No hardship; they're sweet and his mum is a brilliant cook.

Keely and Viri visit Keely's parents every other Sunday. That's an altogether stuffier affair. Her dad still works in North-wick Park Hospital as a stroke consultant and she has no idea what they'll do when he retires. How they'll cope. The job is his and, by default, her mother's life. Neither of them understands why Keely chose to work in the Met and not go into medicine like her sister. Sometimes neither does Keely. But those times are rare. Cases like Cameron Todd's keep the flames of interest flickering. Part of the reason why she hasn't rushed to climb the ladder. After DI there's DCI and that would mean much more of a desk job than out and about in the meat of investigations. Some would say slog. Keely knows she bucks the trend by enjoying the hands-on stuff. Even if it means having to wash the dirt off with industrial strength disinfectant a lot of the time.

She glances down and opens the file. 'So, Cameron, what can I do for you?'

'As I said, I've started driving. I visited Emma's old surgery at Woolwich. The doctors say I should revisit old places. Someone there gave me what was left of Emma's stuff. Wasn't much, just an old folder, but there was a notebook and Emma had written something and I... it made me wonder about us.'

'You and Emma?'

'Yes.'

'What did you wonder?'

He has a slight tremor in his left hand, and he holds his left thumb in his right fist to quieten the movement. 'My memory is like a lost hard drive. What's happened to me is in there, but I can't access the damned thing. Like having a search engine at your fingertips but with no keyboard to type in a request.'

'Do you mind me asking what she wrote?'

'No. I don't mind.' He pauses and for a second Keely wonders if he's being literal, missing the nuance of her questions, but then he reaches to his pocket and adds, 'I've written it out for you.' Cam hands over a sheet of paper. On it, in capital letters are the words:

14TH OCTOBER. CAM'S DO WITH QUANTIPLE.
PANTS ON FIRE?

Keely reads it twice and then asks, 'Does the date mean anything to you?'

'No. But I did some research. Turns out the company I worked for had an annual meeting. I was meant to attend.'

'Can you remember attending?'

'No. But I realise what pants on fire means.'

'Okay. So what do you think the two things taken together mean?'

'After I read this, I thought perhaps we, Emma and me... I had this impression that things were not as perfect as people made out they were between us.'

Keely frowns. She has a ton of work to do. The last thing she needs is a half-recovered trauma victim telling her he's had a *feeling* about a case that most people accept as a tragic accident. She recalls the statements from Emma Roxburgh's family describing Cameron Todd. They'd said nothing that might be classed as an outright accusation, but it was clear they had not liked Cameron much. Thought that Emma should have done better than a nerd. They weren't snobs, but they'd lost their middle-class golden girl and needed someone to blame. Keely has seen enough of grief to realise it distorts logic and renders the most rational mind an emotional shipwreck. Still, their attitude to a very damaged Cameron Todd had not endeared them to Rhian Keely.

'I realise how this sounds. All a bit wishy-wash-up. I meant wishy-washy. You've looked into Emma's life. Was there anything to suggest she was involved in anything?'

'Like what?'

He shrugs. 'I have this weird idea that she got involved in something to do with the hospital. Some person who was dealing drugs.'

Keely puts down the file. 'Can I ask where the hell all this has come from so suddenly?'

Cameron's gaze is steady. 'All I can tell you is what my brain is telling me.'

'I can recall nothing in the file that suggested Emma was anything other than a first-class citizen. She was not in any trouble with us. No record of any wrongdoing.' She almost adds, *as opposed to you and your misspent youth. The feckless student reprimanded for possession of cannabis. The festival arrest for drunk and disorderly.* But what's the point. He doesn't remember.

Cam's head shifts away, searching the room. Small, jerky movements that remind Keely of a bird. 'Is this being recorded?'

'No.'

'So can you find out if there was something like that going on at the hospital where she worked? See if someone was abusing drugs maybe? I have a suspicion it might have been an anaesthetist.'

Keely sits back. This is not what she's been expecting. 'That's remarkably specific.'

Cameron nods. 'It's what I recall.'

Keely taps the file with her pen. 'Even if there is, how does that affect what happened in Turkey?'

Cam flattens the flesh of his left cheek with the palm of his hand and runs his fingers along the angle of his jaw. 'Might be nothing. Might be everything.'

'But all you have is a feeling?'

'No one knows what happened in Turkey. Feelings are all I have to go on for now.'

Keely looks at the file and then up. 'If visiting her place of work has helped, it might be an idea to visit Turkey...'

Cam hesitates and then says, 'You are probably right. But given the travel restriction the FCO are putting out daily I doubt that this is the time to visit anywhere.'

Good answer. And he's right. Still, the copper in her can't help wondering at the convenience of it all.

'I'm sorry if I've wasted your time,' Cam says.

'You haven't. This is an ongoing investigation. And I did say to you that if you ever had any fresh information, I wanted to hear it.'

'This is all I have.'

Keely shuts the file. 'Okay. I'll look into it.'

'Thank you. Do you think it is worth me contacting Harriet and asking her?'

Keely stifles the urge to laugh out loud. *Not unless you want your head bitten off, chewed up and posted back to you in a brown parcel.* She says instead, 'I'd wait if I were you. No sense in upsetting Emma's family if this has no legs.'

Cam blinks, his gaze unflinching.

She sees him out and fetches a tea before heading back to her desk. Messiter is concentrating, doing his utmost to appear busy and not catch her eye. 'Any joy with those calls, Daniel?'

He's been tasked with following up on another suspect in the Peckham killing's alibi. A thankless time-suck. Especially when the people you're trying to engage consider talking to the police tantamount to stabbing themselves in the eye.

Messiter rotates his hand in a gesture of frustration.

Keely writes the words *Guy's* and *anaesthetist* on a Post-it note and sticks it on the rim of Messiter's screen.

'I want you to go to the hospital and chat with whoever runs HR. Ask them about disciplinary actions against doctors abusing drugs in 2018.'

Messiter turns a quizzical face up. 'What about the stabbing–'

'Think of it as a lesson in time management, Daniel. And there's no need to thank me. The pleasure's all mine.'

19

March still has blustery winter hanging on to its coat-tails as I walk back to the flat from Borough High Street. I ponder my visit to the police. Sergeant Keely was always polite to me. I could see that she was confused by what I said, but I hope she believed me. And now we'll see if she can dig up anything about this anaesthetist.

I didn't mention Nicole because I don't want to tell anyone about her yet. Not until she sorts out her own life. At least, that's what I keep telling myself. But of course, there is another reason. I'm wary of what people might say. And by people I mean Rachel. She's a mother hen on acid when it comes to me. She'll say that I'm being naïve. That I'm gullible. She's right to a degree. When you have bugger all recollection of what's happened to you in your life you have no option but to take everything at face value. It's my life, though, and I need to get on with it.

Like they say in that film of ordinary prison folk – Josh's pithy description of *The Shawshank Redemption* which is so far one of my all-time favourites – it's a question of 'get busy living'.

I always leave out the other part when I repeat this mantra to

Rachel because if I ever said, 'or get busy dying' she'd yell loud enough to shatter all the glass in a three-mile radius.

I've been in limbo for months. I've tried to embrace the fact that I'm part of a bigger tragedy, but the truth is I have only me to measure my experience against. I'm not Emma, nor her family. I empathise, I do; the Roxburghs lost a daughter and a sister. But I'm Cameron Todd who had to relearn how to tie his shoelaces and how to wipe his own arse. Just a confused crock of a bloke into whose blighted life walks Nicole Grant. A pretty, sympathetic, breath of fresh air. Too good to be true has crossed my mind many a time since yesterday. But fate can be a strange mistress. And, as Josh would say, usually in a shit American accent, 'About time you caught a break.'

I perceive that I am no catch. Not now. One glance in the bloody mirror confirms that in spades. Perhaps I never was a catch. Harriet has a firm opinion on that if I ever need confirmation. Though her sister, Emma, must have thought differently.

I'm one-eyed, shaky on my feet, too thin, and have a tremor that rules out neurosurgery as a career (Josh again). No oil painting doesn't even come close. But Nicole remembers me from before. Stronger, fitter, relatively undamaged if you accept thirty-odd years of drinking a bit too much and eating a lot of crap as not too damaging. And it was definitely me kissing her in that selfie she showed me. She's watched me from afar. Seen me survive, too scared to come near me because I might not be the person I was. Terrified that I might reject her out of hand. Not remember anything about her. How much courage has it taken for her to finally reveal herself to me?

She's been remarkable. She's been brave. In return I owe it to her to play things cool. Even if I get a little warm under the collar whenever I think of her.

~

I spend the afternoon doing my thing again. A bit of work for Josh, some TV. A lot of reading; technical stuff in the main. I'm playing catch-up with the developer side of things, but the internet is an amazing source of more or less everything. So I'm knee-deep in some articles on artificial intelligence when the doorbell rings at quarter past five.

I press the intercom.

'Hi there. Remember me?' Nicole's voice is tinny through the intercom. 'I'm not staying, but I wanted to see you so badly I thought I'd call on my way home from work on the off-chance–'

I buzz her in before she can finish the sentence.

I put the kettle on. But she doesn't want tea. She declines the offer by saying, 'Drinking tea in bed can make such a mess.'

She knows her way to the bedroom by now. I follow. No complaints. We fall into my made bed. A pulse-surging repeat of last night but more measured because I've learned what she wants me to do to her. And I'm an apt pupil, so it seems. We don't speak, but there are giggles and a little laughter. The day before it was nervous. Today, sheer abandonment. She's lithe and moves with gymnastic grace. Sometimes she's under me, sometimes above, active and dynamic and exciting. I don't have to ask her to do anything. Nicole has skills. She's patient and tantalising but I read hunger in her expression. Nicole likes to be fed.

I will have to remake the bed.

Wash the sheets, too.

Later, I make tea. We sit at the kitchen table to drink it. Me with my shirt out and feet bare, Nicole in my old rugby jersey again with the sleeves hanging over her hands like mittens.

'I went to the police today,' I say.

'What?' Nicole blinks at me over the rim of her cup.

'I spoke to the sergeant who's assigned to my case. To my and Emma's cases. Both still open because the Turkish police haven't totally accepted it was an accident. Sergeant Keely is the link between here and there. A lesson.'

'Liaison?'

She says it nicely. As a question. I nod.

'What did you tell them?' Nicole asks. She's intrigued.

'I asked them if they knew anything about Emma being involved in something iffy at the hospital.'

Nicole leans in, eyes wide. 'Oh my God. Really?'

'Yes. It was news to them. They knew nothing, but Keely says she will look into it. And I believe her.'

There's a pensive pause before Nicole replies. 'If anyone could find out what went on they could, couldn't they?'

'I trust Keely.'

'Weren't they surprised at you just turning up?'

'I told them something had come back to me. A shard of memory from visiting the surgery. I even showed them what Emma had written in her notebook. I didn't say anything about you.'

But Nicole looks eager. 'I'll speak to them any time if they want me to.'

'They will. Once Keely comes back to me, if she finds something out, we can see her together.'

'Perfect.' Nicole's eyes sparkle. But then her expression becomes uncharacteristically serious. 'I need to get this next week out of the way. There's a wedding. One of my best friends. And she knows Aaron – that's the bloke I've been going out with – too. Otherwise, I'd walk away now. But it would devastate her and I'd get blamed for ruining her day. Drama queen doesn't even come close. She's been planning the thing for fourteen months, going large on the day. I've already refused to be a bridesmaid in a dress the colour of a cow's womb. Yesterday she was hysterical at the thought it might be called off because of the virus. And this weekend there's another hen do. The third.' Nicole rolls her eyes. It makes her look cute.

She catches me watching her intently and her face dissolves into sympathy. She grabs my hand. 'Don't worry. Once the confetti's thrown I am walking away from Aaron for good.'

'You don't have to do that for me.'

'It's not just for you. This' – she bouquets her hand up and out – 'has made me realise how much I need to. Seeing you has made me understand how much of a deep hole I'm in. If I don't start digging myself out... Aaron and me...' She shakes her head. 'He's the last in a long line of men I've just stumbled into looking for another you. And I am not a bitch. Not usually. I'm even guilty about coming here tonight.'

'Are you?'

She nods. Tiny movements in an unhappy face. 'A bit.' But her smile is only a couple of heartbeats away. 'I just couldn't keep away. I wanted to make sure I hadn't dreamt the whole bloody thing.'

'I'm real,' I say.

She kisses me. I kiss her back. She tastes wonderful. We sit and talk and she asks me about why I have a notebook by the side of my bed.

'I use it to record my fugues.'

Nicole blinks, her expression blank. So I tell her about the rooftop bar and faceless Emma and Ivan and about how I relive Emma's death and my accident over and over. When I've finished, she's still blinking. Pumping away the tears, trying to avoid a deluge.

'It must be horrible to go through that over and over,' she whispers.

'You'd think so but it's not like a nightmare. I know these people. I spend hours with them. And the end... the falling... is all part of it. An ending of sorts.'

She clenches her teeth together as if a sudden pain has shot through her.

I put my hand on her arm. 'It sounds mad but I'm hoping that one day I might find an answer on that rooftop. You never know.'

She gets up and gives me a hug.

'Can I ask you what perfume you're wearing?'

She tilts her head, delighted that I've asked. 'Bandit by Robert Piguet.'

'French then. Great name. It smells expensive.'

'That's because it is. My little indulgence. Do you like it?'

'I do. Very much.'

Nicole leaves at a little after seven but I can still smell her in my bed that night. It keeps me awake. I ponder Keely and the look she gave me when I told her about the anaesthetist. The look you give a sick dog you feel sorry for. I wonder if she will do anything. Maybe she'll file it away under wild imaginings. I suspect it'll carry more weight if she hears it from Nicole, too.

But that will have to wait.

Instead, a new idea nudges Keely aside. There is someone else who might know all about Emma. And it isn't Harriet. Rachel would get me sectioned for even contemplating the thought. But the time for procrastinating is long gone.

I turn over. Nicole's perfume oozes out from the pillow.

I'd like the bed to smell of Nicole every day.

But I owe it to the both of us to sort out exactly what the hell happened to Emma and me on that night in Turkey. Keely is one step in the right direction. Now I need to take a running jump.

20

There is a place somewhere between sleeping and waking. Adam calls it a hypnagogic state. The dark cupboard in your head where hallucinations usually live. Sometimes vivid and troubling, often the sensation that there are other people in the room. More disturbingly, an awareness that you are awake but unable to move. Most commonly, they occur when people suffer from narcolepsy, sometimes Parkinson's disease, occasionally schizophrenia. I'm up on all the jargon.

But sometimes they happen in normal people as part of some great subconscious jape. That awful sensation of falling that jerks you awake. A smell or a taste or, even more creepily, a feeling like something is touching you. If you ask a hundred people over half will tell you they've experienced something like it in their lifetime.

But what I have is very different. My hallucinatory fugues are a genuine rarity. The trouble is that the hypnagogic state that can give ordinary people the heebie-jeebies is also one that is an almost perfect breeding ground for my fugues, too. So as well as daydreaming on lengthy walks I often get to visit the rooftop bar just before I wake up. When I fugue, I don't stay in bed. I get up and do things I am completely unaware of. If it wasn't so bloody tragic it would be funny.

But I gave up laughing a long time ago.

And this morning, this ordinary Friday morning – how appropriate that today is the thirteenth – I experience a humdinger as I drift up from the depths of unconsciousness.

For a change, it isn't night-time on the roof. It isn't exactly daytime either, but there is daylight – of sorts. A kind of ominous grey that leeches through the cloud-heavy sky to give the scene a sepia tint. The music is different too. Light, daytime jazz. Nothing Cam recognises but full of cool, ethereal, sparse chords. The Russian is on the far side of the roof. No girls with him this time. Impossible to tell what he's doing but it looks like he may be taking photos with his phone. Cam turns away from Ivan to look around and see that for once he's not sitting in a booth. He's sitting up in a bed. Faceless Emma is pouring coffee whilst all around staff in white aprons are dusting tables, collecting glasses, cleaning up.

'Time to get up, Cameron,' says Emma.

'Why?'

'We need to get ready to jump. Take a shower, get dressed.'

'Do we need to dress up to jump?'

'We need to look our best.'

'Do we?'

'You know we do. And the maid is waiting to clean our room.'

A girl in a black and white uniform stands next to a cleaning cart near the bar, patiently waiting. She shimmers like a bad hologram, vague and insubstantial.

'Besides, there's a storm coming.' Faceless Emma points over

Cam's shoulder. He turns to follow. There, in the distance, on the edge of the fugue city of minarets and domes that waver in a heat haze, a wall of boiling ochre and black clouds is tumbling towards them, buzzing and hissing like a plague of insects.

'What kind of storm is that?' he asks. But when he turns back, the wind sweeps in and carries in its hurling fist a spattering, hammering payload of sand and gravel. Cam feels nothing as the wind howls about him, but Emma gets blasted, though she appears not to notice. Even as he watches, she is erased from the rooftop along with everyone else, except the weirdly shimmering girl. And now he sees she is immune because she's made of stone.

From somewhere, a distant scream rents the air, a sudden noise immediately whipped up and away by the wind.

It takes several seconds for Cam to realise that the screaming voice is his.

I snap out of it and am instantly aware that I've poured myself a bowl of muesli and am standing in front of the fridge with my nose inches from it. A carton of milk is open on the table behind. My heart is thumping in my chest.

I look down to see I'm clutching a spoon in my hand. No point arguing with fate. I use the spoon to eat the muesli as I crunch around the flat, waiting for my brain to clamber down from wherever it's been.

Adam has explained, in scientific terms, what the fugues are and that they are causally related to my SBI. But he admits that little is known about their origin within the brain. They are not real – hence hallucinatory – but I remember them as if they are. Sometimes they feel more substantial than my waking hours. Sometimes, like now, I end up wondering if the rooftop bar is reality and me padding around my Bermondsey flat holding a bowl of muesli is the fugue.

But Adam has told me what to do if I felt like that.

Inject a dose of reality.

I go back into the bedroom. Find a box of DVDs and some games that Josh has given me. A seminal back catalogue of gaming and cinematic experience garnered from his formative years and, given what he knows about me, mine too. Underneath the boxes of Super Mario 64, Street Fighter, Sonic, Myst, Quake and dozens more is a shallow box that once contained a shirt. One Josh's mother bought for him to wear to his brother's wedding. The box is made of thick, strong cardboard and has the name of a Jermyn Street tailor embossed upon it. The shirt has long gone. Instead, inside is an inch-thick collection of cuttings documenting an outsider's view of what happened to Emma and me.

Josh has collated these. He gave them to me almost solemnly some four months ago just after I moved in. He looked earnest when he said, 'I think you're ready for this now.'

I keep the box hidden so that Rachel doesn't see it. But Rachel, I remind myself, is home-schooling her kids in Cardiff. She will not appear at the door of my flat. I realise I'm tarring her with a secret police brush. That's unfair.

I pick out a handful of 'L'- and 'T'-shaped strips of floppy newspaper cuttings amidst the odd full page and spread them, crinkling, over my bed. The headlines shout back at me.

Horror ordeal of British couple in Turkish paradise resort.

Woman plummets to her death from cliff in Turkey. Partner suffers life-changing injuries.

Police investigate mystery of UK couple's cliff tragedy.

I've been through these before and arranged them in date order. At first, the press is almost factual in their account and the lurid headlines last for just three days. After that, the reports are sporadic. But the one I'm after, the one I want to read, comes almost twelve months after Emma died and I fell.

Emma Roxburgh inquest finds no answers to the mystery of her death.

An inquest has heard how a British woman fell to her death from cliffs. Thirty-two-year-old Emma Roxburgh from London died while on holiday with her partner, Cameron Todd. Thirty-three-year-old Mr Todd was also severely injured and hospitalised for several months after the incident.

It was revealed that the couple had been staying in Cirali, a resort on the Antalya coast of Turkey in October of 2018. The inquest in Southwark Coroner's Court heard that the hotel owner was the last person to see Dr Emma Roxburgh – a GP in Woolwich – alive when she walked out of the hotel and headed north on a beach road towards the cliff path. A few minutes later, Mr Todd was seen to follow after asking the owner if he had seen Dr Roxburgh leave.

The hotel owner, Eymen Tabak, giving evidence through a translator, reported that Dr Roxburgh seemed to be in an anxious state as she hurried out to the beach road. Mr Todd's injuries were so severe that he could not give evidence as to the circumstances leading to the couple's ordeal.

Another holidaymaker who was in a beachside bar earlier that evening said that the cliff path at the north end of the beach was well walked but unfenced and, though safe in daylight, would be very treacherous in darkness.

Pathologist, Dr Alison Barnet gave a medical cause of death

as blunt force trauma to the head and trunk including bilateral pelvic fractures, skull fracture and a broken shoulder and arm.

Coroner James Quigley said: 'The Turkish police continue to investigate the tragic case, but there is no evidence at this time of foul play. We may never learn the full circumstances of what transpired that October night and I am therefore obliged to record an open verdict.'

I know what an open verdict is. Coroners use this when there is not enough evidence to reach any other conclusion. That means that no one is wholly convinced it was accidental. Emma's death remains suspicious in the minds of the public, the authorities and, as DS Keely has already reminded me, the Turkish police.

And therefore in mine. But of course, I should know because I was there.

But I can't remember. The only thing I am certain of at this point is that Emma wasn't sandblasted to death by a hurricane on a rooftop bar, even if my brain suggests otherwise. But what I'm also sure of is that something is changing inside my head. Because my fugues are. For months, faceless Emma and Ivan and I have sat around, chewed the fat, and then the woman I am supposed to love has fallen off the roof. With me following a moment after her.

Because of this, I am convinced my fugues must have an underlying meaning. They're mental ciphers. Must be. Otherwise I have to accept that they're nothing more than random synapses firing off and colluding together to taunt and tantalise. And if that is the case, what's the difference between a fugue and pure madness?

I wait for the answer, but my stubborn psyche leaves the question hanging. Big joke. No punchline.

So I choose to believe the rooftop bar and faceless Emma

and the storm are cryptic crossword clues which, at present, I have no idea how to unravel.

I don't know where to look for answers either. Other than the obvious places.

I've tried Josh. I've tried Keely. I've gone for the safe options. Time I lived a little more dangerously.

I walk to the kitchen, reach for the landline handset and dial a number I'm familiar with, but I've never dialled before.

From somewhere in the caverns of my mind, I hear Rachel screaming, 'NO.'

But I dial the number anyway and leave a message.

Now we wait and see.

21

Friday at 5.30pm I meet Josh for an after-work drink as arranged. We're not going overboard; Josh has a girlfriend – Lisa – to go home to and I'm not a big drinker these days. I used to be, according to Josh, but since Turkey and all the drugs I'm on, two pints maximum for me. Adam says alcohol and quetiapine isn't a good mix.

As always on a Friday, the pub is busy; though not as full as usual. Some people are taking note of the government's request to implement some social distancing. Avoid restaurants and limit our visits to the pub if we can. Common sense says the only way to enforce that is to shut places down. Because people take such requests as optional. And Friday after work is more than a bit of a tradition with the young professional crowd. Tonight, the end of a normal working week, restrictions must be for other people because here there are as many drinkers outside as in. Not only sad smokers cram the pavements on a Friday night.

The weather is hardly conducive either. Yet the cold and wet is the price you pay for an after-work drink in a city of almost nine million. But what most revellers in the Grey Goose in

Shoreditch are unaware of is that there is a mezzanine with half a dozen tables inside the pub accessed by a stairway just past the toilets. Most punters, keen for a swift Chardonnay or a pint of Doom Bar, never get that far down the corridor. I'm not complaining. Josh and I usually meet in this secret spot and tonight we make a beeline and squeeze through to grab the last available chairs. Fifteen minutes later there's standing room only and by six we have to shout to be heard. Hardly congenial, but as I say, no such thing as a quiet pint on a Friday night in London.

I scan the room. If there is a virus in here, its birthday and Christmas has arrived all rolled into one. Brad Pitt would have apoplexy. Josh senses my anxiety. 'Think of us doing our bit for herd immunity.'

'You think?'

'No, I don't think. And I don't know what to think. That's the trouble. South Korea seems to have a handle on it whereas Italy is in meltdown, so I hear. Perhaps we're all on the deck of the Titanic listening to the band play on as we slide beneath the waves.'

'Delightful image.'

'Cheer up,' Josh says. 'So long as no one in here prefers face flesh over pork scratchings, we're safe. Just wash your hands and practise sneezing etiquette. If your inner elbow looks like a snail has crawled across it, time for the launderette.'

'Nice.'

'What the hell else can we do?'

I take a sip from my pint. Josh is right. What the hell else can we do?

'Get everything sorted the other evening, did you?' he asks.

'Some things,' I reply.

Josh grins. He finds my pedantic responses amusing for many reasons. 'Some things is dead right. Everything would include world peace, a Covid vaccine and solving the thorny issue of fusion reactors. My bad.'

He's fishing for a response. I don't take the bait. 'Do you remember the last time you saw Emma?'

Josh's grin freezes and his throat makes a two-tone buzzer noise. 'End of banter warning.'

'Do you remember?'

'It was a few days before you went to Turkey if my mind serves me. We had a drink. Not here, but somewhere like this. The Drum or maybe even The Marlborough–'

'How did she seem to you?'

'Normal. Looking forward to going away.'

I nod. 'I suspect that she wasn't normal.'

'We know that. She was going out with you for a start.' Josh waits, but I don't laugh. He gives a slight shrug. 'What's all this about, Cam?'

I tell him more or less what I told Keely. But once again, I don't mention Nicole. I don't have to because I've told Josh I met her. He doesn't need the extra intimate details. Not yet. Nicole needs time to sort out Aaron.

I pull out the small notebook. Josh looks at the entry:

14/10/18. Cam's do with Quantiple.
Pants on fire?

'What do you think it means?' I ask.

Josh shakes his head. 'I remember the Quantiple thing. They had a recruitment bash. That was two months before they opened their new offices. You were supposed to go, but you cried off because you were struck down by some kind of intestinal malaise. A bad lamb bhuna if I remember rightly.'

'I don't remember.'

He studies the notebook again. 'But why the pants on fire?'

'Liar, liar.'

Josh looks up, frowning. 'You or Emma?'

'That's what I'm trying to find out.'

He makes a troubled, sceptical face. 'This could mean nothing at all.'

Josh is right. It could all mean nothing. Just a hasty scribble in a throwaway notebook.

'What makes you suspect things weren't normal?' he probes. 'There must be something else? Have you remembered something else?'

'Nothing concrete,' I say. And it is the truth. I haven't remembered anything. Nicole has filled in the blanks. 'Just an impression. Something was off. Either with Emma... or me.'

Concern crumples Josh's brows. 'You and Emma were tight, mate. I can't remember seeing anything off. That's the truth.'

'But what if something was off? What if something happened between us in Turkey?'

Josh puts a hand on my shoulder. 'Bloody hell, Cam. What's brought all this on?'

'Pants on fire has brought this on.'

Something chimes and Josh reaches into his pocket for his phone. 'Here we go. News alert. Latest from our headless chickens – I mean, great leaders. Apparently, we're going to be asked to avoid all non-essential travel; curtail visits to pubs, clubs, theatres and restaurants, and vulnerable groups will need to self-isolate.' He looks up, stricken. 'Imagine not being able to do this of a Friday evening.'

'Voluntary though, right?'

'So far.'

'You think things could get worse?'

Josh drains his pint, puts down the glass and smacks his lips. 'Worse, no not at all. And just by way of reassurance, I know which book you need to read next. I take it you haven't read Cormac McCarthy's *The Road*?'

I shake my head.

'Then that's definitely one you should dive into. It will ease your troubled soul and fill you with positivity and hope for all mankind.'

Josh has that look in his eye. A mischievous glint that tells me everything.

'Can't wait,' I say.

'It was even made into a film. None other than Viggo Mortensen. Amazing performance. He has them rolling in the aisles. Read the book, though, and tell me what your take is. Oh, and drink up. Come on, my shout.'

'We don't usually drink more than two,' I say. Adam and Rachel both warn me constantly about the risk of mixing too much alcohol with my current drug regimen. But I don't overdo it and have worked myself up to a maximum of three pints and or a couple of glasses of wine without losing it. My liver may not be dancing a jig, but mentally, I can cope. Says he.

Josh has no qualms. 'Well, we ought to this evening. We're celebrating the fact that I am about to introduce you to the laugh-a-minute world of dystopian literature as per McCarthy, and, not to put too much of an Orwellian spin on things, this might be the last chance we get to do this.'

'Make mine a half.'

He's grinning as he gets up to jostle his way to the bar. Josh takes my empty glass and wriggles his way through the packed crowd, leaving me to ponder my anxieties. I can't imagine not being able to enjoy a pint together on a Friday night. What the hell will people do?

There are two beer mats on the table. I arrange them so they are centred, and equidistant two inches from the edge. Seeing them there like that is pleasing. I wish I knew why it helps.

'You and Emma were tight, mate.'

Josh is genuine. His recollection of us as a couple is an accurate reflection of how he saw us. And perhaps he's right. Perhaps that was the impression we projected. But it doesn't feel tight to me. Not anymore.

My hand falls and knocks the table, disrupting the pattern of the carefully-arranged beer mats. They spin into a random arrangement. One on top of the other, their perfect alignment destroyed in an instant.

Is this what happened to me and Emma? If we weren't in harmony, if we were drifting apart, could we have argued? Could we have gone for a walk on that beach after dark and ended up in a fight? Could a moment of chaos have caused both our lives to implode?

Josh comes back and we drink but somehow the evening is soured and, once I down the half, I make my excuses. He doesn't object. He knows my tolerance of social situations is low. But I don't share my thoughts with him.

These are way too dark. Labelled 'personal consumption only'.

22

There's a message on the landline when I get home at a little after 8pm. I press the play button and listen.

'This is John Stamford. Thanks for returning my call. Best we meet face to face because I don't discuss anything over the phone. How about The Pommelers Rest. I'll stand you a Wetherspoon's breakfast. 9.30 tomorrow morning. You can text your answer to this number.'

I write the address down. I've never been to The Pommelers Rest, so I flip open my laptop and surf to the website and up pops a pub on Tower Bridge Road. A big pub from the looks of it. And not only the building; the breakfasts look gigantic.

While I'm in the shower, Rachel messages me. She wants to FaceTime. I change and go into the kitchen where the wifi is at its strongest and call her up.

Rachel answers on the third ring. She's sitting in her kitchen with a glass of red wine on the table in front of her. I recognise the Welsh, patterned oilcloth and note the flotsam of plates and soup bowls pushed to one side ready for the dishwasher. I can hear some extraneous noise. The sounds of children laughing punctuated by a rich fruity cough. The backdrop is a kitchen dresser painted in cream with natural oak tops. Rachel did the painting. It's her thing. A life's project given that the house they live in was built in 1889, has five bedrooms and views over the Bristol Channel to Weston-super-Mare and North Devon on good days. Brown water and Channel fog on bad ones. Rachel and Owen are working on the house room by room. They hope to finish by 2060. I suspect that's a joke but given the size of the place I would not be surprised.

'Hi, Cam, cariad.' Rachel looks a little tired in jeans and shirt.

'Hi, Rache. Aren't the kids in bed?'

'I wish. No point much before ten. We'll dose Rosie up with Calpol and hope for the best. But Ewan's cough is better.'

'Is that him I hear or a dog barfing? I mean barking?'

Rachel gives me a long-suffering look. 'Barfing works just as well after Rosie's performance last night. She was up half the night.'

'Poor her. And poor you.'

'They're playing games with their dad.' Rachel turns and shouts. 'Hey, you two, come and say hello to Uncle Cam. Yes, now. FaceTime.' The scene shifts and spins before a face dips into view. My brother-in-law, Owen.

'Cam, how they hanging?'

'They are hanging well, thanks. Several feet off the ground as always.'

Owen grins. He always talks to me this way. As if nothing has ever happened. I like it. His way of coping. He hasn't said so, but Rachel has. In whispers when Owen's flippancy annoys her. Which is often, though I suspect she affects that annoyance. Owen makes Rachel laugh. After what she's been through – thanks largely to me – humour is a gift not to be scoffed at. He, on the other hand, tells me it is his role in life not to mollycoddle.

'How are things in the big smoke, Cam?'

'I'm stocking up on essentials with my one eye on the zombie apocalypse. I also have garlic and wooden stakes.'

'You need to work on your mythology, but otherwise that all sounds good. We, too, are replete when it comes to toilet rolls and handwash. Costco was like a war zone.'

'Are you okay, Owen?'

'You know me, Cam. Enduring, as always, under immense pressure.' He flinches as my sister clips him a playful one around the ear.

'Work?'

'Yeah, well I'm working from home for the foreseeable. Now that both kids are ill.'

The phone is jostled again. Owen steadies it with a, 'Whoa, savages at six o'clock.' Two more faces cram together to appear on-screen. My nephew, Ewan, and niece, Rosie. Rosie's cheeks appear eponymously flushed and she has slight shadows under her eyes. Ewan looks like his dad. For five minutes I listen to a breathless account, in Welsh, of their day at home with Rachel. Making posters, pice ar y maen (Welsh cakes), and playing hide the teddy with Sibli, their dog. Behind them, Rachel makes rabbit-ear fingers above Rosie's head until their performance becomes too competitive and some pushing and shoving enters the scene. At that point, Rachel calls a halt. 'Okay, that's enough. Back to the dungeon.'

Ewan, with the pedantry of a six-year-old, objects. 'We don't have a dungeon.'

'You sure about that?' Owen says and drops his voice into cartoon Dracula. 'Would you like to find out?'

More squeals and I see Owen's blurred form chase the kids from the room.

Rachel takes a slug of wine and puts the phone back to its stable place on the table. 'As you can see, despite casualties, we are fine. But how about you? Are you okay? I got your text. So the drive and the visit to Emma's practice turned out well?'

I've thought hard about this moment. About what to say to Rachel. No point lying. She's a human polygraph.

I say, 'It was good. I met someone there who remembered me. A colleague of Emma's. But I didn't remember her. We had a toffee. A coffee.'

'That sounds good. You had no trouble finding the place then?'

'Google Maps found it for me.'

'But it was worth the trip, was it?'

'Yes, definitely. Afterwards, I remembered going through the barrier at the reception desk to a room that Emma must have used. I didn't recognise it at the time, but the memory came back later.'

Rachel is smiling. 'That's just the way Adam said it might happen. Visiting old haunts will push some of these memories to the front of your brain. Anything else happen?'

'Josh says the last piece of work I did for him was good.'

'That's amazing.'

'He says I should consider doing some freelance stuff. He'll help with it.'

'Are you sure you're up for that?'

'I need to do something.'

'True, but remember what Adam said about overdoing things. Stress is not the friend of recovery from brain injury.' Rachel's head snaps up and to the left. She yells, in Welsh, 'Ewan, do NOT play quidditch in the passage! Do you hear me?' When her face appears in shot again, she shakes her head. 'They are so wound up. Owen is reading them *The Prisoner of Azkaban* and they're obsessed with Hogsmeade and Butterbeer.

He's told them that if they don't behave, they'll get turned into chocolate frogs. I swear he's worse than they are.'

'I don't think it's me that's stressed, Rache.'

'Ha, bloody ha. Anyway, baby steps, Cam.'

'And don't forget the nappy, yeah, yeah.'

That's an unpleasant in-joke from the time I was in a coma. One that both of us would prefer to forget.

She assures me again that she is available any time if I need her, adding that I can come down and stay with them until this virus thing is all over. I decline.

'Understandable,' she says. 'Chances are the kids have or will have it so Owen and I are toeing the line.'

'When did Owen self-isolate?'

'Today. We decided it was the right thing to do. Even if we were extra careful with the kids and the dog... Sibli knows sod all about social distancing and if there was ever a perfect vector, she's it.'

Sibli, the Griffiths' golden lab, wavers into shot as Rachel swivels her iPad towards the floor. A wet nose and smiling eyes appear two inches from the camera.

'Hi, Sibli,' I say.

Then Rachel is back, veering into shot. 'Look after yourself. Cadwa'n saff.'

'I will.'

I text John Stamford and agree to the meet at The Pommelers Rest tomorrow morning. It feels impulsive. I suspect the two-and-a-half beers I've had has helped.

Later, I watch one of Josh's recommendations. This one is, 'A simple tale of a mother and son relationship gone apeshit. With a bit of the supernatural thrown in. You'll love it because it blurs the lines between reality and the unreal. In fact, if it was ever remade, you'd get a part no trouble, given your talent for mental wanderings.'

It's only when Haley Joel Osment says, 'I see dead people' that I realise just how much Josh has excelled himself with cryptic sarcasm this time. Later, when Bruce Willis finally realises his mistake, I wonder if whoever wrote the film had fugues too. After all, faceless Emma who always appears with me in the rooftop bar must be dead. Perhaps everyone there is. Or there's the possibility that I am Bruce Willis, and that I'm dead already, but I won't admit it to myself.

I text Josh and tell him that. His reply is:

No mate, you're not in *The Sixth Sense*. You're the lead in No Sense.

I text back an emoji of a bell and the word end.
Josh texts back: ROFLOL.

At 11pm I hear three rapid pips. Nicole has suggested we use Snapchat for photos and messaging. I downloaded the app. That way, even if she forgets to delete them, messages will disappear. I'm there as Cam. Easy for her to claim it's a Camilla. Safer to do that for now. Aaron is paranoid she says. She suspects he looks at her phone even though she's password-protected it. She tries not to leave it unlocked ever.

I open the app and scroll to messages. I read, *Missing you* signed *N*. That's also the letter I've used in my contacts folder. There's another signal. The photo that materialises shows Nicole dressed in a tight party frock, waving at me with a sad face. The photo counts down from ten seconds and disappears. I know she's at her friend's for another variation on a hen shindig this weekend and it looks like the celebrations have begun. But I'm glad she's texted. Filling my mind with Nicole gets rid of all the weird feelings I've had about not being alive. Of being trapped in some kind of limbo like good old Bruce Willis in *The Sixth Sense*.

But Nicole is real. To prove it, I go into the bedroom and pick up the pillow. I can still smell leather and musk.

Bandit.

That's how I remember her now.

23

W hat hits me the moment I walk into The Pommelers Rest on Saturday morning at 9.27am is how bustling it is.

So much for voluntary social distancing.

The bar is open and there are three people standing nursing pints. Everyone else, and there must be a hundred people in there, are sitting at tables, eating. I stand in the bar area looking around at a thriving business. The place is well-lit with lots of windows looking out to the street. There's a jolly, patriotic red-and-blue carpet on the floor and the place is buzzing. Thirty seconds later a man approaches. Big, around six-one, carrying a good few extra pounds that start at his neck and spread down-wards so that his cable-knit jumper bulges taut under a waxed jacket. He holds out a hand.

'Cameron? John Stamford.'

He hands over a card. No frills. Black print on white paper with his name at the top and the words *Private Investigator* beneath followed by a phone number. I put it in my jeans pocket and then shake his hand, vaguely discomfited by the fact that I shouldn't be doing that, and acutely aware that if I now wash my hands it'll look embarrassing. I'm saved by Stamford fishing a little bottle of sanitiser out of his jacket pocket and squeezing out a thumbnail-sized dollop into my palm before doing the same himself.

'No need to throw away years of social etiquette because of a little cough,' he says in a voice that goes with his bulk.

From what I've seen on TV of the people in China and Italy, wearing personal protection gear and dealing with dying patients, it's hardly a little cough. But I don't argue.

'I've never been in here before,' I say, still a little awestruck.

'Used to be a hotel. Course, doesn't suit the craft beer brigade who turn their noses up at the cheap booze. But more than one Spoons has been a welcome haven after a long night of surveillance. It's a pub. A place for a bite to eat and a drink for travellers. Plus, on occasion, a bloody useful site office for me. Walk in here mid-afternoon and you'll see why some Spoons are social hubs for poor beggars fed up of staring at the same four walls. That's what pubs are meant for and the staff in here are great. They take a tolerant view of letting the homeless people in for a cuppa, too. Within reason. This place used to be a hostelry. Named for the leather workers that worked in this neck of London as far back as the fifteenth century. Got a bit of a soft spot, me.'

'Some of my friends won't come in on pencil. Sorry, principle...' I see Stamford frown. I explain, 'I sometimes get words wrong. Anyway, as I was saying, some of my friends don't come because of something to do with the owner's politics.'

Stamford's smooth, broad face has light-coloured eyebrows that need trimming. His bald head is shaved. Different from the photo on my wall. He shrugs. 'I voted remain, but I still eat breakfast in here. About time people accepted their fate, I say.' He opens his hands by way of excusing an indulgence. 'A Spoons' full English every Saturday is my fix. We're over there.'

I follow him down some steps to a table for two under a print of the Thames from days gone by: sepia images of sailing ships and mudlarks on the banks. Stamford takes off his jacket and sits with his back to the wall. 'Thanks for coming. I admit I was surprised to get your message.' He has a raw voice. A local accent scoured by either overuse or cigarettes. He doesn't look fit enough to be yelling at kids in a coaching capacity, so I presume that tobacco is the culprit. 'What brought on the change of heart?' he asks, his gaze penetratingly direct. He looks comfortable and I surmise he's done this before. Then I remember that he was once a policeman.

'I'm remembering some things. They are vague but each new memory triggers questions that I can't answer.'

Stamford nods and picks up a menu. 'Let's order. What do you fancy?'

I don't feel much like eating but he insists. I go for a smashed avocado bagel; Stamford orders a traditional full English. We're both presented with large steaming mugs of tea. Stamford takes two sugars. The food comes quickly. While we eat, Stamford does most of the talking. 'Just so you know my bona fides, I was with the Met for ten years and then a DCI with Essex police for another fifteen. Drug squad to start with, then major crimes.'

'And now you are a private investigator.'

'That's it. The two M's. Missing persons and marital indiscretions. Bit of debt-tracing as well. But now and again something unusual pokes its head up. Like you and Emma Roxburgh.'

'So you are still working for Emma's family?'

'I am. Engaged to find out what happened that night.'

'I still can't remember anything.'

'But you remember something. Otherwise you wouldn't be here, right?'

'What about your messages. The financial issues.'

Stamford has bacon, egg and hash browns skewered in

layers on his fork. The load pauses halfway to his mouth. He smiles. 'Yeah, that's a bit of artistic licence. Mentioning money usually gets a response. It hasn't in you. Not so far. Unless that's what's got you out of bed this morning.'

I shake my head. 'So that's a lie?'

'Not exactly. You are the beneficiary of Emma Roxburgh's will and insurance policies.'

'And you think that's a good enough reason to throw myself off a concrete jetty and almost die in the process?'

Stamford puts down his fork. 'No, I do not think that. But other people have put forward the possibility. That you miscalculated.'

None of this is news to me. Rachel has been through this ad nauseam.

Stamford chews, takes another gulp of tea and reaches for the ketchup. 'So what's made you contact me, Cameron?'

'A nagging itch. The notion that perhaps all was not well between Emma and me. I found a notebook with something written in it.' I show him a copy of Emma's entry and then explain about Quantiple.

'What's your take on what this means?' Stamford asks.

'I should know everything there is to know about Emma. But I don't. You, on the other hand, know more than anyone, I would guess.'

There's a lull. A door left open for me to get to my point.

'Was Emma having an affair with someone?'

Stamford looks surprised and then lets out a throaty laugh. 'An affair? What makes you say that?'

'There was someone at Guy's. Someone she worked with. I think she was involved in stealing drugs.'

'And you honestly believe Emma was part of that?'

'I don't know. I hoped you might.'

Stamford's eyes light up with interest. 'And if she was, how would that play out with what happened in Turkey?'

I don't get a chance to answer. Stamford's head snaps up and he pushes his chair back. 'What the–'

'Jesus, John. Is nowhere sleazy enough for you.' A woman's voice, confident and shrill, coming nearer. I have my back to her and I don't turn around because the mask of horror on Stamford's face is mesmerising.

'What the hell are you doing here?' Stamford demands, getting up and causing the table to shudder, almost spilling both mugs of tea.

'I needed to speak to you, and your charming assistant was very helpful when I told her how urgent it was. You're a creature of habit, it seems.'

Stamford lunges past me. He drops his voice. 'This is not the best time.'

'It will only take a few minutes.'

The other diners are turning to watch an altercation. A bit of drama.

'Give me five minutes. I'll meet you in the coffee shop across the road.'

The woman laughs and her next words are a whisper. 'Have I stumbled on an assignation.'

'Harriet, please.'

I turn around, recognise her immediately. She looks a little like the image of Emma on my kitchen wall, but thinner in the face and with longer hair. She's lost some weight and there are dark circles under her makeup-free face. I should have recognised her voice. But I've only had Harriet Roxburgh talk to me half a dozen times since Turkey. Her voice has either been a sob, or a berating screech. She is on Rachel's list of no-nos. Guilt flares in my brain. That's two people on Rachel's blacklist in one venue. Must be my lucky day.

Harriet's face freezes and her eyes go from slits to ovals in two seconds flat. She looks from me to Stamford and back before breathing out, 'You.'

Stamford puts himself between us. Too late. Someone has lit a fire under Harriet. She points an accusing finger at me.

'You bastard. You utter bastard. How dare you use Emma to post those disgusting things–'

'Harriet,' Stamford tries to intervene. 'This is not good–'

'You are sick, you know that. You're not fooling anyone with your bloody memory loss bullshit. I know what you did, you despicable monster.'

'Right, that's enough.' Stamford holds his arms out wide.

Two pub staff members clock the fracas and are hovering. One walks over and says, 'Is everything all right here?'

I want to say something, but I can't because I'm frozen to my chair.

'I'm going to the police about this,' hisses Harriet.

But Stamford has turned her around firmly and slides one big arm around her, marching her to the nearest door while she resists like some errant child. She fights him all the way, craning to get her face around to hurl threats at me and to Stamford.

'Let go of me. Why are you even talking to that piece of filth?'

They reach a door. Stamford opens it using one large hand without letting go of Harriet. Then he grabs her by the elbows and shakes her firmly. He leans into her face and says something no one else hears. She stops shouting and sends me a glare that makes me shudder before they both leave through a side exit. Stamford keeps hold of her elbow as he crosses the road to the coffee shop. I turn back to my bagel. Smashed avocado spills over from the surface and the sight of it almost turns my stomach. My appetite is shot. I sit, sipping tea, pondering whether to leave, waiting for my pulse to subside. I'm at the point of standing up and putting on my coat when Stamford comes back in and sits.

'Right,' he says, pushing away his half-finished plate. 'So that just happened. Can I tempt you with another cup of tea, Cameron?'

24

I toy with getting up and walking out. My heart thumps like a trapped bird in my chest.

Stamford leans in. 'I know that was unpleasant but take it from me it was not planned. Harriet has... issues. I can hardly blame her but what she did there was uncalled for and I apologise.'

I stay silent. It prompts Stamford to continue.

'What can you tell me about Harriet Roxburgh?'

'That she blames me for her sister's death.'

Stamford lets his gaze drop to the table and eases out a sanguine, 'Hmmm.' When he eventually looks up, I can see that there's a sharp intelligence swirling behind those pale eyes of his. 'So we understand one another, the Roxburghs have employed me to find out what happened to their daughter. It decimated them as a family and their theories about what took place are... fixed. But they're distorted theories twisted out of shape by grief and the never-ending mental quicksand that is not knowing.'

'I can't help them with that,' I say.

'No. And that's where Harriet and I differ. I know you're

telling the truth about not remembering. I've talked to half a dozen experts and they all say that your physical recovery from your injuries is pretty remarkable. Could be sheer luck, could be sheer bloody-mindedness. I don't know which because I don't know you. But what I'm certain of is that those experts all tell me that your memory of events, or lack of, is kosher given the degree of brain injury you've suffered.'

'Do you want me to say I'm grateful?' It slips out before I can stop it.

Stamford's mouth flickers into a brief smile. 'They told me you were straight. And my answer would be, truthfully, no I do not. But I genuinely think we can help one another.'

'Or perhaps this is a set-up for me to be ambushed.' My heart is still racing but now more like a fluttering moth than a struggling bird.

'I'd be a lousy trap-layer to choose a Spoons on a Saturday morning. But I admit that Harriet can be very persuasive. My assistant is new. Keen as Dijon but young and more than a touch naïve to let Harriet play her. The nature of my job is such that I let her know where I am if I'm working. For security purposes. I've been accosted in car parks and sleazy hotel corridors more times than I've had a full English. But she's not supposed to tell anyone else where I am unless I give her the nod. We will have words.'

I sit back and glance across at the coffee shop.

Stamford sees it. 'Don't worry. I'm watching too. She's promised to stay there for fifteen minutes. So, how about it?'

I waver. He senses it. 'Have another cup of tea and let me explain why she is like she is.'

The Roxburghs are on Rachel's bargepole list of people I am not supposed to go anywhere near. Or talk to. Possibly even discuss. I'm supposed to direct any contact through her. So though I spoke to Harriet and Emma's parents while I was recovering, I remember it through a fog. They visited me in hospital but there has been no exchange since I moved into the flat, other than the uncomfortable episode at the cemetery. I can remember that one well enough. Rachel's words of warning were stark. 'They're too damaged. They don't really care about you. All they want is for you to tell them about Emma and you can't. It's becoming vexatious.'

Rachel is right. Seeing Harriet, hearing her accuse me, was unpleasant. Is unpleasant. But now, since I found Emma's notebook, I'm intrigued. And, despite Rachel's warning, I guess I'm beginning to like John Stamford's matter-of-fact approach.

'Okay,' I say.

Stamford calls the waitress over, asks her to warm up the food left on his plate, orders more tea. Breakfast recommences.

'One reason I took this case on,' he explains, 'is because of the way the Roxburghs' lives imploded after Emma died. If you read it in a book you'd never bloody believe it. You know about all that?'

'Not really.'

Stamford takes a sip of his old lukewarm tea, grimaces, puts it down, wipes his lips on a napkin. 'Six months after Emma died, Peter Roxburgh, Emma and Harriet's father, was found hanged in a wood near the family home. He'd been missing for two days. You were aware of that, I assume?'

I shake my head. Was I aware of that? My memory is shot for the distant past but recent events, stuff that's happened since rehab, is fine. There was a lot of space there to fill if you consider my memory bank like some kind of chest that had been emptied. So I would remember if I'd been told. But I do not remember and therefore I can assume that I was not told. I offer the only explanation I can muster. 'My sister, Rachel, she's very protective.'

The waitress comes back with fresh mugs and Stamford's

reheated plate. He tucks in, filling me in on the Roxburghs in between mouthfuls.

'It came as a complete shock to the family. He'd been out walking the dog. There were no clues. He was a fit and healthy man. There was no note and again that isn't unusual. The dog, strangely enough, was never found. Having said that, it was a spaniel with a liking for rabbit holes and the wood was vast. Who knows, someone might have found it and taken it in.'

I can see that Stamford would like this to be true.

'You a dog lover, Cameron?'

That was one of the things that threw the doctors. 'Ble ma Champ?' One of my first slurred sentences, uttered in Welsh, a language spoken by less than a million people in the far west of Britain, was me asking about a dog that had been dead for twenty years. No wonder it confused them.

'I had a dog when I was growing up. His name was one of the few things I remember from my childhood. Even before I was shown a photograph.'

Stamford pours a two-inch diameter mound of tomato ketchup on his plate. 'Dogs will do that to you. But her husband's death on top of Emma's was too much for Cora Roxburgh, Harriet and Emma's mother. She plunged into a deep depression. A black one. I've spoken to one of her doctors and they're clear that these two horrific events, losing a daughter and then her husband, triggered a major depressive episode. Reactives have a better prognosis they say, but if Cora is anything to go by, I'd say the jury is still out on that one. She's been in and out of hospital for a fragile ten months. That's left Harriet carrying the emotional can.'

'She doesn't look well.'

'Harriet is a doctor, like Emma. She was in training. A haematologist that had almost ticked all the boxes on the way to consultancy when Emma and then her father died. But she coped with it pretty well. Much better than her mother did. Until a year ago. You were still in hospital so I'm not surprised you know nothing about that.' He looks up. 'You don't, do you?'

I shake my head. I know only to avoid Harriet Roxburgh like the plague.

Stamford starts buttering toast. 'Just under six months ago, for the first time since her father died, some girlfriends cajoled her into a night out. She was driving and not drinking. She drove the other girls to a club to drop them off, planned on spending an hour there and going home. She drank nothing but Diet Coke all evening. But they filmed her at the club berating and racially harassing one of the bouncers two hours later, obviously intoxicated. She tested positive for MDMA. She claims that her drink was spiked.'

'I've read that can happen.'

'But the real damage was done by the video of her behaving very badly. Harriet was arrested and charged with affray. And the video escapes into the world. We all know how careful and willing to accept nothing but the truth the denizens of social media are. She had to report the charge to the GMC just at the time when she was about to apply for consultant posts. In short, that one incident – and I have no reason not to accept her version, that her drink was spiked – derailed her career. She's been doing locums ever since, looking after her mother and trying to find out what happened to her sister. All in all, I'm surprised she's looking so well.'

I sit back. This is a great deal to digest.

Stamford reads my disquiet. 'I wouldn't blame you for wanting to walk away right now but it would be a mistake. We share a mutual interest, shall we say.'

I let the dull anger that's brought heat to my face since Harriet started yelling, slowly subside. 'How?'

'I'm not at liberty to tell you everything that I know. But I wouldn't be sitting here unless I understood there were questions that need answering.'

'Like what?'

'Like why Emma walked out of your hotel on her own that night.'

'What about the anaesthetist and pants on fire?'

'That too.'

He looks at me. I return his gaze. 'Tell me you didn't post anything about Emma on Facebook.'

'What?'

'It's why Harriet was so animated.'

'Emma has a memorial page and Harriet is the page administrator. The legacy contact. I have no access. Harriet is the gatekeeper. I'm not allowed to post anything, even as a friend.'

'She says this wasn't a friend's tribute on Emma's memorial page. This is a fresh Facebook page pretending to be from Emma. Someone alerted Harriet to it.'

I stare at him while my mind tries to understand what he's just said. But my thoughts are like leaves in a wind getting blown in random directions.

Stamford's gaze doesn't waiver. 'Harriet's convinced you're responsible.'

The fluttering bird is back in my chest. The bars of its cage are my ribs. 'I can't remember Emma's mobile number. I can't remember her email address. Why would I pretend to be her on Facebook? How would I even begin to do that?'

Stamford keeps looking. Can he tell when someone lies? I hope so, because I am telling the absolute truth. He eyes his watch and then glances over at the coffee shop. 'Twelve minutes. If you're willing, I'll have a shufti into this anaesthetist business. Then I'll be in touch. I'll tell Harriet it isn't you who is posting as Emma.'

'It isn't.' I reach for my wallet to pay for breakfast. But Stamford puts his big hand over mine.

'My shout. The way things are going this might be my last Spoons breakfast for a while thanks to this sodding virus.'

'Will they close the pubs?'

'I'd put money on it. And sooner rather than later.' He glances out of the window once more. 'Just go before she comes back. I'll be in touch.'

We shake hands. Follow up with sanitiser. Stamford grins when he squeezes a dollop into my palm.

'Brave new world,' he says.

As I walk out and turn towards the flat, I see a female figure leave the coffee shop. I dip back into a doorway and watch Harriet Roxburgh cross the road.

She reminds me of a leopard hunting its prey.

25

T he first thing I do when I get back to the flat is open up my laptop and bring up Emma's memorial page. It's exactly as I remember it. The profile picture is of Emma and her family BT. There is no sign of me anywhere. Underneath an image of Emma is a Timeline and Tributes section. I open these up and read again the outpourings of loss and grief that now, thankfully, appear to occur only when significant dates loom, such as Emma's birthday.

Nothing I've tried to contribute has ever appeared. So this can't be the page Harriet is talking about. I type Emma Roxburgh into the search box. Not a common name so only half a dozen people appear. I scan their profile pictures. And there at the bottom is one I recognise from my wall. The name is Emma 'Roxy' Roxburgh.

I click on the name and a page opens. This time the banner image is of Emma on a beach, leering playfully at the camera. I scroll down. On the left is a collage of a dozen photos. Of Emma dressed to the nines on a night out, or in a bikini with a long drink, two of her pouting at the camera. And to my surprise I see myself in a couple of these images. And from the way we're entwined, there can be little doubt that Emma and I are in a relationship.

There's a pinned post on the top of her timeline dominated by another photograph. A candid shot; Emma in a revealing top with a tiara in her hair. The girl next to her wears a garish sash. The photo's cropped but there's enough sash showing to read the words *Birthday Girl* emblazoned across it. Emma's makeup is smudged, and her eyes have a slightly glazed look. The birthday girl, whoever she is, looks very much the worse for wear.

Under the image are the words, *Party time over here beyond the veil. Love you all.*

There are some comments under the image.

GLEN

> Msg me your number. Parteee time.

TOMTOM

> Classy. You're the sort of girl I could take home to mum...
> for a 3sum.

BAWBOY

> Want to swap photos? I got Extra Large.

Bawboy obviously doesn't do subtle. I quickly scan the remainder, stop after twenty-five.

I can see why Harriet would be upset. I don't know why she would think I would have done this. But then I check myself. Of course I do. The look I'd seen on her face was that of a cornered cat hissing threats. She thinks I killed her sister. And she doubtless thinks me capable of taunting her and her family with this sickening little game. It's an unpleasant thought that leaves me anxious and needing to speak to someone. Maybe I could try explaining all this to Harriet. But as soon as I think it, Rachel's voice in my head screams, 'DON'T YOU DARE.'

But then a new thought intrudes. One that makes the hair on my neck stand up to attention.

I pick up my mobile and scroll to a name in the contacts list. Press the call button. Adam answers on the fourth ring.

'Hey, Cam. How are you?' There's extraneous noise. Adam sounds as if he isn't at home.

'Is it possible that during one of my fugues I could post something on Facebook?'

'What?' Adam's voice goes up an octave.

'Posting on Facebook–'

'Hang on. I'm in IKEA queuing for Swedish meatballs with the kids. Let me find a quiet spot. Just hang on...'

I wait for a minute and a half and then Adam says, 'Right. Start again.'

I tell him I went to The Pommelers Rest to meet a friend and bumped into Harriet by accident. I tell him about the Facebook page that is pretending to be Emma 'Roxy' Roxburgh. Then I ask him again. 'Is it possible that I did this during a fugue?'

'No,' says Adam. 'Your actions during a fugue are all automatic. Putting random items in a bag. Rearranging books–'

'Yesterday I poured a bowl of muesli.'

'Okay, a little more elaborate but still something you've done a hundred times before. Creating a Facebook page and account takes time and is way too demanding and sophisticated.'

I wait, weighing up his words.

'Cam?'

'I'm here.'

'Forget it. It wasn't you. No way.' He pauses, then asks, 'Is there a problem with the page?'

'Not very tasteful. In fact, I'd say downright suggestive.'

'For God's sake, why would anyone do something like that?'

'Sickos,' I say.

'I'm sorry you had to go through that with Emma's sister. Couldn't have been pleasant.'

'It wasn't. It was very unpheasant... unpleasant.'

I hear a tinny announcement over a PA system in the background. Adam talks over it. 'Put it out of your mind, Cam. Do something else today. Something that'll cheer you up. Like not going to IKEA.'

'I will. Thanks for talking to me.'

'Any time. You know that.'

'I do. I'll expect an IKEA pencil the next time we meet.' But he's rung off before I can get a response to my attempt at a joke.

I only ate half of my Spoons breakfast so I take my medication, slice up a pear for lunch and eat it with some Gouda. Another one of Rachel's little standbys and one I've adopted when I'm not that hungry. Whenever he gets the chance, Owen says it's as Gouda lunch as any. It always makes Ewan laugh so who am I to argue.

Then I take all the books I've read since Turkey happened off the bookshelf. They're in alphabetical order. I rearrange them by colour of spine. Then I arrange them by alphabetical title. Then by spine size. It helps.

I watch another episode of *The Night Of*. It helps too, but I can't stop thinking about what happened today at The Pommelers Rest and Emma 'Roxy' Roxburgh's Facebook page. I told Adam I think it must be a sicko. That's one of Leon's words. But it is a good one. I also know that I am the only one who truly understands what this all means. It isn't me that's pretending to be Emma. But I think it may be only me that noticed a comment halfway down the list of thirty under Emma's pinned post.

GASMAN

We had good times, Ems. Hope you're flying high as a kite.

When I was in hospital, I underwent lots of operations. I have a titanium plate in my orbit to support my almost blind eye. I also had some wiring in my jawbone. When they went back in to take out some of those wires, a doctor came to see me. He was cheerful and reassuring. He introduced himself by saying he was the gasman for the following day's operating list and that he'd be the one putting me to sleep. I didn't laugh. He didn't care. That's what you call rapport.

I don't for one minute think it was he who posted on Emma 'Roxy' Roxburgh's Facebook page. But thanks to him I know that gasman is a term doctors often use for anaesthetists.

We had good times, Ems could mean anything. But, knowing what I know, *Hope you're flying high as a kite* could only mean one thing.

Emma's supposed affair was with an anaesthetist.

I bounce around questions that rebound against the inside of my skull and none of them land with an answer. I have no proof that my suspicions have any real, hard foundations. But I know one thing for certain. I will work with John Stamford to find out.

26

C anfield Brain Injury rehabilitation unit is a stone's throw from Greenwich, tucked into a quiet lane behind the busy A2 as it runs east towards Woolwich. Every Sunday I go back and visit. My way of paying back, or forward – I'm never quite sure which applies. Most of the patients who were there when I was have moved on through physical therapy, practising assisted daily living and a goal-oriented care plan. I know because I've been through it. I'm lucky. But not everyone is.

Vanessa is almost twenty now. She was on a section of the M25, heading home after landing in Gatwick. They'd been to a family wedding in Crete. That section of motorway is a smart motorway with no hard shoulder. It was dark when their Renault lost all power and stalled. They drifted into the inside lane with no lights on and no juice for the flashers. Vanessa's father was speaking to the AA when the Renault was rear-ended by a forty-four-ton juggernaut.

Vanessa's parents and younger brother were killed instantly. Vanessa, asleep in the back, catapulted out through the windscreen and over the crash barrier into the wasteland to the side of the road. Her injuries were severe. Life-changing is a term that seems to have leaked into common usage. But I don't like it; too much room for manoeuvre. I mean, if you're a pianist and you lose two fingers, that just might qualify as changing your life. If you're a budding model, a scar on your forehead might even sway a jury.

But being smashed into by a truck transporting eight cars doing sixty miles an hour does more than stop you playing the piano or get anxious about a posed selfie.

So life-changing, yes. But catastrophic would be the word I'd more likely have chosen. Vanessa required a craniotomy to relieve the pressure on her swollen brain and a fusion procedure to stabilise her damaged spine.

She is paralysed below the waist.

Both of her parents were only children. There are a handful of distant second cousins, but, to all intents and purposes, Vanessa is alone in the world. She is also in a wheelchair, unable to stand without help.

Her speech is slow and slurred. Her coordination poor. More often than not, when I call, I am her only visitor. I'm there because I'm one of the few people who knows what she is going through. She calls me the big brother she never had. She thinks I am the only person, apart from the brilliant therapists at the unit, who treats her as a human being.

To everyone else she's a wobbly freak in a wheelchair.

She should have known not to tell me that, because now, when she gets uppity, that's what I call her. VW. Vanessa the wobbly.

But that's okay. She gives as good as she gets. She calls me Cam-a-one – referencing my blind eye – when we trade these affectionate insults.

All the staff recognise me. I greet them as old friends. But I'm here for Vanessa.

The sky is clear and even though March isn't over, the sun is pleasant on my neck as I wheel her out into the street, and we head to a pub for a drink and a sandwich lunch. Unlike the clientele at the Grey Goose and The Pommelers Rest, some people are heeding the request to minimise social contact. For a change we have no difficulty in finding a table. I ask, 'The usual?'

'Onleeifyourhavinone.' Her words slur and tend to run together. But I have no trouble understanding. I'm attuned.

'Today I think vodka and lime on the rocks.'

'Then a double rum and Coke it is. No ice. But I want an umbrella and a cherry.' Vanessa smiles, and lifts her chin, which shakes faintly from side to side. She has a glorious smile. 'Make it happen.' The last sentence comes out as 'Makeitappn.'

'You sound half pissed,' I tease.

'I'm a cheap date.' She waves her fingers in the air, laughing at her own joke. She does that a lot. Sometimes she laughs when she should be crying. But that's just disinhibition. She'll get over that. Just like she got over the enormous halo frame screwed into her skull which was present when I first met her. It was there to stabilise her spine. But she said they'd attached it because they finally worked out that she was a fallen angel.

An iron halo for an iron girl.

We overlapped at the unit for only about three weeks. When I got out Vanessa stayed. That's why I'm here.

I bring back the drinks. Diet Cokes with ice and lemon for the both of us. The rum and vodka are just our little joke.

It's a friendly pub. They even dare to use the word 'gastro' which adds an acceptable level of pretentiousness. So the shared lunch 'sandwich and chips' becomes chargrilled rosemary focaccia with pesto and balsamic-roasted tomatoes, and kachori lentil fritters. While we wait for our food, we talk about her week. Her progress is slow, but she's doing great. She's still in the unit because she's in the throes of selling her parents' house and buying a flat for herself. One adapted for her needs. That takes a lot of courage, a lot of money and a lot of time.

'The insurance money is coming through,' says Vanessa in response to my requesting an update. 'Takes for ever.'

'You could always move in with me,' I say.

'I'm having enough trouble looking after myself. I'd be hopeless having to look after you, too.'

'Hilarious.'

'Anyway, thanks for the offer, but no thanks.'

Rachel's been helping Vanessa with a financial plan. Sorting out the house and arranging investments for the insurance payout that Vanessa got. All so that she can live comfortably while she recovers. She's buying a flat in a new development in Elephant and Castle. That's not far from me. I've told her that means all my friends will be able to help.

'That's another two people then.' Dry as a bone is Vanessa.

She wants to get back to finishing her course at university. But what I want is to see her walk again. The docs tell her there is no chance. She can't stand unassisted. But we've both seen the YouTube videos of the robotic exoskeletons that people with lower-limb paralysis can strap on and walk with. It's sci-fi writ large but they are astonishing and in the marketplace. The trouble is, they're also monstrously expensive. Around £100,000 for the machine, software training, etc. Cost means that these things are not available on the NHS. I think it would be great for Vanessa.

But we don't talk about it much because that kind of money is no joke.

Still, I'd love to see her try. So I'm on it.

'What about your week, Cam?'

'I drove for the first time.'

'Wow. How many dead?'

'Yeah, yeah, laugh it up. When I've done a bit more we'll be off to Brighton for lunch. Just you and me.'

I see her face change and realise with a pang that perhaps she may not want to go for a trip in the car. Not mine nor anyone's.

'If you want to, that is,' I add with haste.

'I do. But not yet.'

'No, no. In the summer. When it's shot.'

'Hot,' she corrects me. And the smile is back.

When the food arrives, I tuck a serviette into Vanessa's collar front and we eat. She's a great kid. I've never heard her complain once since she arrived in the unit. One day, she will walk into this pub with me. I have a plan. We chat and drink another Diet Coke for a couple of hours and then I take her back to the unit because I can see she's getting tired. I kiss her on the cheek when I leave. Promise I'll be back next week.

27

A t 7.53 that evening, Nicole calls. Her voice is bright with anticipation.

'Hey,' she says.

'Hey yourself.'

'I finally managed to get away from Mia – she of the never-ending hen do. I told Aaron I was going back to my flat for a soak in the bath and an early night.'

'Sounds like a tough weekend.'

'I'm tired of wedding talk. But I'm not tired. How are you?'

'A lot has happened since I saw you last.'

'Good or bad?'

'Both.'

'Do you want me to come over?'

'Is it far? I don't have a clue where you live?'

Nicole laughs. 'Minor detail. A flat-share with two other girls in Wandsworth. Converted council accommodation. In other words, the pits. I can be there in half an hour.'

'Didn't you want a bath?'

'Don't you have hot water?'

'I don't have a bath.'

'No, but you have a shower. Much better for the environment. And big enough for the both of us if I remember.'

Later, when we've had two showers, one before and one after Nicole has been her wonderful, generous and experimental self again, we sit with a glass of wine (just the one for me) and I tell Nicole about what's happened with Stamford and Harriet. She listens, both surprised and horrified.

We're on the sofa with just a table lamp lit. She rests her head on my arm, her fingers playing with a loose thread on my shirt. 'I feel awful that you've had to do all this alone. Why don't you wait until I can help you? Emma's sister sounds like a real cow.'

'She isn't. She's still very upset about Emma.'

Nicole sits up and stares at me with eyes muted to the colour of a stormy sea in the room's shadow. 'You won't say anything bad about anyone, will you?'

'I only wish I could feel some of Harriet's pain. Her sense of loss. But I can't. Emma's death is like any stranger's death to me. Awful, yes. But distant. Like reading about some terrible disaster that's happened on another continent. You're sympathetic but too far removed for it to have real impact. And it sounds like Emma's family have been through hell.'

'What would you call what you've been through?'

'An unsteady walk in the spark... park.'

Nicole snorts and snuggles up to my arm again, her small hands wrapped around my bicep. Leon would be proud that there are some to wrap around. Nicole's hands are like a child's. But when she's in bed, they're one hundred per cent adult in what they do.

'Once the wedding is over, I promise I'll come with you to see the police and this private detective. Sounds like he knows what he's doing.'

'That would be great. But it's easier for me to talk to him now with Rachel not being on my case. She's tied up with the kids and she would not approve. Besides, I've lit the blue touch scraper.'

'Paper,' says Nicole. But her voice is tender, not mocking. 'I hope you're not doing this just for my sake,' she says into my arm. 'I don't want you getting into trouble for me.'

'I'm not doing it only for you. I need to clear a path for the future. For me as well as for us.'

Nicole tilts her head up. I study her face. Her skin is the colour of mellow ivory. 'I like it when you say us,' she murmurs. She buries her head and snuggles into my arm like a cat. 'I never thought I'd hear you say it.' Her hair is clean and smells of cucumber. 'I can't wait to get this wedding over. I promise we'll spend the whole of the weekend after next together.'

'That sounds nice,' I say.

'All I have to do is get Aaron out of my hair.'

'Will that be difficult?'

She squeezes my arm with nails painted pillar-box red. 'It shouldn't be. He thinks of himself as God's gift and tells me at least twice a week that I am lucky to have him.'

'Is he?'

'No on both counts.'

'Okay. So he'll be happy to be a free agent then?'

'You'd think so. But I know him. He's like a big kid. As soon as he knows he can't have something, he's mad for it.'

'Anything I can–'

Nicole tilts her face up once more. She smiles, but not before I glimpse the worried look it replaces.

'There is nothing you can do but be patient. I'll sort it out. I promise.'

She calls an Uber at eleven and I'm left alone in the flat with my memory boards and heady Bandit hanging in the air, hoping that Aaron, whoever he is, is willing to be a grown up.

Nicole seems confident.

The trouble is, if I was losing someone like Nicole, I know I wouldn't be.

28

D S Keely knows Harriet Roxburgh well enough to be on first-name terms. That's what being the FLO in a case such as Emma's does for you. There is nothing Stockholm syndrome about it, though she'd spent days at the Roxburghs' house in the immediate aftermath of the horrors of Turkey and it was difficult to not sometimes feel that they were all being held hostage to dreadful circumstances.

But a link had been forged and it was now a question of continued contact and a wary respect. Not a friendship as such. At least not from Keely's point of view. And she isn't sure how Harriet might classify the arrangement. Given what Keely has seen of Harriet's nature, she doubts she makes friends easily.

Keely checks herself and wipes the thought. Opinion, not fact. It's still a bit of a tightrope walk when it comes to dealing with the Roxburghs though. Harriet deserves empathy but tempered by a degree of toughness. Especially when everything becomes messy and she blows up into a rage, accusing the police of not doing enough, of incompetence, of not giving a 'flying fuck'.

Keely never quite got to grips with knowing what a flying

fuck is even meant to be. But you learn never to sever the ties when there's an open verdict and an ongoing investigation. The relatives deserve no less. Even when said investigation has hit a roadblock if not a complete dead end. And Keely is not a great believer in coincidence. So she understands the nagging itch that comes from seeing Harriet turn up at the station just days after Cameron Todd. An itch that will need to be scratched.

But not yet. First, she listens to what Emma's wound-up sister has to say.

'I brought it along in case you wanted to do fingerprints and such.'

Keely stares at the envelope inside a sealed, clear plastic bag held in Harriet's hands. The envelope is manila, A5. Already opened, a brown smear on the inside of the ripped flap tells the story. She hopes, for Harriet's sake, that she used a letter opener and not her finger to do the ripping. Even though the plastic bag is a barrier, the unpleasant sweetness of its faecal odour is unmistakable.

'And you think Cameron Todd did this?'

Harriett looks aghast. 'Who else?'

'Any reason you suspect him?'

'We argued.' Harriet's lips are wafer thin as she delivers this little sweetmeat.

They're in the corridor at the station. Harriet is dressed in jeans and a padded gilet over a woolly jumper. She has scuffed trainers on her feet. She looks as if she's come straight from home after discovering the post without passing go. Keely finds an empty interview room, ushers Harriet in and closes the door.

'What kind of argument?'

'A tiny altercation. In a pub. We bumped into one another. These things happen. Did you know he's opened a new Facebook account in Emma's name?'

Harriet has no accent, other than the one that comes from

attending a good school that ensured a lot of stars got added to her first letter of the alphabet exam results. The ones that smoothed the way into medical school. Her sentences are clipped and assured. Keely has long since discovered that though bluster and confidence might get you a long way in the outside world, they count for sod all in the sceptical eyes of the law. She composes her face into a questioning pout. 'No, I didn't. He told you that, did he?'

'No, of course not,' Harriet answers. 'But who else would do such a filthy thing?'

'So he denied it?'

'Yes he denied it. But then this appears.' Harriet waves the bag. 'As good as admitting it was him, isn't it? I needed half a litre of Hibiscrub to get my bloody hands clean. I'm sorry, but he should not be allowed out on the streets unsupervised.'

Keely tilts her head with raised eyebrows. 'That's a little extreme, no?'

'Opening Facebook accounts in the name of your dead girl-friend and posting shit through her sister's letterbox I'd consider pretty damning. God, how much ammunition do you need?'

Ammunition, thinks Keely, for a firing squad no doubt. No accident in that word choice. In another universe Harriet Roxburgh would happily shoot Cameron Todd if she had the chance.

'Did you see him do it?'

'No.'

'And he denies the Facebook thing?'

'Yes. That's why I brought the envelope. Fingerprints. DNA.'

'DNA? For a dog turd? I can tell you now we have no Alsatians on the database. Though I read that Southend council are considering testing pavement sausages and some village in Essex has been doing it for a couple of years. I even think there's a company you can register your hound with called PooPrints.'

Harriet's face sets hard. 'I'm glad you're finding this funny, sergeant.'

'Ooh, sergeant is it? We being formal now?'

'Rhian, this is no joke.'

'Agreed. The smell of that envelope certainly isn't. But unless you saw him do something there is no case. Did Todd say anything else to you during your argument?'

'No. He was doing his rabbit in the headlights act. Again.'

'I don't think that's an act, Harriet.'

'Don't tell me he has you fooled too?'

Keely sighs. 'Did Emma ever mention anything about a colleague at Guy's who was in trouble over drug abuse?'

Harriet frowns. 'No. Why?'

'Something's come up, that's all.'

'You can't say that and not explain.'

'I can. And I will. You'll be the first to know if it has legs. Once we've made our enquiries.'

'Emma was allergic to other medics after what happened to her in Bristol.' Harriet issues this as a statement in a low hissing tone. 'You know that.'

'I do. But it would be remiss of me not to ask.'

'In a way, I wish she had been involved with another medic. Rather than that Cameron bloody Todd. Please tell me you'll bring him in and talk to him.'

Bring him in. Keely hesitates for three seconds, toying with not wanting to give Harriet the satisfaction of believing she's Queen of the Nile. But then realises that for once she's one step ahead in this little game. 'I promise I will. Talk to him, that is.'

'Soon?' Harriet waves the bag again.

'Today.' Keely folds her arms. 'As soon as I can arrange it.'

29

Leon has me doing a kettlebell circuit. Swings, then figure of eight, alternate swings, upright rows, squat to shoulder presses then single arm lifts. When I told Josh about kettlebells – he'd never heard of them – that they were like cannonballs with handles you swing between your legs and over your head, he almost had a fit laughing.

'Anyone had a billiards injury, bell against ball?' He was giggling hard when he said this.

'I'll ask Leon,' I replied, but Josh didn't hear because by that stage he was making small mewling noises and holding his stomach with mirth-pains.

But Leon tells me kettlebells are great for coordination and core, combining weights with movement. In between sets I rehydrate.

'How are you then, mate?' Leon asks as I gulp water from a metal bottle. An odd question. It isn't as if I've just walked into the room.

'I'm good,' I reply, warily, in case his question is a lead into an extra set.

'Noticing a bit of a spring in your step today. Know what I'm saying?'

He's fishing. He thinks it's got something to do with my love life. Maybe it does. Time I dropped the 'M' bomb. 'Think I'll be fit enough for a half marathon in three months?'

Leon does a theatrical double take before his face breaks into a huge grin. 'No reason at all. In fact, I got two clients in the same aspirational boat, man. I worked out a wicked programme for them, yeah? We're on the same wave. Mostly roadwork as it gets closer. But three months? No worries.'

'Even with my gammy leg?'

'Compensate. If it's safe, we'll deal with it.'

'Will you sponsor me?'

'You got a sheet. I'll sign up.'

'No, no sheet. I'm going the web way. I'm on JustGiving.'

'Cool. You have a target?'

'Twenty k.'

Leon dips his head into his shoulders as his eyes go wide. 'Oh my days. Are you buying a Ferrari, Cameron?'

'No. But it is to do with transportation.'

'You could buy a Tardis with that, man.'

'That's precisely what I'm doing.'

Leon slaps his thigh. 'Hah. I like that. Okay, let's get another kettlebell set done and dusted. Then we'll get you treadmilled up.'

'I see you're going to enjoy this.'

'Gain is pain, Cam.'

'What if they close the gyms?'

Leon looks offended. 'Why would they do that? I mean this virus lark needs fit people, you know what I'm saying? Where else are clients going to do weights and shit?'

'Agreed, but if you watch the news it looks inevitable.'

'That would be so not cool.'

'If it happens, we could still do this online.'

'You got some bells at home?'

'No, but I can get some. A 10 or 12 and maybe a 14kg. Skipping rope. Use a chair as a step.'

Leon considers this as if I'm contemplating going to the moon. 'Not cheap, Cam.'

'Well, I reckon there'll be a rush if a lockdown kicks in. I'll get some ordered today.'

'You're giving me the blues, man.'

My phone is on my towel on the edge of a mat a few feet away. It chimes out a text alert. I hold a finger up for Leon and check. A message from Keely. She wants to see me tomorrow.

Leon watches with disapproval all over his smooth face.

'Anything interesting?'

'Just the cops asking me to go in.'

Leon, mouth gaping, blinks before he erupts with another guffaw. 'You crack me up every time, Cam. Every time. Keeping it real like always. You ready to work now?'

I pick up a kettlebell. Put on my game face.

Leon says, 'In five, four, three, two, one...'

30

Keely sends Messiter down to greet Todd. She meets them in the room that she'd used to speak to Harriet Roxburgh the previous day. Todd is in sweatshirt and pants and holding an aluminium drinks bottle in one hand. She's suggested Messiter sits in. Like it or not he's a part of this now.

'Any news of the anaesthetist?' Todd asks, direct as always.

Keely is sitting with a file in her hands. She offers Todd a seat. But it isn't the sergeant that answers his question. Instead, she turns to Messiter. 'Dan, tell Mr Todd what you found out.'

Messiter takes the file and, still standing, pulls out a sheet. 'First off, there was no evidence of anyone dealing drugs. The hospital wanted to make that very clear. But they suspended a female anaesthetist for stealing drugs. Dr Roxburgh was involved only as someone who spoke up on behalf of this doctor. She was a close friend, apparently. The doctor concerned, an Alison Barnet, was disciplined. She's just finished eighteen months of rehab and a phased return under supervision. She's now back on the medical register and working in a drop-in centre in Manchester.'

'So there was no charge?' Todd asks.

'The hospital did not want to press charges. They dealt with the issue internally and reported it to the GMC. They're the ones who police doctor's fitness to practise, not us.'

'Even doctors fall off their pedestals sometimes,' Keely adds. 'Could it be this is what your notebook message was about?'

'Liar, liar,' Todd mutters. 'Possible, I suppose.' He sends Messiter one of his glares. 'And there was no talk of an affair.'

'I got this from the hospital's Human Resources department. They weren't exactly keen to talk. They take confidentiality very seriously. But from what I understand, Dr Roxburgh and Alison Barnet were old friends. In med school together.'

Todd waits.

'Anything's possible.' Messiter squirms. 'But Barnet was in a relationship with a male colleague at the time.'

Todd is massaging his forehead. 'And all this took place just before we went to Turkey?'

'Barnet's suspension was in September, the month before,' Keely explains. 'And I've spoken to her. She denies any kind of sexual relationship with Emma. Became very upset that I even suggested it. She considered Emma a very good, loyal and supportive friend. I suppose Emma might have told you about this. Perhaps that's what you remember. It would be easy to get confused.'

'Two and two make five. I know,' Todd says.

Keely watches him flit his eyes around the room, searching. She's seen the exact same move countless times from desperate people with nowhere else to go. Whether the parent of a lost child, or a caught-out thief, there are no answers anywhere on these featureless walls. And yet she can't help wondering if he's holding something back.

'Confused is my Lidl name,' Todd says and then adds resignedly. 'Middle name. I thought it might be important, that's all.'

'Fair enough,' Keely says. She pauses for a beat before speaking again. When she does, it's phrased as a question. 'I hear you bumped into Harriet Roxburgh?'

'Who told you that?'

'She did.'

Todd looks away and lets out a moan of dry laughter. 'She thinks I've posted something on Facebook about her sister.'

'Have you?'

He gives a brief shake of his head. 'Why would I do that?'

'I don't know. Perhaps you were confused...' She wants to add the word 'again' but stops herself at the sight of Todd's face stiffening.

'I'm not that confused. I was right about Emma being involved in something at the hospital, wasn't I? It's only the details I got wrong.'

'Harriet Roxburgh brought in an envelope that someone posted through her letterbox,' Keely says.

'Okay...' Todd is wary.

'It was full of dog excrement.'

'And you think I, in my confused state, did that, too?'

'Did you?'

'No.'

'You are still in therapy, are you, Mr Todd?' Messiter asks.

Keely is too late to suppress the little smile that brushes her lips. She hides it by glancing down at the desk. Messiter has come in with the sucker punch at precisely the right moment. As they'd rehearsed.

'You know I am,' Todd says. 'I fractured my skull, constable. It wiped my memory of who I was, where I came from, who I knew and loved, and left me incapable of even the most basic tasks. But it didn't make me mad.'

'I spoke to Dr Spalding. He tells me you still get fugues,' Keely says.

'You spoke to Adam?' Todd looks affronted.

'I did because it's my job. And the question still holds. You still get the fugues, yes?'

'I do. I told you all about them before.'

'You have. I'm just wondering if you remember what you're doing when one of these fugues happen. Could that cause your confusion?'

'I'm not confused. Adam will no doubt have explained to you how I can't perform complex tasks when I fugue. Opening a Facebook account isn't something I'd do on automatic.'

'What about posting dog shit through a letterbox?' Messiter asks.

There's a long beat while Todd gives Messiter a stony stare. Eventually though, he responds. 'Yes, well, that's automatic, obviously. I mean, I do that every day.'

Neither of the police officers speak.

Todd gets up. His face is flushed. 'Are we done?'

'I think so,' Keely says.

'Thanks for your help,' Todd says.

'If you remember anything else, we'd be happy to help.' Messiter puts his sheet of paper face down on the file.

He's a good goader, thinks Keely. Knows which buttons to press.

'Or perhaps I'd be better off finding things out for myself,' Todd replies.

'I wouldn't do that, Mr Todd. Too many raw wounds.' Keely doesn't want things to end on a sour note, but it looks like they failed on that score.

'Wounds need to close if they are to heal, sergeant.' Todd opens the door.

'I'll see you out.' Messiter follows.

When they've gone, Keely puts the sheet of paper back into the file and arches her back. A ligament clicks and there's a delicious release as a muscle relaxes. Bloody Zumba class. Her phone beeps. A message from Viri telling her they've just had a heads-up from the governors at his school that they're shutting up shop. There are still a few weeks to go before the Easter break, but they pulled the plug early to give students, many of whom are from abroad, a chance to get home if they can. It means Viri will work from home from now on setting up online work schedules for his pupils, attending virtual meetings, standing two metres behind people in the queue for milk and bread. They already know that A and O levels are off for this year. And that means much more detailed and intensive teacher assessments for the universities to filter through entry forms. It might mean a freebie into uni for some students. But it'll mean a heavy workload for sixth-form teachers.

She sends back a message saying that maybe that spare room in the house will get painted at last. She receives a rude reply by return.

Keely puts her phone down and brings her mind back around to Todd. She must write up this little chat. File it away until the next time Todd turns up with one of his half-baked memories. She doesn't blame him. How can she? The bloke is damaged.

She's still sitting when Messiter comes back in.

'Poor bloke,' he says.

'Yeah.'

'Do you think he posted that turd?'

Keely shrugs.

'By the way, what's a fugue anyway?'

'You'll need to google that one for the official answer. But from what I know, it's a kind of hallucination. A type of waking dream in his case.'

'What, like literally off with the fairies?'

'I doubt you'll find that definition in any of the textbooks, Daniel, but more or less. He hallucinates while he is doing other things. As if he's split in half. Like his body is in one place and his mind is somewhere else. He remembers the hallucination but not what he's actually physically doing.'

'Wow. So he could have posted that turd without knowing.'

'I doubt that. Posting turds takes special skills, like finding one for a start. If he posted them, he did so deliberately.'

'Should we test the envelope?'

'Done. I think I'm off the lab's Christmas card list.'

Messiter shakes his head. 'Still, rough deal getting your head smashed in and not even remembering your dead girlfriend.'

'Trouble is he is remembering. Or thinks he is.'

'That's harsh.'

'Perhaps. But this case has destroyed a family.'

'What about him?'

'He's still alive, isn't he?'

Messiter says nothing and his silence draws Keely's gaze. 'What?' she asks.

'I still think he's had a rough deal.'

'Not as rough as his girlfriend or her family. What would help them, not to mention the rest of us, is if he told us what happened.'

'You think he knows?'

'If he does, he's the best damned actor I ever met. The trouble is, amnesia is too...'

'Convenient?'

Keely smiles. 'See, now you're starting to think like a detective, constable.'

Messiter remains silent. Keely's words zip his mouth shut. He picks up the file and walks out of the door. As he does, she hears him mutter, 'Harsh.'

31

I don't hear from Nicole at all on Monday or Tuesday. I'm not bothered because she has a lot of baggage to sort through, what with Mia's wedding and the Aaron problem. She'll get back to me when she can, I'm certain.

On Wednesday, I get up at 7.45 and do my usual thing. Drink a glass of water, brush my teeth, stretch – lots of sometimes painful stretches because my muscles and their tendons, in all those long months of inactivity, shortened and stiffened. No breakfast, not yet. I'm on the 16:8. Adam's idea. Eat food within an eight-hour window only. The other sixteen hours I fast. A way of controlling intake and prevent snacking to which I'm prone. Rachel, for once, was very keen.

'We do it most days of the week. Never on weekends. And booze can properly bugger it up. Empty calories and all that,' was how she'd explained it with the zeal of the converted.

Not that my skinny malink of a sister needs to worry about obesity. She never stands still long enough. But a 16:8 is another way of trying to control her universe. And if there's one thing Rachel craves, it's control.

After the stretches, I shower. Then I tidy my bedroom and

clean the bathroom. Not that it needs it. I never let it get dirty. I saw an admiral once give a TED talk about how, as recruits, they were made to make their beds perfectly first thing in the morning. The first task of the day, once completed, sets the tone for what's to follow. A small thing, but by doing the little things correctly, there's hope for accomplishing bigger things. And added to that is the fact that a made bed is a splendid thing to crawl into after a grim day at the office, the gym or, as in my case, the clinic. So I make the bed and clean the bathroom.

Today I need to keep busy because I must let the other half of my brain think. To analyse what's been going on. Keely's questions about Harriet and her vague accusations upset me more than I was willing to admit.

I posted nothing. Not on Facebook. And certainly not through a letterbox.

At a little after nine, my mobile rings. I check the number, pause for a second, and then answer. I hear gravel.

'Hi. It's John Stamford.'

'Yes. Your number is in my contacts.'

'I appreciate you taking my call. I was worried that after Saturday–'

'Harriet was upset.'

'She was out of order.'

'She's been to the police because someone had posted dog ship... shit... through her door. She thinks I did it.' I wait for him to ask if I did. He doesn't. I like Stamford a little more.

'She's angry.'

'I understand that. And not just about Facebook or the dog stuff, right?'

'No. Still, I'm sorry she dragged you into it.'

'So am I.'

There's a pause and then Stamford asks, 'I'm ringing to see if we can start again? We didn't talk properly.'

'We were Harrieted.'

I hear a noise that might be a mini guffaw. 'We were. Plus there's news about your anaesthetist.'

'Alison Barnet?'

Stamford laughs again. 'You continue to surprise me, Mr Todd. Not many people can do that.'

'Cameron,' I say.

'Okay, Cameron. I'm working from the office this morning. Why don't you come over? I'll get some coffee on.'

He gives me an address in New Cross. 'Do I need to bring body armour?'

'You can borrow mine.'

I don't drive. I walk to Tower Bridge and get a train to New Cross Gate. From there it's a quick stroll along New Cross Road. I pass betting shops and hair and beauty salons, cafes and the odd restaurant. I take a right at The White Hart. One of two big pubs I spot in the area. But half a dozen businesses are boarded up, windows nailed over with swollen sterling boards pasted with for sale or rent signs. This is not high-end London. This is unfashionable, ungentrified, South East London. The few places that are open don't strike me as capable of surviving a complete closure as has happened in Italy or Spain.

Locate Intelligence is Stamford's business address. A grand name for a not-so-grand premises above a defunct sports shop with graffiti on the door and a steel grille over the window. I press the button marked L.I., and I'm buzzed in.

The stairs are narrow and wheelchair unfriendly. I can smell something unpleasant from a closed door to my right. Stamford comes to the half turn in the stair and says, 'The sods buggered off back to Karachi and left a fridge full of food.

It's been removed, but the smell hasn't. It lingers. In fact, it follows. Like in that horror film of the same name. Come on up.'

I take the turn and follow Stamford. The stairwell fills with his big backside covered by black trousers that are shiny over the rump. His shoes have rubber soles, his white shirt has the cuffs rolled back to reveal thick forearms. One, on the left, has a tattoo.

I follow him into an office with open windows facing the busy street outside. The room we enter has a paper-cluttered desk, filing cabinets, corkboards and three computer monitors. In the corner is a kettle surrounded by a handful of mugs and canisters. Beneath it is a mini fridge. The office chair is empty.

'Mandy's day off. She goes to college.'

'Is she your assistant?'

'Yeah. My sister Lucy's girl. Purple hair and nose rings. Mandy, that is. She'll grow out of that if she sticks. She says she has a taste for this. Before her it was all temps. We'll see.'

Stamford opens another door into a second room. This one has better furniture, a pale desk, the chair behind is more substantial and padded. Two armchairs squat on the other side of the room.

'Take a seat. Coffee?'

'Okay.' I suppress the urge to ask what kind he has.

Stamford disappears back into the outer room and talks to me with the volume up a notch through the open door.

'It's only instant.'

'Fine,' I say. No point being a coffee snob in New Cross.

'Sugar and milk?'

'Yes, to both. One sugar.'

Certificates and licences pepper the wall behind the desk. Association of British Investigators. Information Commissioner's Office registration number. Plus a photo of a younger, thinner Stamford in his Met uniform. All hung like hunter's trophies to inspire confidence in the punter this side of the desk.

I presume.

Stamford brings the coffee, hands me a mug and then sits in an armchair. I follow suit. There's a coaster on the desk and I dock my mug.

'Biscuit?' asks Stamford.

I shake my head. This is cosy. We're doing informal.

'Thanks for coming,' he says. 'And once again, I apologise for what happened last Saturday. I assure you it was not an ambush.'

'But you still work for Harriet.'

'I do. But what happened was... unacceptable. Unprofessional. Mandy and I had words. Though how many of them stuck is anyone's guess. She's feisty.'

'Mandy or Harriet.'

'Both,' says Stamford.

The coffee is nothing like my bean to cup. But it is warm and wet when I sip it.

'So,' continues Stamford, 'I looked into the anaesthetist business. Not much joy, I'm afraid.'

'No. I got it wrong.' I tell him about my visit to Sergeant Keely and DC Messiter. About what they told me about Emma's friend, the drug user.

'More or less what I found out,' Stamford says.

'The police think I'm becoming confused.'

'Are you?'

I smile. 'Why don't we stop playing games? You know all about me. Even if you don't, Harriet does. She must have told you about my fugues.'

'You suffer from hallucinations.'

'Very specific kinds of hallucinations. They're highly repetitive. The people I meet in these hallucinations are always the same people. The place I meet them is the same place. I'm awake, but not fully, and I'm not aware of what I'm doing physically.' I pause and then add, 'but lately they've changed.'

Stamford's expression is neutral, wanting me to explain and I'm happy to oblige. I let the words pour out.

'I had what they call an SBI, a severe brain injury, that left me with total amnesia. Ever since I became fit enough to walk and feed myself, I've been trying to fill the huge void in my head. Most of everything I do and have done for the last year involves trying to remember. I do this in several ways. The first is listening to people. Asking them to tell me, or better, show me photographs or videos. Most of the time these might as well be of a stranger. I can tell from looking in the mirror that these images are of me. But it's like looking at someone else. Occasionally, a word or a sentence works. Something will click and I'll remember a fragment which leads to another. Like dominoes.'

Stamford sips his coffee. His mug is charcoal-coloured with the words GET SHIT DONE in big white letters.

'Then there are things I find out for myself. One of the best ways is experiential memory. Going back to places I'm supposed to have visited in the past. Seeing people or buildings again. Sometimes that works.' I toy with telling him about Nicole. But that can wait. 'And then there are the fugues.'

I tell him about the rooftop bar, and Ivan and the dancing girls and faceless Emma and plunging off the roof into the water below. In my head I sound like a stuck record. When I finish, Stamford's expression is pained.

'Are they significant, these fugues? Can you make sense of them?'

I shrug. 'They're more abstract than logical. But I'm convinced they mean something. Who is Ivan for example? And why did a statue I haven't seen before suddenly appear and survive being sandblasted into oblivion by a storm whereas everyone else around her didn't?'

'Must be very frustrating,' Stamford says.

'Or a very convenient way of a guilty man hiding behind his illness.'

He smiles. A thin, knowing smile that tells me he's read the Harriet textbook of accusations. 'It must be tough. Not knowing.'

'Sometimes I clutch at drawers.'

He frowns.

'I meant straws. That's another quirk of mine. My friend Josh calls me Captain Quirk of the sadship Mentalprise.'

Stamford winces but is still smiling. 'Josh sounds like a character.'

'He is.'

'You're never tempted to go back to Turkey? To where it all happened?'

'I've thought about it. I had a lot of sinus pain for a while. Long plane journeys at altitude were not recommended.'

'I'm sure the Turkish police would like to interview you.'

I nod. 'We've spoken. Sergeant Keely said I should. She was present when I did, but I couldn't help them.'

Stamford locks eyes with me. 'I've been to Turkey. To the beach where Emma died, and to the hotel you stayed in. I taped it all. Do you want to see?'

'Experiential triggers are one of the best ways to remember.' More stuck record.

'Okay.' He walks around to the business side of the desk and jiggles a white wireless mouse. 'Give me a second to set up.'

I wait and sip the coffee. It's too sweet. I think Stamford was generous with the sugar. Are teaspoons of a standard size, I wonder? Did he use heaped or level? Three minutes later, Stamford sits back from hunching over the screen. 'Up and running.'

He swivels the screen so that I can see it. For now it's frozen, a smeared image of sand and sea. It could be anywhere. But it isn't. It's Turkey. Where Emma died and where I almost died.

'Ready?' asks Stamford.

'Yup,' I reply.

Stamford presses play.

32

I watch the video, shot, Stamford explains, on a GoPro attached to a baseball cap on his head. There's no sound, but Stamford provides a voice-over. He bobs along a stone and pebble beach that seems to go on for ever with the sea aquamarine and flat in a shallow bay beyond. Ahead, sand stretches in a long lazy yellow arc. He turns 180 degrees to face north. Here, the sand ends in some barren rocky cliffs. Then the view turns away from the sea, back towards the scrubby foliage behind, bordering a road that runs the length of the beach. Stamford walks forwards and stands at the edge.

A car goes by; a dusty old Mercedes. A family walk past. Blond-haired children with towels around their waists and backpacks with snorkels poking out from the flaps. They look hot. Germanic or Scandinavian, I guess.

Opposite is an entrance. The sign above an archway reads, *Mavi Pansiyon*.

I see the world from Stamford's viewpoint. But nothing is familiar.

Not the little garden with the outdoor seating area under a

canopy: 'This is the breakfast area,' Stamford commentates as the video rolls.

Not the pathway leading down past the office and through the garden with hammocks and swing seats in discreet areas walled off by tall plants: 'Guest area.'

Not the small blue bungalows lining the pathway where the video halts at number 31: 'This was your room.'

A hand reaches for the door handle. I glimpse a tattooed forearm. The door swings inwards to reveal a white room with tiled floors and a double bed with a blue eiderdown. Stamford enters, looks around, steps into a grey, tiled bathroom with modern chrome fittings.

'Anything?' he asks.

I shake my head. On-screen, Stamford fast forwards the video. Back out to the road, right, and then back over to the beach. To a bar with scattered tables and chairs arranged haphazardly under parasols on the beachfront. I read Flames Bar on sun-bleached signage. On-screen, Stamford sits, the view out to sand and sea, then swinging left up the beach to the north end and the cliffs.

'You were both here the night it happened,' Stamford explains. 'I've spoken to two couples who were also there. One, a German couple with good English, were on the next table. They said you and Emma were relaxed. Together until Emma got up and walked up the beach alone. You stayed seated for ten minutes after she left. Then you got up and followed.'

I've heard all this before. On-screen, Stamford is looking at the bar, which, in reality is more a small shack with bar stools and bottles on shelves and a chest freezer under an awning. Very basic.

'Why did Emma leave the bar alone?' Stamford asks.

I don't know. I communicate that with a shake of my head.

Stamford continues. 'You were maybe forty yards from your hotel back over the road. You could have gone there for a drink.'

'But it had no sea view,' I say.

'No.'

'Maybe Emma forgot something.'

'But you'd been out to eat. You were seen in Cirali village at a place called Yoruk's. It was about ten when you arrived at the Flames Bar. My guess is you were calling in for a nightcap. Emma left her beer half drunk.'

'Did they play music?'

'Yes. The owner was Dutch. People go for the view and the music. Chilled-out jazz funk. I think I heard some Leonard Cohen when I was there. Not an oud in sight.'

'Oud?'

'A kind of traditional guitar. You'd know it if you heard it.'

His words distract me. From somewhere, from the deep dark depths of my mind something shifts. 'Toilets,' I say.

'What?'

'They have no toilets. Emma wanted the loo. That's why she left me alone.'

Stamford freezes the video.

'Are you sure?'

'No. But something came back to me then.'

'It would make sense.' Stamford grabs a pen and scribbles something down. 'It also might explain why the German couple thought you became restless and kept looking at your watch.'

'When she didn't come back, you mean?'

'You left half your beer, too.'

'But then what?'

'North. To where it happened.'

33

He presses play and the video speeds up again. The beach flies past as he heads up towards the north end.

'Quieter up here. Farther away from the village. Mostly campsites. Boats moor in the bay here, too.'

He slows the video to normal speed as, on-screen, he approaches the jagged stones that make up the sea cliffs jutting out into the bay and cutting off the beach. A few yards from where the cliffs begin, he turns inland, follows a path in and then up along a very narrow switchback sand trail to the very top. There's a superb view of the beach to the south and the mountains behind. Then the scene shifts forwards towards the cliff edge. Finally, we're at the precipice and the camera view tilts dizzily down towards the water and the rocks beneath. Where Emma was found.

'If you want me to stop at any time?'

'No,' I say.

The camera pans right, back towards the incongruous, fractured stone and concrete jetty standing proud of the water along the beach. A different view of it from the clifftop. I've seen this view many times before but only in police photographs. Seeing it in real time like this is very different.

'That's what I fell off. They found me somewhere around that jetty.'

'You were in the water, bleeding from a head wound. Emma's body was washed up against the rocks at the bottom of the cliffs below where I am standing with the camera.'

Stamford freezes the frame. The jetty is rough and ready, patched and uneven, the rocks on which it is built piled beneath it. A high, jerry-built platform with no barriers or fencing. I've seen images of the party boats tied up here. Brigs with sails that are never unfurled, disembarking passengers from their top decks along wooden gangways they keep on the boats on this jetty. But never images of anyone jumping or diving from it. Too dangerous because of the other, older collapsed structures beneath it. Not big on health and safety is this part of the Turkish coast it seems.

Stamford unfreezes the video and lets it pan back to the viewpoint from the cliff, freezes it again. I stare at the screen for a long time; at an azure sky and parched rocks, the blue-green sea below. 'It makes no sense either of us being anywhere near that path.' I shake my head.

Stamford looks at me, his head bobbing. 'No. Not in the dark. Would have been pitch black.'

'It seems mad. But we must have had a reason.'

Stamford checks his notes. 'Emma left the hotel before you got back. Maybe fifteen minutes had passed. When you saw she wasn't there, you asked the manager's son if he'd seen her. He told you she'd turned left out of the hotel and walked north.'

'Did I follow?'

'Yes. Two hotel guests saw you running up the road. You went onto the beach. A short time later, someone moored on a boat forty yards out in the bay hears a scream and splashing.

Then more shouting. They used lights from the boats and they saw you floating. Someone jumped in and fished you out. By the time police arrived, they'd found Emma's body too. But it was the rocks that killed her.'

I squeeze my eyes shut. Try and remember. The story is one I'm horribly familiar with but all I see behind the blackness of my lids is more blackness. A void. I open my eyes.

'Harriet thinks Emma and I had a fight. That I was chasing her.'

'That isn't how I read the narrative. It's more that you were worried about her, trying to find her.'

'But what if she's right? What if we fought and I pushed her?'

Stamford stares. 'Did you?'

I want to believe that I couldn't do that. I avoid answering with another question. 'Did the German couple at the bar think we'd been fighting?' I ask.

'No. They didn't.'

'Then why did Emma leave that hotel alone?'

'Why do you think?'

I shake my head.

Stamford prompts me. 'Why does anyone go anywhere in a hurry?'

I run with it. 'Either to get away from someone or something, or to meet someone or something.'

Stamford looks pleased. 'Deductive reasoning. Ying and Yang. So if Emma wasn't trying to get away from you–'

'Perhaps she was meeting someone.'

'Exactly.'

'But who? Cirali is a sleepy beach resort. Emma wanted a complete break. She was searching for her inner hippy. At least, this is what I've been told.'

'Go on.'

179

'If she wasn't running from me, and I hope she wasn't, if she was going to meet someone, who could it have been?'

Again Stamford nods. 'You were in the middle of nowhere. I will state the obvious now, but I find it sometimes helps to vocalise these things. If she was meeting someone, then it was either a local or a visitor. The Turkish police did a good job of eliminating locals. Cirali isn't an enormous place without tourists. They knew everyone who lived there.'

'Then that leaves the visitors.'

'And everyone who stayed in Cirali had to show their passports. They've all been traced and more or less ruled out.'

'So where does that leave us?'

'With the one group of people you haven't mentioned.'

I ponder. My research on Cirali suggested it attracts all sorts but those that spend any time there fall into two camps. The younger set: Scandinavians, Russians and other Europeans, looking for the simple life. Perhaps hiking the Lycian Way with backpacks. Or hippies and surfers willing to go off-grid and camp out on one of the many beaches further along the unspoilt coast.

And then there's the other lot. The socks-and-sandals brigade. An older set decked out in safari suits with wide-brimmed hats. History buffs clutching guidebooks as they clamber over the crumbling stones of the ruins of Olympos; the ancient city that sits incongruously at the south end of the beach. A mecca for Marcus Aurelius fans hoping to pay homage to his burial place. This same group would also be drawn to the Chimaera. The eternal flames that burned all year round from trapped gas escaping up through fissures in the rocks. Greek mythology there, as it was then, still doing its thing for all to see. I've read that one thing to do in Cirali is to trek up to the Chimaera to see the flames still alight after dark. Some people in the YouTube videos I'd seen were even toasting marsh-mallows.

As you do.

So Cirali wasn't just a laid-back beach. It attracted day trip-pers by the score. I share this with Stamford. He listens, impressed.

'Correct. And people who came for the day in coaches and minibuses would not need to show identification to anyone. But the busloads from Antalya had long gone by the time you were sitting in the Flames Bar on the beach. Too dark to visit Olympos then.'

My heart slides. But Stamford has a light in his eyes. 'But what if you weren't a part of an organised tour? What if you had your own car?'

'Then there's no hope of finding anyone–'

The expression in Stamford's face stops me. 'That's the thing about car hire. You need to show ID. And these days, a lot of hire cars possess navigation systems. A few, the more unscrupulous hire firms, can track where you are and how far you've driven their battered Yaris along the dirt roads.' He pulls out a printed spreadsheet. 'I've got to know the Turkish police reasonably well. Worked hard to gain their trust. Several bottles of Glenfid-dich later they came up with a list of foreign nationals who hired cars and travelled to Cirali in the forty-eight-hour period leading up to Emma's death.'

He takes out a sheet of paper and slides over a printed-out list of thirty names.

'I only received this a week ago in a handwritten letter. That's what prompted my call to you. I tried to whittle it down, take out the outliers – a couple of Japanese and the Turkish and Greek ones. Take a gander. See if anything rings a bell.'

I rotate the sheet and pore over it, but they're just names.

Black letters on a white page. Mandy has typed them out in alphabetical order.

```
Abbot
Ascher
Burdge
Collins
De Vries
Duchon
Francis
Ganz
Howard
Jaune…
```

Several have a line through them. I count twenty in all not crossed out. 'But none of these are connected to Emma, nor to me?'

'No.'

'Then how do they help?'

'I don't know yet.'

'Yet?'

Stamford doesn't answer. His silence gives him away.

I ask, 'What are you not telling me?'

He studies my face, his gaze unwavering. 'Look, I have no idea if anything that I've told you is of significance. But the answer must be on that beach in Cirali. What made Emma leave the hotel and rush off like that? Someone else must be involved. What I've shown you is my way of explaining that I retain an open mind.'

'But I still could have killed her. That's what Harriet would say.'

'And she does. Frequently. But the timeline of events doesn't support that, does it? Emma could have gone anywhere to get away from you. She'd given you the slip at the bar. Does it make any sense that she'd go somewhere isolated? With no people around? If she was scared of you wouldn't she find a public place where she could find allies, or at least witnesses? Emma was a bright woman. Hiding at the end of a beach doesn't add up. My impression is that she went there to meet someone.'

'But who? Who would she know in Cirali? And why would she want to meet anyone without me?'

I ponder these self-imposed questions. But they're hydra-headed. As soon as I find an answer, another conundrum pops up in its place. What if she had set up a meeting with someone? Perhaps a quick getaway in a quiet part of the resort. A moped or a car perhaps. What if she was meeting up with a lover and they were planning to run off? What if I caught her before that could happen? I'd be angry, a little drunk, confused. All the ingredients necessary for a calm, considered, rational discussion.

Not.

Jesus.

They race around in my head, these snaky thoughts, but the chequered flag in every scenario only has one podium finisher. That's me. Finding Emma. Challenging her. Losing it...

'The people who told you about Emma, do you think they've told you everything?' Stamford's question puts the brake on my ruminations.

I stare at him and shrug. 'Unlikely. My sister is overprotective. My friends... they're not sure what to say. They're scared of hurting my feelings. None of them understand that I have no feelings to hurt.'

'So the name Mathew Haldane means nothing at all to you?'

I shake my head.

'No one's mentioned him?' Stamford persists.

My pulse ticks up a notch and I try to recall the name from my threadbare memory banks. 'No, definitely not. Why?'

'Why indeed? Someone like Emma should not have had any enemies. But then the world is a strange place.'

My eyes flick from the sheet to Stamford's face. 'Who is Mathew Haldane?'

'I'm going to get into trouble for telling you this. I get the impression it's been decided you're better off not knowing.'

'Decided? By whom?'

Stamford clicks the video off, stands and turns to a shelf. He pulls down a box file and finds a photograph. He holds it out to me. I study a male face. A stranger's face.

'Dr Mathew Haldane,' Stamford says. 'Before they struck him off for stalking a colleague.'

When I swallow, there's no saliva left in my mouth. Stamford puts me out of my misery.

'That colleague was Dr Emma Roxburgh.'

34

For a moment everything freezes and the world spins.
Haldane?

I've never heard the name before.

As always when I'm confronted with something so big, so barn-door obvious from my previous life, doubt rears its malicious head. Could someone have told me? Shouldn't someone have told me?

'You okay?'

Stamford's question drags my racing thoughts back to the starting line. I manage a muttered, 'Fine.'

But Stamford isn't fooled. He has a masters in reading people. 'As I say, it's feasible no one's mentioned it because they wanted to protect you,' he offers.

'From what?'

A shrug. 'Unnecessary pain. Your sister's been a strong gatekeeper as far as all this is concerned.'

'But I need to know. If it involved this man, Haldane–'

'Whoa.' Stamford holds up both hands. 'That's not what I said.'

'Then why mention him?'

'To illustrate the fact that we all have things tucked away in the dark crevices of our past. All of us.'

'But–'

'No. No buts. What happened between Emma and Haldane was bad, but–'

I cut him off. 'In what way?'

Stamford closes his eyes. I can see he's refereeing a mental battle between telling me unpleasant truths and wanting me to tell him what I can remember.

Quid pro quo, baby. I hear Josh's voice clear as day in my head.

Stamford decides. 'This all took place years ago. Emma's first junior post. She could not have been more than twenty-three or four. It turned very nasty. She was the innocent party, he was her senior and, it turns out, a card-carrying... weirdo.'

I suspect that Stamford would prefer to have used an alliterative four-letter word in lieu of weirdo. But we don't know each other well enough for that. There's such a thing as decorum.

He barely pauses while I register this, before pressing on. 'There was nothing between them. But in Haldane's mind she was the one for him and he became obsessed. It ended up with him being prosecuted under stalker laws. He also lost his licence to practise and ended up in jail.'

'So was it him in Turkey?'

Stamford let's his head drop before bringing it back up to contemplate me with a wry smile. 'No. There's a restraining order against him still being anywhere near Emma or the family. He's still not allowed to leave the country. Believe me, if I thought he had anything to do with it I'd have dragged him kicking and screaming from whatever stone he lives under. I'm telling you about him only because if you dig, you're bound to come across his name.'

I should be grateful. I gaze again at the long-shot list of people that hired cars and realise it's incomplete. Some cars might not have had satnav. Not been tracked by GPS. I check the Hs. There's a Howard but no Haldane.

Something else catches my eye. Underneath the list separated by an inch of white paper is another name.

`Berend Rusink.`

'Who is this?'

'That shouldn't be there. That's the Flames Bar's owner. The Dutchman.'

Perhaps the shock of learning about Haldane is what jolts my subconscious. But I'm aware of a new thought emerging. Synapses fire, a pathway opens, a connection is made.

'Do you have a photograph?'

'Of who?'

'Rusink.'

Stamford shifts the mouse, clicks a few times, calls up his albums on-screen. More clicks and I'm looking at the image of a tall, rangy man with dirty-blond hair and a light stubble. He's lounging in a chair, eyes squinting into the sun. Sand and sea provide the background. He's very tanned. I suspect that the blond tips in his hair did not come from a bottle, but from the bright sunlight above. His shirt is open to the navel showing a big gold chain...

'Rusink,' I say. 'Sounds a lot like Russian.'

'Does it?'

'To a damaged mind it might. I know this man. I speak to him two or three times a week.'

'Really?' Stamford sits up.

'Don't get excited. All this happens here.' I tap the side of my head. 'I must have met this bloke. Knew his name. Ivan.'

'I don't follow.'

'In my fugue I visit a place that's a figment of my imagination. A bar. The same bar every time. A rooftop bar. I've concluded my fugue is an amalgamation of recollections. It must be the Flames Bar but my brain has moved it somewhere else. A rooftop. Somewhere high like the top of the cliffs you were standing on with your camera.'

'He's not Russian,' says Stamford. 'He's Dutch. At least he was. He died last year. Cancer of the lung.'

Another ghost.

'But his name was Rusink,' I say. 'Ivan is Berend Rusink, the manager of the bar. My brain has taken his name, twisted it, and moulded him into a stereotypical Russian drunk.'

'Does knowing that help?'

'Perhaps. Another part of the jigsaw. Only even more cryptic than I thought it might be.'

'But progress, right?'

I don't answer. I watch Stamford's video again. It triggers nothing new. No more synapses fire up or hold hands to make a connection. When it's finished, I ask for a copy of his hire car list of names.

He hesitates. 'How is that going to help?'

'I could do some digging.'

Another wry smile. A Stamford trademark. 'Ah, that's where we need to draw a line. This is sensitive information. The data protection people would have my head on a pike if I let this out of my sight. They'd have yours too. So no can do the list. Best that enquiries all come from me because I can function under the radar.'

I start to object but decide he's right. Best I leave that side of things to a professional. But I've seen the list, stared at it. Impossible to unstare.

My coffee has gone cold, but I turn down Stamford's offer of another.

'It's been edunational,' I say.

He doesn't correct me. He gets it. 'Glad I could help.'

'I'm not sure you've done that. But it's made me think.'

We shake hands. Stamford does his thing with the hand sanitiser and offers me a blob. I accept. I'd forgotten. He doesn't do elbow touching, thank God.

When I get back into the street the sun is brightening the day, and I wish I'd remembered to bring my sunglasses. I squint, breathe in diesel-perfumed air and retrace my steps back to New Cross station. I get back to my flat half an hour later. My stomach says lunchtime, but this is no time for food. I sit at my desk and open up my weapons cache. Laptop, mouse, Google.

While I wait, I open my notebook and write down as many of the uncrossed-off names from Stamford's list that I can remember. I get eighteen.

Then I open up a search engine and type. One name.

Mathew Haldane.

35

Haldane's image is all over the internet. I click on a few. He is tall with boyish features, and in most of them he sports a fashionable stubble that lends him a scruffy vibe. In profile his nose is bigger than it looks straight on, slightly hooked. It reminds me of a bird. Nothing majestic; more vulture than hawk. There's a variety of candid snaps. Some with him in tennis or squash gear, some of him with a stethoscope slung around his neck in a jaunty, badge-signalling, look-at-me way. And one, more tellingly, of him leaving what might be a law court looking older, drawn, guilty.

But when I pull up the lurid press reports, Haldane's true nature is revealed as the headlines glare back at me. There are red tops and broadsheet reports. But I plump for a reputable online medical journal for the facts.

Surgeon struck-off for sending over 300 messages in one week to a junior doctor. His 'relentless obsession' led to prolonged sexual harassment.

Mathew Haldane was today found guilty by the Medical Practitioners Tribunal after the panel heard how the 35-year-old locum senior registrar bought his victim some tea on her first shift and immediately suggested that sleeping with him would ensure she got the best rotation.

The victim, who cannot be named, was subjected to repeated unwanted physical abuse, having her bottom squeezed on several occasions and repeatedly being touched by Haldane in situations where it was difficult to escape.

General Medical Council lawyer, Jane Smedley, explained how Haldane was in a position of some power when the victim began her first job at the Royal Infirmary in Bristol.

She admitted that she had been warned about his lecherous approaches but explained how she thought that his blatant propositioning was nothing more than a prank to begin with. 'It was so over the top, it could not have been real,' she said. 'But then the texts started coming through. Even though I told him over and over I had a boyfriend and was not interested.' When she eventually reported the harassment which took place over an eight-day period she had become too unwell with anxiety to work.

But Haldane was relentless in his pursuit, Smedley explained. He was overheard on more than one occasion asking the victim, 'How much do you want to get naked with me?' Things escalated when his continued texting became explicit and he sent a video of himself in a shower performing a sexual act.

Haldane, who studied medicine in Birmingham before progressing to his position one rung down from being a consultant, showed little remorse. During the hearing, he told the panel he was convinced that what took place was nothing more than a 'consensually flirtatious relationship. I was popular. She knew a good thing when she saw it'.

After Haldane, originally from Upton in Gloucestershire, was struck-off, the chair of the tribunal, Michael Linklater said, 'Mr Haldane demonstrates a complete lack of appreciation of the effect his extreme behaviour had on the victim. A lack of understanding of the power imbalance in the professional relationship and of how this severely limited the response of the victim is evident. She was a completely innocent party to his predatory behaviour, even when she repeatedly declined his advances and explained that she was in a relationship. She did nothing to encourage him, contrary to his obviously misguided appreciation. Added to the almost unbelievable number of lurid texts he sent her, it cannot be denied that Haldane's behaviour harassed the victim both sexually and professionally. His judgement is patently impaired and there is a strong likelihood of repetition of his behaviour. His professional and clinical misconduct are fundamentally incompatible with continuing to practise as a doctor.'

I scroll down another page and find a report of a court case. This time on the website of a national broadcaster.

A surgeon who made 'sexually motivated' advances to a fellow doctor has been given a suspended sentence for stalking

Mathew Haldane, who sent over 300 text messages to another doctor, some of them sexually explicit, was simply 'flirting', Bristol Crown Court heard. The doctor, a woman, had only begun working as a junior house officer a few days before Haldane began his texting and aggressive behaviour. She contacted hospital authorities who referred the case to the police.

Haldane admitted the charges on the third day of his trial in December 2011.

Prosecutor Denis Axon told the jury that Haldane 'has abused his position as a mentor to the trainee doctor and persisted in his harassment despite repeatedly being told to stop by the woman'. Haldane, from Upton in Gloucestershire was a locum general surgeon at the Bristol Royal Infirmary in 2010 when the offences took place. During the trial the court heard how the woman suffered great distress and became too ill to work as a result of Haldane's actions. He was found guilty of stalking, causing harm or distress and received an 18-month suspended sentence.

His case has also been referred to the General Medical Council and a tribunal will sit to consider his fitness to practise. The female victim needed six months off to recover before she could recommence her career.

I push back from the screen, my scalp crawling. I was not the boyfriend she'd tried to fend this prat off with. Not then. I first met Emma when she was twenty-seven. What I've read is horrific for all kinds of reasons. First, that Emma had to suffer all this. Second, that someone like Haldane got into a position, a senior medical position, without someone finding out what kind of predatory monstrous arse he was. And third, perhaps most important of all, is the fact that until today, I had no idea this had happened.

I recall Stamford's placating words: 'It's feasible no one's mentioned it because they wanted to protect you.'

I don't like it, but I understand because it smacks of Rachel's modus operandi. As my guardian angel, she would have considered telling me and thrown the consideration out as not helpful. After all, this was history. Years before I met Emma. Still, it rankles.

Especially given what Stamford has told me. He's a no-stone-unturned type of bloke. What he's explained, the way he's investigating the case, has given me a lot to weigh up. Not least of which are the things he didn't say.

Namely, that all the theories he's discussed are based on the fact that someone else was involved.

But there are other theories. The one favoured by Harriet for a start. That there is no one else involved. That I'm the one responsible.

I open a folder labelled Emma on the laptop. Find another folder called Vids. This was a present from my brother-in-law, Owen. They're video-files, MPEGs and MOVI files. He installed a universal player so that whatever format the files are in, I can play them. There are only a few of Emma before I met her. In university, partying with her pals, gowned and capped at her graduation. But most of them are of the two of us. Holidays in the sun, family Christmas get-togethers, various friends' weddings. I've watched them as much to see what sort of person Cameron Todd was as I have trying to get a handle on Emma. I, there is no doubt, was a bit of a smart-arse. Always ready with the funny quip, the rude comment, the dry put-down. I don't find my old self hilarious. Because I'm way too much like Josh in these clips. We must have been insufferable at university. But the odd thing is, other people seemed to find me funny. Especially Emma.

There's one video I go back to. We're with friends, a group of eight of us. Josh is with a girlfriend and we're playing games. From the number of wine glasses and bottles, it's a post-dinner party or a very lazy lunch. Pale faces and scattered tinsel anchors the timeline at Christmas.

A drawing game; someone sketches the word they see on a card, then passes it on to a partner who has to guess what it represents, who then passes it on for someone else to interpret. We're at the reveal. Emma's meant to have drawn 'dumbbells'. Somehow, my written interpretation of this has become 'elasticised testicles'. Crude, even puerile, but when I hold the drawing up to the camera, they do look worryingly misshapen, unequal, organic.

Emma's a little drunk because when she sees this, she erupts with laughter. And she gives in to it wholly. First, a dribbly giggle thanks to a mouthful of wine, descending rapidly into something else altogether. She tries to bow her head, as if she knows what's coming, but that just makes everything worse. Her laugh starts out loud but peters out into a whistling vibrato that leaves her helpless and almost unable to breathe. It's a contagious laugh and she can't stop it; her amusement strings well and truly plucked by my one silly comment. Soon the entire group is helpless because watching Emma lose it is hysterical.

I watch the clip and smile, not because I consider myself especially funny or to revel in my devastating wit. I watch it because I was the one who made Emma laugh. Of all the photos and videos I've seen, this is the one that makes me wish I could remember Emma the most. The way she collapses into me, thumps the floor, moans in agony. Her hair is mussed up, she's almost weeping with mirth but still managing to look pretty.

I wish I remembered that girl. The one who laughed at my stupid jokes. Why would anyone want to kill her?

Why would I?

I close the laptop and send Nicole a Snapchat message. I need to see her. She texts back.

Around 7?

That will do.

I realise it's after two. I grab a sandwich and text Josh.

Fancy a coffee? I have news.

K. Arabicadabra's. Minton Street. 3.30-ish?

Are they open?

For today, yes. Tables separated by a couple of metres. We should be fine.

Of all the people close to me that are likely not to lie to spare my feelings, Josh is the hands-down winner. I text back a thumbs up. Then I turn back to the screen to find out more about Mathew Haldane.

36

J osh has ordered me a flat white when I arrive at Arabicadabra.

The place is quiet, playing soft music. I like it.

'Carrot cake?' he asks as I sit next to him.

'Turnip pie,' I reply.

'Not a culinary competition,' Josh says. 'An offer. Me being nice.'

'Why?'

'I reckoned you needing to see me mid-afternoon meant a development. I was smoothing the way.'

'No to the cake,' I say.

'Hm. Must be serious.'

'Were you aware that Emma had a stalker? A Mathew Haldane?'

'Haldane?' Josh's face wrinkles. 'That's an unpleasant blast from the past. Short answer is yes. We all knew. But Emma didn't talk about it much. She only ever opened up once. After we watched the Robin Williams film, *One Hour Photo*. We had no idea at the time, but she went quiet and started to cry in the final half hour. It really got to her.'

'I don't know it.'

'Worth a watch. An everyday story of delusional obsession. Robin Williams of all people. Genius casting. Who would guess *Mrs Doubtfire* could make a good lunatic stalker? Bit old-school now but he is good in it. I say old-school because the premise comes from the days you took your camera film to a lab to get the thing developed.'

'Shades of Thomas Harris' *Red Dragon* then.'

'Absolutely.' Josh grins. 'You watched that one, did you?'

'Read the book too. Number four of the top ten you sent me.'

'Glad to learn you're taking notice.' Josh looks pleased. 'Anyway, in *One Hour Photo*, Robin Williams sees some holiday snaps and gets obsessed with a family. Begins to fantasise about them. Won't leave them alone. I remember us sitting around afterwards and everything poured out. What Emma'd been through with Haldane. Not exactly the same, but close enough to be a trigger for her. Wasn't news to you, of course. She'd talked to you about it.'

'Why have you never told me?'

Josh flinches.

'Did Rachel ask you not to?'

'No. I never even considered it until now. I mean, not the sort of thing you bring up in a conversation with someone recovering from severe brain trauma.' He adopts a faux American accent reminiscent of a hundred cheesy sitcoms. 'Say, Cam, remember that time your dead girlfriend got stalked and harassed by a creep when she was starting out on her career?'

I don't react.

'Come on, mate. I assumed.'

'Really? You assumed? I can't remember the name of my first pet goldfish.'

'Moby. You showed me pictures once.' Josh tries a lopsided grin. I ignore it.

'It would have been nice to know about Haldane.'

'I assumed Rachel would have told you...' Josh frowns, but then sits forward. 'Why the sudden interest in Haldane? What's happened?'

'I spoke with John Stamford today.'

'Stamford?'

'The private investigator hired by Emma's family.'

Josh sits back in his chair. 'Why?'

'Because I asked him about the gasman. I wanted to find out what Stamford knew.'

'And?'

'Nothing that the police hadn't already told me.'

'The police?' Josh's mouth now actually hangs open.

I tell him all about my meeting in Wetherspoons, Harriet, and the Facebook page and the gasman post. I tell him about Keely and about Stamford. I realise there's a lot to tell. The only thing I don't tell him about is Nicole and me. The way things have developed. A promise is a promise. When I finish, all Josh can do is stare. 'Jesus, Cam.'

'If your next sentence is "does Rachel know?", I'm leaving.'

'No, I wasn't going to mention Rachel. I'm just... shocked.'

'That I'm finally trying to find out what happened?'

'Well, yeah. I suppose that's part of it. But you said Stamford said Haldane had nothing to do with what happened in Turkey because he's not allowed to leave the country.'

'No. But hearing about him has rattled me.'

'I can see that. Bloody Haldane... such a weird na–' Josh stops in mid-sentence. I see the signs. A lightbulb moment.

'What?' I ask.

'Haldane. It's an unusual name.'

'You said that once. Come on. What's exploded in that brain of yours.'

Josh knows he's got no escape. 'Physics, man.' He has his

phone out and is googling. 'Yup. Haldane rang a bell. John Scott Haldane, his namesake, was a medical researcher. Nineteenth century and into the First World War. He was big into sorting out protection for the troops in the trenches.'

I wait. Josh was never any good at getting to the point quickly. And today he seems especially obtuse.

'Anyway, this Haldane was into masks.'

'Masks.'

'For the trenches.'

'You mean gas masks?'

'I do.'

'So what's the big deal–' I almost hear the clunk as the penny drops. The Facebook entries Harriet has assumed are from me on the Emma 'Roxy' Roxburgh site. One had a sobriquet that I'd assumed came from an anaesthetist. But if your name is Haldane, it could equally be a reference to a namesake.

Gasman.

Josh and I chew the cud for another ten minutes, but it gets us nowhere. Josh has to get back to the office. He's had a text about departmental discussions relating to working from home. As a senior team leader, he's involved in transitioning all that for the staff of Whoneedspensions.

'Text me,' he says as we say goodbye.

Outside, the afternoon sun beams down. Still spring. Once again the river draws me. I get on a number 78 bus and get off at Tower Bridge. Half an hour later, I'm standing next to where Banksy painted a child fishing syringes out of the river. Faded now, yet Japanese tourists still wander up, disappointed at not finding it, bemusedly asking locals if they're in the right place. I stand a little further away, leaning against a whitewashed wall to gaze out across the barges moored to the south bank. The wind has dropped. There's no one around. A good time and place to do what I've decided I must. I have a list of labelled forbidden numbers from Rachel. Ones I should not respond to if they ring me. I scroll down, find the one for Harriet and dial it.

'Hello?' Her voice is wary.

'Harriet, Cameron Todd.'

No reply. The silence lasts so long that I ask, 'You still there?'

'What do you want?'

'To talk.'

'I'm listening. For now.'

'The other day–'

She cuts me off with a sharp, 'If you're expecting me to apologise, it's not going to happen.'

'That's not why I'm ringing.'

Another silence. Looks like I'll need to do most of the talking.

'Not me that posted crap through your letterbox and not me who posted on Emma's pretend Facebook page.'

More silence.

'I did some digging,' I say. 'Spoke to the police and to John Stamford.'

She snorts. 'I noticed.'

I tell her about my initial gasman idea. About asking Keely. I'm halfway through having just mentioned Alison Barnet when Harriet breaks in, her voice seething with anger.

'How could you think that? Alison was one of Emma's med school friends. She made a mistake. A ghastly mistake but Emma stood by her. Alison would never post anything horrible about Emma.'

'I know that now. But I had to ask someone to find out. My memory is not what it was.'

A muffled sound. Harriet snorting.

'What can you tell me about Mathew Haldane?' I ask.

I hear air being sucked in before exploding back out of her. 'What?'

'Haldane. How come no one ever told me about him?'

The answer pours out in a tirade. 'Why would anyone in their right mind mention that maggot's name? He almost ruined Emma's life and her career. He's a sick predator. She was newly qualified. Full of hope and promise and he almost snuffed that out. It took her years to get over him. There were times when we thought she never would. Her job saved her. Her commitment to medicine.'

'And then she met me.'

'Yes she did. And look what happened.'

Harriet's bitterness scours my ears. Another pause.

'Why are we even talking about this?' she asks eventually.

'Because I'm trying to find out what happened. Struggling to put things together.'

'Oh well, that's all right then.' Her words are acid. 'Never mind about my lovely sister who deserved none of this. And Haldane was just the start of the rot. But it's you who screwed everything up. You who took her to Turkey. You who argued with her and threw her off that cliff.'

'I don't remember doing anything like that. And the police–'

'Are useless. But one day we're going to find out the truth, Cameron Todd. And when we do, I will be outside the courts when they lock you away for good. I'll be the one waving a flag and singing "congratulations" at the top of my voice. You're not fooling anyone with this memory-loss twaddle. And I know you're just pretending to help John Stamford. I warned him about you. And dragging Haldane into this when he isn't allowed to come within a hundred miles of Emma's bloody gravestone is pathetic. It cannot be him that's posted on Facebook. His restraining order forbids any internet activity involving Emma. He'd go to prison if he did. Why are you stirring this up? Sod off back to Wales, why don't you. You are pathetic, you know that. You are–'

I end the call before my ears start to bleed. Ringing Harriet was a mistake, though I am wiser about Haldane than I was. But like Stamford, Harriet is sure he could not have been involved in Turkey.

As soon as I think I'm getting somewhere I get the legs cut from under me. But there is one more call I need to make.

37

I'm still standing with my back to the Thames. There's 4G and a full battery on my phone. At 4.40pm, I FaceTime Rachel.

She answers within ten seconds. She always does. Her face swims into view. In shadow with a bright window behind her. She shifts so that the light falls on her face. She's got some colour back in her cheeks. I tell her so.

She smiles, pleased. 'And where are you? Outside getting some exercise? Is that the river I see behind?'

'Yes. Been to see Josh. I'm walking back to the flat.'

'So you thought you'd do an outside broadcast?' Rachel laughs.

'The sun sometimes shines in London too. Thought you might want to see it.'

'How is Josh?'

'Same as always. We had a good chat. About Mathew Haldane.'

Rachel's mouth slides into a quizzical, troubled smile. 'Mathew Haldane? Why on earth were you talking about him?'

'His name came up.'

'How?'

'My brief trip to Emma's old practice seems to have shaken my memory tree. I met someone who knew Emma. She's nice.'

'She? Who's she?'

'She's called Nicole.'

Rachel blinks.

'Don't look so surprised.'

'I'm not. It's... good. That's good.'

I can almost see Rachel's antennae twitching as she slips into mother hen mode. Though mother ant would be a better analogy if she has antennae. I concentrate.

'It is. And after talking to her, I had a chat with Harriet about... things.'

'Ca-am.' She splits my name into two horrified syllables.

I plough on, needing to get it all out. 'That was interesting in a car wash type of way... I mean car crash. But not half as interesting as talking to John Stamford.'

'WHAT?' There's a sudden movement as Rachel shoots up out of her chair. I see she's in a T-shirt and running pants.

'Rache. He's okay.'

'No he is not, Cam. Oh my God, I knew this would happen.'

'What does that mean?'

'It means that you shouldn't be speaking to these people alone.'

'Why? I have nothing to hide. And it's helping. I remembered some things and I'm understanding others.'

'Like what?'

'Like how my memory is jumbled. Just like I mix up words when I speak, my brain has twisted my recollection of certain things.'

'Clear as day,' Rachel says with a little shake of her head.

'Oh, come on, Rache.'

Rachel takes a deep breath and finds the chair again. 'Go on.'

'In my recurring fugue, my rooftop visits, I assumed that

someone was Russian when he's actually Dutch. I twisted a Dutch name into Russian.'

Silence. Rachel's worried stare is augmented by a confused furrowing of brows.

'Look, gobbledegook it may be to you,' I say, 'but for me this is progress. And Stamford is working on what happened in Turkey. He's not trying to get me to confess anything.'

'You shouldn't trust him, Cam. He works for Harriet and the Roxburghs.'

'Is that such a bad thing? How can finding out what happened to Emma be a bad thing?'

'Because... you're vulnerable, that's why. And Harriet's made her mind up about what happened.'

I can't argue with that. Even so, Rachel needs to understand that things are changing. Evolving. 'But I'm also a grown-up,' I say. 'And I need to work through this stuff to get to a point where I can move on.'

'Agreed. But as Adam has said, it takes time. Trying to run before you can walk can lead to a nasty fall if you're not very careful.'

'There's a difference between walking and crawling, Rache. I am not a bloody toddler.'

'Fine. Once the kids are better and I'm out of this self-isolation, I'll set up a meeting between us and Stamford.'

'You don't need to do that. If I need to speak to him again, I'll do it.'

'No, Cam. Don't. He's a detective. He has... techniques. I don't want you getting yourself into any trouble.'

'I'm always in trouble, Rache. Have been since I fell on that metal stanchion on Cirali beach. I need to find some answers. For myself as much as for everyone else.'

'You didn't do anything wrong, Cam.'

'Didn't I? How do you know?'

A fresh silence mushrooms between us.

Rachel shakes her head slowly. 'Please, Cam. Don't do anything rash. I've got another week here with the kids. I'll speak to Owen. He can hold the fort for a few days and I'll come up.'

'No non-essential travel. Haven't you heard? Everything's going to get much worse.'

'I consider you essential, Cam.'

'You don't need to mother me, Rache.'

'I'm not mothering you. I'm only looking out for you. And all this... it's too much too quickly. You are worrying me, Cam.'

'Telling you this was a mistake.'

She backtracks. 'No, no it's not. I'm glad you're telling me.'

'But it's going to give you a headache, isn't it? Instead of looking after the kids you're going to be preoccupied with your messed-up brother.'

Her face falls. 'Don't say that. You are not messed up.'

'That is so not true, Rache, and you know it.'

'Why are you being so hard on yourself?'

'Perhaps it's time I was.'

Rachel sighs. A lock of hair falls forwards and she strokes it out of her eyes with a finger. 'This must be hard for you. I realise that. You've lost so much, and I can see how desperate you are to get some kind of closure.'

'No, not closure. I'm not grieving, Rachel. I can't because I don't feel I've lost anything. That's the trouble. A line has been drawn for me. There's no going back, only forward. This is my way of moving forward.'

Rachel's voice softens. 'I won't be anxious if you promise me you will not do anything... silly.'

I don't answer. I love Rachel. I love her kids. I think the world of Owen. I'd be lost without them or him or her. She's been my anchor. But I can't help wondering sometimes if all her rules and anxieties are what's been holding me back.

'I'll be careful,' I say.

'Promise?' There's a tremor in her voice and I'm regretting this call.

'Promise. I have my wall and your number.'

'Maybe I should ring John Stamford.'

'Don't do that. This is my gig, Rache.'

She nods, blinks, I can see she's weighing up all I said. 'What you found out is good. It is. We can go through it all. Sift out what's important.'

'We will,' I say and attempt a swerve. 'But now you need to look after yourself and the kids.'

'All the schools are shutting now. Except for key workers. Their kids are going to school. Glorified babysitting if you ask me.'

'I heard.' She's angling for time. I suspect she'll try to convince me not to do anything rash again at any moment. Probably ask me if I'm taking my meds. 'I'll keep you in the loop,' I say.

'Talk to Josh and Adam about this. See what they say.'

'I will.'

'You know where I am.'

'I do.'

'Promise me you'll be careful.'

I end the call with my best winning smile. I turn back to the river, enjoying the cool breeze on my face. Rachel wants me to use Adam and Josh as my sounding boards. Of course, there's some validity in that. But they are not the only ones I feel I can open up to now.

I turn away from the flowing waters of the Thames and head back to my flat, enjoying the faint flutterings of anticipation.

38

There's wine breathing when Nicole arrives a little after seven. Her preference is white. Chardonnay, unoaked. The buttery kind.

She kisses me with shining lips as soon as she's through the door, kicks off her shoes and sits next to me on the sofa.

Heady Bandit fills the surrounding air. I tell her everything that's happened since I saw her on Sunday. She listens, owl-eyed, brows crinkling first in curiosity, and then with increasing horror as I reveal all about Haldane.

'Poor Emma. That sounds awful.'

'You didn't know?'

Nicole shakes her head. 'I don't suppose that's something she'd broadcast to staff at the surgery. If anyone knew they didn't say. If it was me, I'd want to try to put it all behind me. Forget all about it.'

'Stamford doesn't believe Haldane has anything to do with what happened.'

'But you do?' She's sitting with her knees drawn up in skinny jeans. Her toenails are painted red to match her fingers and the lips on her pretty face that is staring intently into mine.

'Emma didn't have any enemies. Everyone has told me that time after time. But this Haldane would surely hold a grudge.'

'Didn't you say there's some kind of restraining order?'

'Stamford said so and Harriet confirmed it.'

'And he can't leave the country?'

'No.' I stretch and loosen my neck. 'I'd let it all lie if it wasn't for this Facebook thing. Someone has set up a bogey... bogus Emma Roxburgh page. It isn't me. And someone on it has posted as *gasman*.'

I have my laptop open. Nicole reads the entry.

GASMAN

We had good times, Ems. Hope you're flying high as a kite

'Sounds very suspicious,' she says. 'There must be some way we could find out who set up the Facebook page?'

I shrug.

Nicole takes the laptop and clicks on the 'about' button. Emma's information comes up.

'We know it can't be Emma,' I say.

'Ugh. This is so mean. Did you ask the private investigator, um, Stanley?'

'Stamford,' I correct her. 'No. He would tell me if he knew anything.'

'You trust him?'

I nod, surprising myself. I do trust Stamford. Rachel would scream.

Nicole gives up and passes the laptop back. 'It's vile, I know, but somehow worse that Emma's sister can suggest this could be you. She must hate you.'

'She blames me for Emma's death.'

'Would you like me to speak to her?'

For a moment I can't answer. My expression must give me away because I see Nicole's cheeks flush.

'I'm sorry. I don't mean to interfere. I only want to help.' Tears well in her big eyes.

God, I'm an idiot. I put my hand on her arm. 'Sorry to be so touchy. My call with Rachel was...' I shake my head. 'She thinks I'm incapable of being careful.'

'She's just worried about you.'

'She mothers me. But I don't want you to do that. That would be weird. So thanks for the offer, Mum, but no thanks.'

'I can't help thinking all this hassle is my fault. If I hadn't said anything about Emma and the anaesthetist.'

'Rubbish. I'm glad you did. I'd never have spoken to Stamford. I'd never have found out about Haldane.'

She brightens. 'So what are you going to do?'

'I don't know yet. But I need to do something.'

'You think he has something to do with this Facebook page, don't you?'

'One way to get at Emma and her family without coming anywhere near, isn't it? Social media is the coward's Kalashnikov. And you can always get someone else to pull the snigger... trigger.'

'I suppose,' Nicole says. I detect a degree of distraction.

'Are you okay?'

She shakes her head. 'No. But not because of you or this.' She waves at the laptop. 'It's Aaron. I think he suspects something.'

'Really?'

Nicole sighs. 'I haven't spoken to him since the weekend. We've texted, but we've both been busy and, to be honest, I'm kind of avoiding him. But today he asked me who I was going to meet after work. I said I was going to yoga and then for a drink with some girlfriends.'

She smiles at the shock in my face.

'Don't worry. They're good friends. I have an alibi.'

'Are you worried about Aaron finding out about us?'

'Yes and no. He's the possessive type. Always has been. Things aren't brilliant between us. I wasn't expecting him to be so clingy, that's all.'

'Sounds like you're the one being hassled.'

She shrugs. 'It'll be worth it. Finding the right moment to cut the cord is the hard bit. I'm not a breaking-up-by-text kind of girl.'

I smile at that. 'If you need to stay here, you're welcome. To get away, I mean.'

'You're so sweet.' Nicole's eyes crinkle and she dabs moisture away from long curled eyelashes with a forefinger.

'If there's anything I can do.'

'I can think of one thing.' Nicole leans in and kisses me.

We don't make it to the bedroom. Surprising how roomy the sofa can be when you're playing doctors and nurses.

Later, at around nine, Nicole puts on her coat. She sees me watching her and tilts her head.

'One day I will not leave, I promise.'

'You need to sort things out with Aaron first.'

'Yes, I do. But what about you? What are you going to do?'

That one gives me pause. I've asked myself the same question many times since talking with Harriet. 'I want to speak to Haldane.'

Nicole stops buttoning her coat. 'Is that wise?'

I shrug. 'He's a piece of the jigsaw. Emma must have told me about him. I want to ask him about the Facebook page.'

'Do you know where he lives?'

I shake my head. 'I thought a phone call. To begin with.'

'Do you have his number?'

'No.'

'You could ask Stamford.'

'I could.'

'Or, you could let me try to find it.'

'How?'

'Did I tell you what Aaron does?'

'No.'

'He works for MobileN. They're a third-party mobile contract provider. He can more or less get anyone's mobile number. MobileN checks when contracts are ending – don't ask me how – and then cold calls to offer new terms. He'll do that for me. He's done it before for work, when older patients can't remember their number. I'll tell him this is one. Someone who's moved away that we need to get hold of. Can't be too many Haldanes. I'll do some research and see if I can find out where he lives too. Which town at least. I'll text Aaron now.'

I watch as her fingers fly over her phone's keyboard. She's quicker than I am. But then who isn't.

'Seems cruel to be using him just before you end it.' Another of my spoken-out-loud thoughts.

She looks up with a mischievous grin. 'Consider this his leaving present to me.'

I frown.

'Oh, don't look so worried. This will all be over with by the weekend. After the wedding, I promise I won't be leaving like this ever again.'

'I'd like that.'

Her smile could melt an iceberg.

An hour later I get a Snapchat message from Nicole with a number. I write it down. When I ask how she's been so quick, she texts back.

There are people in his office 24/7. Someone is always ready to ambush unsuspecting phone contract holders :)

I take my pills and switch on Netflix. Another Josh recommendation. This one, a series called *Firefly*. Josh says it's a cult classic. Dystopian sci-fi future in an almost Western style. Josh says I'll love the flesh-eating Reavers. I give it a go. But I've drunk a little too much wine with Nicole. I should have delayed taking my medication. As it is, ten minutes into episode one, I drift off and fall asleep immediately.

39

I van stands at the bar. There are no girls with him this time. He's smiling at Cam.

'You find out my secret.'

'Je bent nyet Russisch,' Cam says. He's not sure what language it is.

Although Ivan still speaks with a hammy Russian accent, Cam now knows he's something else. Not that it matters. Not here. On the far side of the room the maid is at it again. This time he sees her making up beds where there shouldn't be any. Cam searches for faceless Emma. She's not sitting opposite him this time. The sky is a dusky magenta, but storm clouds are gathering on the horizon. He looks around and she appears from a stairwell, her features, as usual, absent. But he recognises her walk and her voice.

'Mine's a Jack and Coke. Make it a Zero,' she says to Ivan.

He smiles and saunters towards Cam with a glass full of amber liquid clinking in ice and a bottle with a quartered lime in its neck.

Faceless Emma is halfway across the room. Behind her, Cam

notices what might be a dog following her. Something low, a dachshund maybe. A dark shape hugging the floor a few feet behind her legs. But on closer inspection it has no legs and now Cam is thinking more mamba than Fido. The movement is more coiling than trot. It triggers an innate abhorrence programmed into the oldest reptilian part of his brain. He wants to move away from it, jump up and run, like a cat with a cucumber placed on the floor next to it. Snake reflexes. But the darkness seems to sense his awareness. It stops, turns and rolls under a booth.

'We need to do something about that,' Cam says to Ivan.

He shrugs. 'It is drains. They say there is something bad there. Yad.'

Emma slides into the booth opposite. Ivan leans on the table. 'We need some romantic music to take away the... how you say, vonyat?'

He walks back to the bar. Music wells up. The White Stripes: 'I think I Smell a Rat'. Ivan is a comic.

Cam natters to faceless Emma. For the first time he notices the statue next to a plant pot is incomplete. There's a missing nose and one eye has been sanded away by wind and rain. Oddly, she's dressed in a uniform like the maid. Emma's worried about work. But he can't concentrate because he has one eye on the statue and the other on the booth where the black coiling smoke has disappeared. He watches it like a hawk. Twice it billows out, only to billow back in. He has no idea what it is, but he knows it isn't healthy. When he looks up, the maid statue is closer, the storm clouds have thickened.

'Stink,' says Emma.

'What?'

'That's what vonyat means. Stink.'

~

I come to myself groggily. I'm up high, just as in the fugue. For a moment I'm badly disoriented. I pivot, seeing a sign that reads EXIT and a door in a small shed-like structure housing the block's elevator machinery. The wind has picked up and I shiver. I pivot back, take three steps forward and look down over a barrier to the street below. There's daylight but what I look down upon is not a street. It's a marked space; resident parking. I take a moment to realise that I'm on the roof of my own building. But I do not understand how I got up here. I hurry back to the exit, walk down the stairs to my floor and through the open door of my flat. This is a fresh departure. I don't remember going to bed. I must have fallen asleep on the sofa. Normally, I don't move far in fugue mode. I do things, routine, mundane things. But I stay within the same room or rooms. Usually.

Not this time.

But with this change comes a kind of understanding. My fugue is like a constant loop. At some point the maid will come closer, the sandstorm will engulf us. Or perhaps our demise comes after the sandstorm. That I haven't worked out yet. Clearly, my awareness of what happens in this bar, my hallucinatory appreciation of it, is not governed by where I left off previously. I can appear at any point. And that has changed. In the past I would always be aware of Ivan and the girls, the music, the long chats, but it would culminate in the inevitable dive we would take off the roof to our deaths.

But for the second time that hasn't happened. Emma and I survive and I've exited the fugue without a swan dive. The script has expanded into a director's cut.

Hayley Joel Osment's voice whispers in my head. '*I see dead people.*'

I think about that when I get into the shower.

I'm still thinking about it when I drink my second cup of

coffee, one eye on the clock. The whisper makes me acutely aware that me getting up to the roof, the real roof, is not a good idea. Not while I'm in the fugue. Best I talk to someone about this worrying trend where reality and the imagined world of my hallucinations seem to be getting ever closer.

40

After breakfast I keep clockwatching, waiting for the minute hand to reach three. For it to be 9.15 which, I've decided, is a respectable time to ring Adam. The number I have is his mobile and so, logically, he doesn't need to be at work or his desk to take the call. But there has to be boundaries, as Josh keeps telling me.

'Ring me any time means ring me any time except between midnight and 7am, you berk.'

He came up with that after I'd rung him several times in the middle of the night. It wasn't that long after I'd moved out of rehab. I'd had no true conception of time then. And Josh loves his sleep.

In my living room, the minute hand has crawled to twelve after the hour when my mobile rings. I pick up and frown. It's Adam.

'I was about to ring you,' I say. 'Why are you ringing me?'

'And good morning to you, too, Cam.'

'Sorry. I really don't like coincidences. It reminds me too much of Josh's theory of synchronicity.'

'Is he a fan of Jung's?'

'No. He's into sci-fi and says that synchronous events are evidence of outside interference.'

'You mean a higher purpose?'

'No. In Josh's case because the lizard people who really run the world have decreed it to be so.'

'He really believes that?'

'After four pints of IPA, yes.'

Adam laughs. 'I am ringing first of all to see how my favourite patient is doing.'

'And the real reason?'

'I have some med students coming for their extensive and exhaustive two-week block. The only time they get during their undergraduate years to learn anything about mental health.'

'That does not seem like long enough.'

'Tell me about it. My job is to educate and titillate. That's where you come in.'

'Never been called titillation before.'

'I thought I'd trot you out in front of them. You are worth three chapters of any textbook.'

I can almost see Adam smiling as he says this.

I pause, think about it and then ask again, 'And the real reason?'

Adam hesitates, but he knows he's beaten. I can tell by the way he softly snorts. 'Okay. The truth. Rachel rang me.'

'Did she?'

'Yes. She has me on speed dial.'

'She mothers me.' Yet more stuck record.

'Nothing wrong with that. It's called continuity of care.'

'She doesn't need to worry.'

'Good. That's good. But she did say you'd had some fresh recall?'

Rachel will have told Adam everything I told her. So I tell him only what's new. 'My fugues have changed.'

Adam says nothing. I recognise it as one of his expectant pauses.

'I'm still on the rooftop at the bar, but now I know Ivan isn't Russian. He does too. There are maids making up beds, and there's a sandstorm. It blows in and wipes everything away – well, almost everything. What's left is a statue that seems to move and something very unpleasant made out of black smoke.'

'Fascinating,' says Adam.

'Glad you like it. Any ideas?'

'Do you feel threatened by these new appearances?'

'They're increasingly becoming a part of the final scene. Emma's fall and mine.' I don't say push. Too close to the bone.

'A statue, you say. Classic? Modern?'

'More classic. Looks weathered. Sometimes wears a maid's uniform.'

'Well that's easy. You were staying in a hotel. As for the smoke, what's strange about it?'

'Ivan says it smells. It seems alive to me.'

More silence. Then Adam speaks. 'You've been doing some research, I take it? On Cirali and where it all happened?'

'Yes.'

'Though you may not remember, it's highly likely that you and Emma would have visited Cirali's more obvious tourist attractions. That means you will have been to Olympos and seen the Chimaera.'

'Probably, though I don't remember doing either.'

'Olympos is at the end of the beach and it has a necropolis. Lots of tombs and ruptured sarcophagi and crumbling stones. Not sure if there are any intact statues, but certainly there'd be carvings. And, as I said, there are the Chimaeras.'

'What about them?'

'The breath of a monster tamed by Bellerophon when he jumped on Pegasus and poured molten lead into the beast's mouth,' Adam affects in a dramatic voice. 'The stuff of nightmares. Legend has it the flames are the beast's breath. And I understand that the seeping gas from somewhere underground contains methane amongst other things. Maybe even a little sulphur? You'd certainly smell that.'

'So, are you saying that what I'm seeing is a melon... I mean melange of my trip to Cirali?'

'It could be. Perhaps the best way I can think of to explain it.'

I pause. It almost makes sense. 'But there's something else. This morning I ended up being outside when I came out of the fugue. I wasn't to start with. That's never happened before.'

'No, it hasn't.'

'What do you think this all means?'

Something that might be a meaningful exhalation escapes Adam's lips into the phone's mouthpiece. In my mind's eye I see him lean back in his chair and steeple his fingers. Classic Adam. 'Clearly, the change in your memory, the improvement I should say, is affecting, possibly informing, the fugue. Feeding into it somehow.'

'That's how I see it too.'

'Much of what you're hallucinating is open to interpretation.'

'I agree. But on the whole, I'd say the lines are getting more blurred.'

'Lines?'

'Between the reality of what I can actually remember and what the fugue, in its own way, is trying to tell me. A kind of cryptic puzzle. Ivan is the giveaway. His real name is Rusink. He was the barman at the beach in Turkey. Looks just like him. But in the fugue, I've mangled the name and stereotyped him as Ivan. The point is, nothing in the fugue is quite what it seems.

Josh has postulated the Second Life theory. He thinks all the people are avatars in a kind of virtual reality.'

'Interesting analogy,' Adam says.

'You don't buy it?'

'Way too simplistic a theory. And, given what I know about Josh, the easiest way for him to process it. But that's the issue. Rationalising. Second Life is a virtual world with laws and parameters. What rational laws are there in your fugue?'

'Not many that I can see. Except that we're not flying or have fishes' heads.'

'Make sure you record the changes. For when we next meet.'

I drift into the living room, still on the phone to Adam, stand in front of my wall. 'What about the physical changes? The fact that I walked outside–'

'You've had fugues out walking before, haven't you?'

True. I may be worrying unnecessarily.

'Let's see what happens next time. This could be a one-off,' he adds. Adam, as always, is reassuring.

'When are your students coming in?' I ask.

'I lied about them.'

'Course you did. I just wanted to make you feel guilty.'

'Mea culpa.'

'If she rings again, tell Rachel I'm fine.'

'I will. And I'm here if you need me.'

Adam's photo stares out at me from the corkboard. I stare back. 'Thanks. What about your clinics? How are they going to work with social distancing?'

'Not easily. We've had a heads-up from our director of clinical services. The grapevine says that by Monday we'll be in total lockdown. No more voluntary restrictions. They'll be mandatory.'

'What does that mean?'

'Enforced closure of all non-essential businesses, I suspect.

We think they'll ask at least 1.5 million vulnerable individuals to completely self-isolate.'

'Vulnerable?'

'At risk. The immune-compromised. Diabetics. Cancer patients on treatment. Known respiratory disease. The list is long.'

Another thought slips into my head. 'What about wedding venues?'

'Something you're not telling me, Cam?' Adam's voice cracks with amusement.

'A friend of mine is a guest at one this weekend.'

'Though we as a unit are gearing up in advance, my understanding is that major changes will come into play beginning of next week. This weekend is the last chance saloon for anyone wanting to tie the knot.'

'Wow. This is the real peel... deal.'

'It is. So you need to stay safe, Cam.'

'I love alone, you know that. Live alone. You know that too.'

Adam laughs softly. 'Things like this can seem unreal, as if it won't happen to you.'

'I'm being careful. I'm handwashing. I own lots of sanitiser and toilet paper.'

'Then you are all set. Even so, any problems, ring me.'

I thank Adam. He's a good guy. But he's right when he says this seems unreal.

I have started McCarthy's *The Road*. What a brilliantly bleak picture he paints. Disconcertingly, I wonder if we're all going to end up in nuclear bunkers.

Half an hour later I get a text from Leon.

Double whammy, Cam my man. Gym is closing tomorrow for the foreseeable. As if that's not bad enough, I've got a bit of a cough, bit of fever. I'm self-isolating but you need to monitor yourself.

I text back.

Stay safe, Leon.

I don't know for certain, but I think I'm okay. I don't feel unwell. I don't have a fever or a cough. But Leon's text has shocked me. As Josh would say, 'This shit just got real.'

41

After a restless night, I get up early and make coffee, this time with almond milk. Rachel says it's good for me. At least it's palatable, not like her other suggestions. Those I have to swallow and some of them are big buggers. Like 1,000mg glucosamine tablets, or the orangy salmon oil capsules. The label for the latter tells me they're full of EPA/DHA fatty acids and DHA contributes to the normal function of brain activity. I'm AFT – all for that. Are they doing any good? Who knows? Sometimes I wonder if they're just placebos. But then they don't seem to do any harm, so I take them, swallow them down with the almond milk coffee. But today the glucosamine gets stuck at a bend in my oesophagus halfway down and I need to chase it with a glass of water.

Then I sit and think about that last fugue. I can't get that coiling black smoke out of my mind. It was almost as if it had a purpose. As if it sensed me. Ivan had used two words. Yad and vonyat. I google them. I start with Dutch, but that doesn't work. Then I go to Russian and yad translates as poison, vonyat as stink. So, though Ivan is Dutch, he peppers his vocabulary with Russian words.

There's no logic to any of it.

Still, these are accurate descriptions. Ivan had mentioned drains, too. He implied that was where the black smoke came from. But what I saw was more than the ooze of a bad smell. It had substance. Volition. Seeped almost like a miasma or gas.

Gas.

I wait until 10. I consider 10am a reasonable time. It gives people the chance to get up and have breakfast. I pick up my phone and scroll to my notes, to the copied and pasted number Nicole sent me the evening before. I memorise it and punch the keypad. The number rings eight times before someone answers. When they do, there's no greeting. Only a terse question.

'Who is this?'

'Hi,' I say. 'You don't know me. My name is Cameron Todd.'

Haldane doesn't reply.

I try again. 'Is this Mathew Haldane?'

'How did you get this number?'

'I'm sorry to call out of the blue. I am not trying to sell you anything.'

'How did you get this number?' He repeats the question, this time more slowly, in a monotone.

'I am, I was, Emma Roxburgh's partner.'

Several long seconds of empty silence follow. I can hear him breathing. Finally, he asks, 'What do you want?'

'I need to know first. Are you Mathew Haldane?'

'Yes.'

'I'm not trying to make trouble.'

'Of course not,' Haldane says, his voice dripping with derision.

'I'm not. You know that Emma died.'

'I read something. Saw it on the news.'

'Then you also are aware that I was injured in the same... incident.'

A three-second pause follows before he says, 'Yes.'

'I lost the vision in one eye. Broke an arm. Smashed one side of my head in and got a severe brain injury.'

'Sounds like fun. Poor you.' The meaning of the words bears no relation to how he delivers them.

'That means no memory of things up to the event. I've been trying to piece things together ever since. Your name came up.'

'I bet it did.'

'Not from Emma. She might have told me about you, but I can't remember that.'

'So?'

'I wanted to ask if she'd had any contact with you before the accident.'

The laughter that follows is prolonged and bitter. When it finishes Haldane says, 'Is this a wind-up?'

'No.'

'You're a sodding journalist, aren't you?'

'I am not. I promise. You can ring me back–'

Haldane cuts me off. 'Okay, let's pretend it is you, Cameron Todd. You've lost your memory and now someone's brought my name up, so you thought you'd ring me up for a chat, is that it?'

'More or less.'

'Okay, *Cameron*.' He uses my name with extra sardonic emphasis. 'If you found my number you also googled me, correct?'

'Yes.'

'Then you've read that your precious fucking Emma got me struck-off for sending her some texts and emails. She ruined my life. I am still under a restraining order not to contact her bolshy family, despite the fact she is long dead.'

'Yes, but–'

'If I do contact them, I could go to prison. So what makes

you think I would go anywhere near Emma or any other toxic Roxburgh with a lit bargepole?'

My turn to pause. 'You've answered my question.'

'Ironic, though, right?'

'Ironic?'

'That the lovely Emma fucked up both of our lives in her own sweet way.'

Her photo is on the wall. Lovely Emma, smiling. I bristle. 'Emma died. How can that be her fault?'

'Good question. But from what I read the case is still open, am I right?'

'That's why I'm trying to find out as much as I can. So I can–'

'Remember? I'm surprised you want to. You didn't ring me for a simple chat. What reminiscences of mine could help you? You rang hoping that I'd confess to some bullshit theory you cooked up, didn't you? Well I have theories too, Cameron, and I've had lots of time to ponder mine.'

He lets his loaded sentence hang.

I take a breath. 'What do you mean?'

'I mean what if there isn't anyone else involved?'

I wait, sensing more. Dreading it.

'What if you and Emma had a fight? What if she told you there was someone else and you lost it? What if you threw her off the cliff and then yourself after her? Maybe you were hurrying to get away and fell. Screwed yourself and Emma.'

'That is not what happened.'

'How can you tell?'

I can't. Haldane, I realise, is enjoying himself.

'I'd be in no great hurry to remember anything if I were you, Cameron, my friend. I'd let sleeping dogs doze by the fire.'

'I loved Emma!'

'Did you? Or maybe she was having it off with someone else and you couldn't stand the thought of it. Maybe you were playing hide the saveloy with a nice little slice of totty on the side and she found out. Maybe that's why you pushed her off that cliff?'

Liar, liar, pants on fire.

He's right on one count. The bit on the side. I had been seeing Nicole. But that was only in response to something that Emma was doing. I begin to wonder at the wisdom of this call. People warned me off Haldane for a reason. I can't let him start messing with my head.

'Everyone says that we–'

'Everyone says?' He hisses out the sentence. 'But only you can know the truth, am I right?'

I don't answer. I want to say something, but I can't find the words because I realise that he's right. Only I can know the actual truth of it. No one else. It's then I hear something that sends a shudder quaking through me. A whisper, barely audible.

'Emma wanted me more than anything. More than you, Cameron. It was only a matter of time.'

I blurt out an exhalation of horror. 'What did you say?'

'I said only you know the truth.'

'No, after that. The whisper...'

'What whisper? Are you hearing things now?'

'You said something about Emma wanting you.'

'Jesus. You need some help, *Cameron*.' Again, the heavy emphasis on my name. 'Do me a favour. Never ring this number again.'

The line goes dead.

I sit for a long while after Haldane has hung up. I drink too much coffee, welcome the buzz, realise I'm an idiot. What the hell was I thinking in contacting him? What was I hoping to achieve? But even as I try to rationalise my actions, the memory of that whispered taunt echoes through my brain.

'*Emma wanted me more than anything. More than you, Cameron. It was only a matter of time.*'

Was it Haldane who said it? Or did I imagine it? Or did I hear a buried splinter of truth worming its way slowly and painfully to the surface of my consciousness? If we'd argued, what if I was the cause? What if Emma found out about Nicole? What if she confronted me on that beach in Cirali and I flipped?

I squeeze my eyes shut. Force myself to imagine what it might have been like. An argument, a scuffle, my temper flaring.

I do need some help.

I glance at the clock on my phone. Half eleven. Rachel has sent me seven messages. The last one half an hour ago.

I don't respond. Rachel isn't who I need to talk to, nor Adam, nor Josh.

I send Nicole a Snapchat message. She answers within half a minute with a sad emoji followed by:

Of course I can meet you. I'll wangle an early lunch. Let's try Bean There at half twelve.

42

The 1940s headscarf woman behind the counter looks flushed and hassled. Bean There is busy.

Finally, people have realised something bad is coming and they're wanting to make the most of things while they can. A last hurrah for coffee and cake and weddings. From everything I read on the news, life is about to change. But I arrive twenty minutes early and find a table for two. I'm already seated with a glass of spring water in front of me when Nicole arrives. She's smart in a knee-length skirt, flats and a white blouse.

Her uniform.

We order soup and she sits opposite me, holding my hand as I tell her about my call with Haldane. She listens avidly. She's a great listener, her eyes drawn down with distaste when I tell her how it went.

'Sounds awful,' she says.

'He hates Emma, that's obvious. But he was telling the tooth. The truth.' I shake my head in frustration. 'What if I'm not remembering because my subconscious isn't letting me? Self-preserving by forgetting?'

'He was messing with your head, Cam.'

'But the whisper sounded... It sounded like it wasn't him.'

'Who else could it have been?'

I don't answer, but we both mull over what the implication is. Haldane wasn't shy to spit out his accusations. That I was hearing things. Voices. From inside my head.

The soup arrives. I'm glad of the distraction because I'm sensing a trend in what's happening to me. First the fugue changes, then I find myself outside in a strange place after suffering one. And now this voice.

'*You need some help, Cameron.*' Haldane's echo in my head this time. Nicole sees me messing with the spoon, the soup slowly cooling in its dish.

'You should eat.'

I try a spoonful. Piquant tomato and basil. But my appetite is shot.

'I really wish I didn't have this blasted wedding to go to,' Nicole says.

'You must,' I reply. 'It could be the last time anyone can get married for a long while. Adam told me a lockdown is imminent. Just like in Italy. No pubs or restaurants. No cinema. No church.' I glance around and drop my voice. 'No coffee shops.'

Nicole sighs. 'Ugh, don't. Mia, the bride to be, has texted me five times in the last hour. At least twenty guests have cried off already, and the list is growing. People don't want to travel. Plus a crowd were supposedly flying in from the States and their flights are all cancelled.'

'All the more reason for you to support her then.'

Nicole squeezes my hand and pouts. 'You are so nice.'

'As I say, this place will likely be shut next week.'

Nicole lets out a heavy sigh. 'So awful. But I will not let that change anything. As soon as the wedding is over I'll tell Aaron we're finished. The reception's in Oxford and I'll be staying overnight. But by Sunday night it will be done. Mia will say I've ruined everything, wanting the drama for myself, but I don't care. By Monday, lockdown or no lockdown, we'll be fine. I promise.'

I smile stiffly.

'Oh, Cam, don't be sad.'

'Sorry.'

'Don't apologise. None of this is your fault. Can't be easy for you. But promise me you won't contact this Haldane again. He sounds like a creep.' She sighs. 'Together we can get this sorted. I'll come with you to see the private investigator chap, and even Emma's sister next week if you want. Two heads and all that.'

'Thanks.'

'Now eat your soup before it goes cold.'

I manage half the bowl before pushing it away. At a quarter past one, Nicole glances at her watch. 'I must go.'

'Thanks for listening.'

'I hate to leave you like this.'

'I'm fine,' I lie.

She leans across the table and kisses me. I watch her go, pay the bill and leave.

I drive back to the flat using a route I planned out. No point paying unnecessary congestion charges. I'm in the process of letting myself in through the main entrance when a voice calls from behind me. I turn around to see Detective Sergeant Keely and the lanky DC Messiter walking towards me.

'Don't look so worried,' Keely says.

'Why? Are you coming to tell me I've just won the lottery.'

'The police don't do that,' Messiter says.

Keely cuts in, admonishing. 'He was making a joke, Dan.'

Messiter flicks me a bemused glance.

I nod.

'Sorry,' he says. 'Must be your deadpan delivery.'

I toy with giving him a mini lecture on the reasons for my altered affect. Adam has a long and jargon-filled list to explain the causes. But life, as Josh says, is waaaay too short.

'Can we come up, Cameron?' Keely asks.

I open the door and let them in. In the flat, I put the kettle on and offer them tea. Keely orders one with milk and sugar. Messiter wants coffee. But he's befuddled by the choices I offer him from my bean to cup machine.

'Instant will do,' he pleads.

'I don't do instant. How about an Americano?'

Messiter looks doubtful.

'Nice with cream.'

'Okay. I'll try it.'

Keely mutters, 'Pleb.'

I make the coffee and tea and we sit in the living room and I watch the two officers study my wall. I explain. Messiter seems relieved.

'At first I thought it was one of those weird obsessional pinboards. You know, the kind you see in TV cop shows with a loony stalker and a wall full of cuttings and photos of the victim.'

Keely rolls her eyes and, seeing it, Messiter blushes and hides his face behind his mug. Then she turns to me.

'Mathew Haldane,' she says, 'ring any bells?'

Messiter is staring at the morning post and the notebook I've left open on the coffee table. The names I'd read on Stamford's list of people who'd hired cars in Turkey are visible. I get up and pick up the notebook and some other flotsam. 'Let me make some more room. I'd have teddied up if I knew you were coming.'

Messiter frowns.

'Tidied is what I meant.' I move the bundle to a stool in the corner. 'There. Haldane, you said, wasn't it?'

'That's right,' says Keely. 'We've had a nice long chat, he and I.'

'About?'

'You contacting him.'

I don't respond. All three of us drink our hot infusions until Keely says, 'As you know, he is under an indefinite restraining order for all things Emma Roxburgh-related. He spoke to his parole officer to report your call. He wasn't in breach of the court order, but because he wants to remain a good boy, they've asked me to find out what the hell is going on. So, why did you contact him?'

I sip tea and formulate my answer.

Keely hasn't taken her eyes off me. She shifts her weight on the chair and smooths down her trousers. 'In your own time, Cameron. If you please.'

43

Messiter gets into the squad Vauxhall Insignia on the driver's side. Keely slides into the passenger seat and senses her colleague's displeasure hovering like a bad smell between them.

'Come on, Dan, spit it out.'

Messiter has his hands on the wheel but has not yet switched on the ignition. 'Okay, honest opinion? You were a bit hard on Todd. Again.'

'Yes, well, I'm all for stopping situations before they become a complete disaster rather than after the event when, more often than not, it's us who are left picking up the rancid pieces.'

Messiter doesn't engage with her. Instead, he starts the car and indicates to pull out. It will take them half an hour to drive the nine miles to the station at this time of day. Despite the government's appeal to people to work from home, judging from the current traffic and the number of commuters cramming the Tube Messiter took to work this morning, nothing much has changed yet. In fact, the Northern line from Highgate, where he rents a room in a flat with two others, was about as full as he can ever remember it. If there was a virus floating about, it must have had a bloody field day on the 7.40 from High Barnet to Morden.

The morning briefing from the super hinted at more draconian measures being brought in, too. Messiter's sister has asthma. She would be very vulnerable to the coronavirus. He's all for making sure people comply. And London is full of idiots in foil hats who think this is another bloody conspiracy, whining about an affront to their personal space and freedoms. They clearly don't watch the same news bulletins about what's happening in China and Italy and Spain that he does.

'Did you see that wall full of photos? Of his mother and his dead girlfriend? Just so he can remind himself of what they look like.' Messiter raises a hand in acknowledgement to the van that has just let him out.

Keely takes a swig from a litre water bottle she keeps in the car. 'I did. But none of that gives him the right to poke his nose into places where it might get bitten off.'

Messiter throws his sergeant a glance. 'I read up about Haldane. He's a creep.'

'Creep he may be. However, he's a creep who does not want the conditions of his restraining order compromised by someone wanting to rake up old manure.'

'Todd is trying to get his life back on track.'

'Really? Is that what he's trying to do?'

'Come on, sarge. Can't be much fun not remembering anything at all about your old life. Your parents, your girlfriend.'

Keely stops mid-swig. 'I'm beginning to think you have a thing for him, Daniel.'

'I'm AC not DC. And suggesting that is bang out of order. What if I suggested you fancied him?'

Keely grins. 'I'd have to caution you for triggering me. For having offensive thoughts. Far too late, matey. You lot lost the battle ages ago. We blew you out of the water with armour-piercing #MeToo shells. It's up to us girls to have all the non-PC fun now.'

Messiter shakes his head and Keely grins at seeing a little muscle clench and unclench in his jaw.

'Besides,' she says, not wanting Messiter in too much of a mood when they get back to the station. He's got a mountain of work to do on top of the pile she's about to give him. 'His sister rang me. She was worried about him. He has these hallucinations.'

'Fugues,' says Messiter. 'I looked them up.'

Keely shoots across an eyebrows-raised glance. 'Whatever they are, they aren't—'

Messiter pulls up at some lights and snaps his head around. 'What? Normal?'

'I didn't say that. I didn't think I had to. He's damaged and vulnerable. Exactly the type who slips off the grid surprisingly quickly through no fault of their own. He needs a little guidance. Rules to know what's safe and what's quicksand.'

'I still say you were too hard on him. You more or less accused him of going off the rails.'

'What if I did? Consider the evidence, detective constable. First, this paranoia over his girlfriend and the anaesthetist. And now he rings Haldane of all people. What has he got to do with anything?'

'Nothing much. Oh, except for the fact that he's the git convicted of harassing Todd's dead girlfriend.'

'Less of the sarcasm, Daniel. That all happened years ago. Okay, Haldane is a narcissistic toerag. But he wasn't anywhere near Turkey when Emma Roxburgh died. And even toerags can feel threatened by nuisance calls from—'

'Don't say it.'

'Come on. We both know Todd isn't... like he was.'

'That's not what you were going to say.'

'I was going to say not firing on all cylinders.'

'Yeah, right.'

'Okay, plain speaking. I do not want to be the one shovelling his brains off the pavement.'

'What?'

'His sister told me his fugues are all about being up high. On a roof, or a cliff.'

Messiter shakes his head. 'I think the guy just wants to get back to normal.'

The lights change and they pull away.

Keely lifts the bottle to her lips but adds one more retort before drinking. 'And I'm with him on that. Then we may finally find out what really happened on that beach in Turkey.'

'You still think he could have done it?'

'Let's say I'm keeping all my options open. And so should you, detective constable. So should you.'

44

I get up on Saturday with my mind jittery from the police's brief visit. At first, I was angry. But then I try to see it from Keely's point of view. Not a pleasant sight.

I do my stretches, drink water and then sit at the table and review everything and remember – hah, sometimes I do – that I didn't take my medication yesterday. I reach for my pillbox and swallow a modafinil. Chase it down with a gulp of hard London tap water, rinse and repeat with quetiapine as I let the dull resentment from the police's visit simmer.

Then I realise that I've taken both together when they should be four hours apart.

Nothing bad is going to happen. At least I don't think so. But they'll probably negate one another and leave me a bit mushy.

Concentrate, Cam.

I sit for an hour, all the while preoccupied by the thoughts of what Keely said. More so by what she'd left unsaid.

She'd warned me off. Suggested I ought to be careful. Suggested I get some help.

Get some help. My new catchphrase.

People are concerned about me. Rachel, Nicole, Adam... I

think about adding Keely but decide against it. She's too abrasive. But like the others, she too, worries I may be losing it. Whatever the hell *it* is. My mind? Control? Ability to reason?

What's left of my coffee has grown cold in the cup. But I don't want another one. My mind is buzzing like a fly at a window despite a sudden wave of tiredness flowing through me like thick oil. I slide over to the sofa and plop, head against the armrest, one foot on the floor. In repose. Is that the term?

I feel languid and useless. So much for the modafinil. This morning quetiapine is three rounds up and in danger of winning the bout hands down.

Damn it. I need to be more careful. For a moment, I ponder that. Usually I am. So what's distracting me? I already know the answer. Despite everything I've done I am no further forward with remembering. I'm a man trapped in a dark cave with no lamp to guide me.

I fish out my phone and open up the photo app. To an album entitled Emma. I lost my old phone somewhere in the sea in Turkey. So did she. Both washed away on the tide. Some fisherman gutting a tuna might get lucky and find my iPhone 6. But even if it was found mine would be useless because I can't remember the passcode. Emma's is a similar blank. If we were comfortable enough with each other, I like to believe we might have shared our passwords. Other people do. Many's the time I've watched Rachel pick up Owen's phone and use it without needing to ask.

I study the Emma album. Somewhere in the Cloud there are hundreds of out-of-reach photos of me, Emma and us as a couple. Rachel told me Harriet tried gaining access to Emma's phone account but was met with a fat refusal.

I correct myself. I mean flat refusal.

Data protection is unmalleable. Even for the dead.

So my album, on my new phone, comprises of images Emma

and I had shared on social media, that appeared on other people's timelines and phones. Images I've been sent by friends and acquaintances after I appealed to them. They number a couple of hundred.

I scroll through and stop occasionally to try to remember. No joy, despite labelled dates and places. But I'm drawn to a series of photos of us taken on a sunny winter's day. The hats and clothes we are wearing hint at the bitterness of the weather. We're obviously not in London. Too much green and a stunning architectural feature stretched over a picturesque countryside. Namely, the viaduct at Hockley near Winchester. I count half a dozen snaps of us walking over the viaduct, and half a dozen more of us looking back towards it.

Rachel told me I had a thing about trains in my other life. Even had a train set when I was a child. I'm thirty-five now. That means I was thirteen when the first Harry Potter book came out. I, like countless others, became a little obsessed. I say that because I've only seen the first two films (an everyday story of a speccy boy wizard and Robbie Coltrane in platform boots according to Josh) and not read any of the books. Not since the accident anyway.

So trains and viaducts were a *thing* of mine courtesy of JK Rowling and Platform Nine and Three-Quarters. The question is, did I drag Emma along or was she a willing victim? But looking at her expression in the photographs suggests no coercion. We enjoyed ourselves. The smiles are not forced; the pleasure seems genuine. Emma looks pretty in her beanie hat. And suddenly I need some of that. Suddenly, I want to stop obsessing about the day Emma died. I want to remember her alive.

I go out for a walk, shop for essentials. But I can't empty my mind of its looping mentation. Time for a change of scenery.

I don't question the impulse as I punch directions into Google Maps. The estimation is two hours in current traffic conditions. I check the time. Almost 3pm. I could be there by 5 and it would still be light.

Why not? Why the hell not?

The phone rings. I don't answer it. My mobile has twenty WhatsApp messages from Rachel. I don't want to speak to her. Not now. Not after the way she'd helicoptered me with Adam and Keely.

I grab my car keys from on top of the small pile of letters and papers I'd moved off the table yesterday to stop Messiter's beady eyes from clocking them. It's a clumsy manoeuvre and the papers fall to the floor. Cursing, I pick them up and stare again at my notebook, at Stamford's list of people who hired rental cars in Turkey and who had been in Cirali the day Emma was killed.

I put the list down on the table with the rest of my spilled pile and head out. I don't want my brain cluttered with all that now. I just want space.

My usual congestion-charge-avoiding route takes me around the Oval and over Vauxhall Bridge, down through Twickenham to Sunbury and the M3. The radio is on and I listen to someone discussing films. I hear nothing in the recent or upcoming releases I want to see. Besides, Josh says I need to watch *Zombieland* next. One of Josh's top ten. Predominantly because of Emma Stone, he said. I caught him reddening up a bit when he said it.

Approaching Winchester, the satnav takes me to the Otter-bourne Road, to the park and ride. Rain is still spitting as I lock the car and head north along a cycle path towards a busy road. I cross near a roundabout and then stroll to the signposted Hockley Link across the main railway line. I may well have been here before but I do not remember any of the turns. So I follow the map on my phone. A few yards further on, the path enters open countryside, and the viaduct opens up on the left half a mile away. From this angle I count fourteen of the thirty-three brick arches. I wait for the rush of pleasure I'm hoping will take me back. But there's nothing.

Not yet.

From the viewpoint it's an eight-minute stroll along the edge of a field alongside the M3 and then up a ramp and onto the viaduct. The red-brick parapet walls are almost six feet high except where the upper few feet have been replaced with steel rails to afford a view of the meadows beyond. I stand at one of these viewpoints and gaze out over the lush greenery below. Just as Emma and I had in 2016.

Rain still pops sporadically against the hood of my jacket. The same jacket I'd worn in the photograph of me and Emma. A deliberate choice. All part of the experiential technique for triggering memory Adam has suggested.

A few cyclists and two dog walkers are all I come across. It's getting late to be out walking and the viaduct is not lit. But something about this piece of remarkable engineering calls to me. An echo of the enthusiasm I'm supposed to have exuded when I was younger? Or of how Emma and I had laughed here?

Benches and historical interpretive artwork adorn alcoves along the way. I read them all, but nothing triggers a response. I walk the whole length and then turn to walk back, warm in the jacket. Too warm. I hear rather than feel the rain stop so I slide off my hood and am met with a sudden rush of traffic noise from the M3 close by on the other side of the viaduct. There's a signal tower on the viaduct path, recognisable from a recall of the snaps I'd studied at a point at which Emma and I took photos. I walk back and read the dedication to railway workers.

I wait to see if something comes. Nothing does.

A little further on is another viewpoint. I go to it and gaze down toward the River Itchen beneath.

I spot a figure in the trees. Looks like he's holding binoculars up to his face. A birdwatcher in the water meadows. I let my gaze drift up to the west to a line of gold where the grey clouds end. Without warning, the red brick of the arches below glow bronze in the rays beaming horizontally from the almost setting sun. A beautiful sight. I realise I'm alone on the viaduct. I want desperately to remember something, but all I can sense here is emptiness and this tranquil moment.

What did we do when we left here, Emma and I?

Did we go to a pub?

Did we visit Winchester and go to a gallery? Something Emma was fond of doing. No point considering that now. Far too late on a Saturday afternoon for galleries. They'd be closing if not already closed. Besides, some of them had put the shutters up in response to the government's precautionary request that all non-essential businesses shut up shop.

I close my eyes and lift my face. Setting sunlight filters through my shut lids and turns the world orange. A promise of summer at the end of a damp, dismal day.

Still, I can't remember.

'Sorry, Emma,' I say. 'Rest in peace.'

Perhaps the warmth of the jacket combined with the buzz of traffic is what lulls me. Perhaps the delicious caress of the evening spring sun on my face. Whatever the trigger, I'm trans-ported, and, without warning, Emma answers me.

45

S he's not on the viaduct, and neither is Cam. They're on the rooftop bar, and for once alone. At the point in Cam's fugue narrative where they stand near the edge. Cam looks over. The river and the meadow are gone. In their place he sees the rocks and the whitecaps of the breaking waves at the northern end of the beach in Cirali.

'We don't need to be here,' he says. 'We could walk back into Winchester.'

Faceless Emma smiles. Only her mouth is visible. The rest, as always, is featureless.

'If only we could, silly. We can't stop this, Cameron.'

She takes a step back, a step towards oblivion. Cam puts out a hand to stop her. She tilts her face down towards the sea.

'It's not me you need to stop,' she says, smiling. 'It's them.'

Cam half turns, sensing someone else. The someone whose hand will push Emma off in this iteration of the fugue. The hand that causes her to plummet to her death. The hand he's come to believe might be his own. He sees, right behind him, the decimated face of the sandblasted statue and behind her a shadowy figure that is black smoke coiling and uncoiling, pushing out two arms like some monstrous amoeba that melds with those of the statue's. Cam takes a step back. He still has hold of Emma, but she is leaning out, accepting her fate.

'You don't have to,' he says, but all the while the statue's hand is reaching forwards, driven on by the coiling smoke.

Cam shouts. 'You don't have to, Emma!'

A whistle brings me back. Harsh, urgent and just in time. I'm not standing on the path of the viaduct. Instead, I'm four feet up on the wall, nearly fifty feet off the ground. I waver and sway, buffeted by a strong breeze, panic threatening as I wonder if this is still a part of the fugue. But my feet are on a solid surface and my lower leg meets resistance. I glance down and to either side, trying to grasp what this is. There is no six-foot viaduct wall here. The upper two feet of bricks are missing, replaced by a single metal rail. Still a barrier, but one that you can look over to the meadow and the landscape.

I've clambered up onto the brick. One leg in front, one leg behind the rail. Standing with my arms out, balancing. Or rather, swaying. I rock forward. The only thing between me and emptiness is my left leg behind the rail. My right leg has stepped over. I sway again as the wind gusts, vertigo threatening to send me head first down into the meadow below. Resistance makes me bend my knee and brings my weight back. But I overcompensate and topple backwards, barely escaping snapping my shin with a foot trapped under the railing. I tumble onto hard ground. My back hits first. There's a jarring pain but then my head follows. Somehow the ruffled hood of my jacket cushions the blow.

I'm winded, but only slightly. Hardly a bruise as I get to my knees and pull myself up. Who whistled? I scramble up and look down. The light is fading quickly but I can make out a shape beneath the trees. Is it the birdwatcher? I raise a hand. A feeble gesture but something moves below in response. A black shape that reminds me of coiling smoke.

I'm not hurt, but adrenaline is pumping, accelerating the shock of my backwards tumble, feeding the frisson of fear that grips me. What if the birdwatcher is not a birdwatcher? What if, instead, the same roiling shadow I'm seeing in my fugue is now here with me in Hockley?

Stupid. Illogical. But I can't shake the weird conviction. Nor can I now dismiss the fact that I am losing control. I clutch the rail to steady myself, let the trembling in my arms and legs diminish.

A fall from this height might have killed me. If I'd landed on my feet, my pelvis and spine would've snapped. I might live but I'd be in a wheelchair again. This time permanently.

But what if I landed head first?

What if I made *sure* I landed head first?

For a moment I contemplate the notion. Let the ramifications permeate.

My demise would put an end to things. I wouldn't be a bother to anyone after that. Not to Rachel, or Josh, or Adam.

No one would miss me.

I squeeze my eyes shut. That's not true. Nicole would. So would Rachel and Josh.

And Vanessa. I mustn't forget Vanessa.

Besides, it's the coward's way out.

I get up and hurry off the viaduct. The birdwatcher was on the other side of the river which means he has to come up that side. Whoever or whatever he is, I don't give him the chance. I half jog back to the car though my shin, where it leaned so heavily against the rail, hurts. I ought to be grateful it didn't snap. Within ten minutes I'm back on the M3 and heading towards London, wondering just what I was doing in coming down here alone.

Experiential triggering.

There is a strong argument for revisiting these places with someone else, I realise. Someone to give a different perspective. Someone who could stop me from doing something very, very silly. I'll ask Nicole to come with me next time.

Next time.

She's leaving Aaron this weekend. Breaking it all off. I won't call her though. Not now. She'll be at the wedding listening to speeches. Maybe getting drunk. I wonder if she's thinking about me.

About her damaged liaison.

Night closes in around me as I drive. I shiver for a good fifteen minutes. Adrenaline, not the cold. Terror does that to you.

But I'm annoyed too. Not only because the fugue might have killed me but the realisation that what just happened is exactly what Keely accused me of – losing control. The lines are blurring. And badly. For a moment, a gut-wrenching second, I'm convinced the sandblasted maid-statue and the coiling smoke figure are sitting in the back seat of the car. I sense a thrill of real fear brushing the hairs in the nape of my neck. I peer into the rear-view mirror but there is no one in the back seat. The maid's sandblasted face is only in my mind's eye. I'm getting more and more certain that only in the fugue do the real answers lie. And I need answers now Haldane has rekindled my fears.

Of how what happened to Emma was my fault.

From my conversations with her, Keely has not dismissed that same idea either. I want to believe I could not have done it.

But my tenuous certainty needs backing up with facts if I'm going to somehow put all this behind me.

Unless it was me all along.

The closer I get to London, the more the need to unburden myself of these poisonous thoughts grows.

46

I drive straight to Greenwich. It's almost eight by the time I get to Heathfield. Vanessa is in her room watching TV. She's surprised to see me.

'Is it Sunday? If it is someone will pay for me missing a roast dinner,' she slurs.

'Not Sunday. I wanted to talk to you.'

'Been expecting something. Rachel's been telling me all about you.' She delivers this pronouncement immediately as I sit down.

I wince. 'Telling you what, exactly?'

'She thinks you've gone rogue.'

I try to fob this off with a joke. 'The only rogue I've been anywhere near is a rogan josh. With Josh. That'll be me the rogue and Josh, another rogue, having a rogan josh. Works on so many levels.'

'With your linguistic skills this is very thin ice.'

'Give me some credit.'

'Rogan josh doesn't work at all, and you know it.' She mutes the TV with the remote. 'You in trouble, Cam?'

I'm sitting on the edge of Vanessa's bed. She's in a powered wheelchair wearing a neck collar. Better than the bloody great metal halo screwed to her skull, but both designed to stabilise her vertebra so that, in her words, 'My wobbly head doesn't fall right off and roll under a bed.' And she's asking *me* if I'm in trouble. I suddenly feel about an inch high.

'Come on. Spillthembeans.' Vanessa manoeuvres her chair with an elegant thumb and forefinger on the armrest joystick so she's facing me. 'Still waters run full of effluent, Cameron. Time to flush.'

'Did you ever consider becoming a poet?'

She ignores me and tilts her head. 'The oracle awaits.'

Vanessa's chair stops moving and with her hair backlit by a lamp on a shelving unit, she looks like some sort of sci-fi queen on a throne waiting for the ambassador of a far-flung planet to present to her.

'You know about my fugues, don't you?'

'Do bears...?'

'I'll take that as a yes, then.'

On the silent TV a DC hero is battling supervillains in soundless scenes of mayhem. I drag my gaze back to Vanessa. I tell her all about Keely and Stamford and Harriet and Nicole and end up with my visit to Hockley.

'My fugues are constant. Identical for months. You know what they're like. I'm on a rooftop somewhere warm. Always evening, always a girl–'

'The lovely faceless Emma.'

'Bingo. The other people are the same too. And the fugue always ends with me and Emma falling off the roof.'

'I love these kids' cartoons.' Vanessa's delivery is poker-faced.

'But now, everything has changed.'

'How?'

'I still can't see Emma's face. Previously she always fell, but now a hand pushes her off. And today... today even stranger things were going on in fugue-ville.'

'Like?'

'A statue. Female, a maid of some sort, and a figure made of smoke. They're the ones who push Emma off and, I suppose, me.'

Now I realise how much I want to believe those words are true. To rid myself of the nagging, sapping alternative. The possibility that the pusher is me.

Vanesa blinks. 'If it's changing, isn't that a good thing?'

The same thought has occurred to me in one of many grasping-at-straws moments. But I haven't told her everything. So I add, 'I think the fugue has my memory locked up in it. But somehow it's become twisted and abstract.'

'That's deep.'

I wait for her to add, 'Like a well full of shit,' but she doesn't. 'It sounds mad, doesn't it?' I say.

'Does it? I thought the head doctors had an explanation for your little mental awaydays?'

'They do. I'm their prime specimen. But...' I swallow, let the words trickle out. 'Today, when I came out of my fugue I was standing on the parapet of a viaduct.'

'Okay.' Vanessa's blinking increases.

'See, I told you it's mad.'

'You're not mad. There's a reason for this. You told me yourself you've been a lot more proactive.'

'So you think this is my memory working itself out?'

'Like the enigma code.'

'Nice analogy.'

'Not convinced?'

'I'm not a big fan of this development, the physical theatre side of it. Viaducts and roofs are both capable of tipping me off. If my fugue wants re-enactments I'd rather dress up in a tunic with a red cross and wield a wooden broad sword with the Sealed Knot.'

On TV, a caped hero throws a fire truck at an eight-armed monster who bats it away like a fly.

'Are you frightened?'

'No.' A lie. 'But when I was standing on that parapet, I saw a figure in the trees. At first, I thought it was a birdwatcher. But later I wondered if it was something else.'

'Like what?'

'I don't know.'

'Something from the fugue?'

'Maybe.' Another hesitation before I take the plunge. 'And when I came back to myself, I did toy with the idea of jumping. As a convenient answer.'

'To what?'

'Everything.'

There's a slight but perceptible shake of Vanessa's head. 'We've talked about this.'

'Yes, we have.'

In fact, we made a pact, Vanessa and me. We promised not to let one another suffer if push comes to shove. She laughed when I said that, given my fugue circumstances. She made me promise how, if she ever ended up unable to move at all, if the multiple surgeries on her spine go wrong, I'd help her find a way out. Smuggle her to Switzerland and a nice end-of-life clinic. And I made her promise me the same. Except my situation would be more mental than physical. If I lost it all, and they threatened to lock me away in some secure unit somewhere, I made Vanessa promise she'd engineer an escape and a syringe full of insulin for me.

All theoretical and maudlin. But we've both stared the Grim Reaper in the face and lived to tell the tale. We're allowed to share things way too dark to share with anyone else.

'We agreed that you can't go anywhere or do anything... permanent until I'm out of this place,' Vanessa says.

'By anywhere, you mean mentally AWOL?'

'Yup.'

I don't answer.

'Agreed?' Vanessa stares me down, demanding I speak the words.

'Agreed. But what do I do about the fugues?'

'Exorcism?'

I laugh. Vanessa doesn't.

'You're kidding, right?'

Vanessa shakes a pair of wobbly jazz hands and hoots out a 'Wooo' before making eyes at the ceiling and adding, 'I don't mean the holy water and green vomit kind. I mean laying your ghosts.'

'As in finding out what happened?'

'Yes. Stamford sounds as if he's onto something. And Nicole sounds amazing. Get her to help you. You're not mad, Cam.'

'That's not what Rachel would say. Nor the police.'

'You're not asking them.'

This is exactly what I needed to hear. I grin. 'You'd like Nicole.'

'I'm looking forward to meeting her.' Vanessa smiles. Though still a little lopsided and not as broad as Leon's, it's just as bright.

47

The kitchen clock says 9.57pm when I get back to the flat and I haven't eaten or taken my teatime meds. On the way home I fix the first part by calling in to Thai Spice – my go-to takeaway. I crack open a beer and eat *pla kapong neung* in the kitchen and check my messages. I finally reply to Rachel and text to tell her I've been out for a meal. A small white lie since I am eating – so what if it's takeout – and that I'm tired and off to bed.

She answers in capitals with:

WHAT ABOUT SOCIAL DISTANCING?

I don't bother answering. Instead, I wash down some quetiapine (I can't be arsed with modafinil now) with what's left of the beer. I'm sure these damned tablets get bigger by the day. Is this particular cocktail helping or hindering my fugues, I wonder? I could try stopping the lot... I can just imagine what Rachel would say.

I try watching a little TV but end up flicking through the

channels because I know I won't be able to settle. I make the mistake of ending up on Sky News.

People have not been listening to government advice. After months of miserable winter and dank and dark weekends, the weather has turned. In the western part of the country the sun is out and, though hardly balmy, the masses have made for beaches and beauty spots, desperate to get out after the dismal February. Like caged animals sensing freedom. But the scientists and politicians warn there'll be a heavy price to pay. Now they're threatening to close parks and put up roadblocks.

It's insane.

I'm Brad Pitt in *World War Z* watching chaos unfold from a distance. Helpless to stop any of it. I resist the urge to look out of the window to check if any undead are loitering in sleep mode, twitching, head down, waiting for a noise or a smell to signal their next victim. Oh yes, I know all the clichés. I'm becoming an expert. *Zombieland, 28 Days Later, The Girl With All the Gifts, Shaun of the Dead* (Josh's number one, needless to say), I've seen them all now.

Pure fiction, right? But I don't look out of the window. I'll sleep better if I don't. I turn off the TV and drag myself to bed. The world is going to hell but oddly enough, after chatting with Vanessa, I'm bathed in a strange sense of calm.

I sleep well. Dreamless oblivion. No hypnagogic fugues tonight.

Sunday, I mooch around, reflecting. Mostly wondering what happened on the viaduct at Hockley, hoping Nicole is okay and willing her to ring. But she's been to a wedding. Her best friend's wedding. Chances are she has a hangover. Best I leave her alone.

I walk down to the newsagent and buy a paper. It makes for grim reading.

Two thousand cases of Covid-19 in London, but the bad news is the rest of the country is likely to follow over the coming weeks. A hundred people have died in the city. The forecast is for thousands.

National Trust has shut its parks. The mayor of London has not yet closed the Tube, arguing that it's vital for key workers, but he fears too many people will use it on Monday. There are photos of people on beaches in Devon and hundreds on the Yorkshire Dales.

At some point in the afternoon I lounge on the sofa, draw the curtain to cut out the light slanting in, bleaching out details on my wall, and think. I try to fit all the bits and pieces I have together into a messy collage of what I know. See if I can make some kind of plan. More a thought cloud than anything, yet somehow it helps. I slide my gaze over the wall and focus in on the people playing the biggest part in my life. I don't include Rachel or Josh because they are constants. This is more about me trying to chart the changes.

The first image I land on is DS Keely. The photo of her is a newspaper cutting from some case that made the papers. She's with another officer but I've snipped him out. I scanned and enlarged the image. Her hair is longer than it is now, but still Keely. Still that unforgiving I-dare-you-to-lie stare.

On a sheet of blank paper I write Keely's name as a heading and scribble my thoughts underneath.

KEELY
Suspicious of me. Still thinks I'm guilty. A person of interest.
Thinks I'm unstable.
Doesn't like me meddling.

Next comes Stamford. His image is culled from his website. He looks more like a friendly financial advisor than a private investigator. Something to do with the side-on shot, the suit and tie and the cheesy grin.

STAMFORD
Has information on the Turkish angle.
Comes across as genuine.
Admits his first loyalty is to the Roxburghs.

Even though I underline the last sentence, I know I want to trust him. He is the only one as keen as me to find out what happened in Turkey. Or so it seems. But there's one more name to add.

NICOLE
Willing to help.
Knew Emma.
Treats me as normal.

I want to cross out the very last sentence as soon as I've written it.

It rankles.

I'm a thousand light years from normal. I shouldn't be expecting anyone to treat me that way. Yet, Nicole accepts me for who I am. Flawed and damaged. She's one of a handful of people who do. Josh does, Stamford and Vanessa do. Adam does too – though I'm his patient and by definition that's a different relationship. Still, with Nicole, she's the first woman since Emma that I've slept with. I may have slept with any number of others before Emma, of course – oh, yeah.

I guffaw. Who the hell am I kidding? I can't remember sleeping with Emma, so there is no chance of me remembering anyone before her even though I must have. So in effect Nicole is my first.

What a way to reboot the system.

I slouch off to bed with Nicole on my mind. I want to message her, but I don't. I promised myself I wouldn't. She may, at this moment, be telling Aaron. Explaining to him how none of this is his fault. That I've reappeared out of her past like a ghost, definitely no shite whining armour involved.

That one stops me in my tracks. My dysphasia normally throws up malapropisms. Spoonerisms are rare, though this one, shite whining, is a classic. I must write it down for Josh. He'd love to see a knight in shite whining armour.

I scribble it down in my notebook and drag my thoughts back to between the tramlines. The point, what my addled brain is trying to explain to itself is, the last thing Nicole needs is pressure from me. The ball is in her court.

I must be patient.

But it is hard.

48

I'm in bed by eleven that night, halfway through McCarthy's *The Road*. Neither the boy nor his father yet have a name, and I'm guessing their anonymity will persist as they trudge through a nuclear winter. At first, the lack of quotation marks bothers me, but the spare style suits the harrowing subject matter. In a self-flagellating kind of way. I text Josh and tell him this. He comes back with a smiley face and:

Read one more chapter and then listen to this.
https://youtu.be/SJUhlRoBL8M

I finish the chapter and surf to the provided URL and a crucifixion scene. This is a bit too much irony even for Josh. Never one to be troubled overmuch by the issues of good taste, sometimes Josh walks perilously close to the line marked crass. But then, on the video, one of the crucified men starts singing. I know who Eric Idle is, but I've never seen or heard 'Always Look on the Bright Side of Life' before.

I close the covers of *The Road* and watch the video five times.

The sixth is interrupted by my phone cheeping. If it's Rachel, I will not answer. But this signals a Snapchat message.

Nicole.

Hi Cam. I spoke to Aaron at his. He didn't take it well. We had a blazing row. He'd had a few drinks and lost it.

I text back.

What do you mean?

There was a lot of noise. Mostly Aaron shouting. His neighbour knocked on the door. Aaron swore at him. The neighbour called the police. It wasn't pleasant. I left before the police came. Better they didn't see me.

What does that mean?

This time, when the phone pings, an image pops up, a Nicole selfie. Only not the usual smiling Nicole. She has no makeup on and she's pouting, but only to demonstrate the bruise around her lip and over the corner of her mouth.

I sit up, heart pounding. I slide to my feet, scattering sheets behind me like a snake shedding its skin.

Let me call you.

No. It's late and I'm at a friend's. I promised her I wouldn't speak to anyone. I promised her I'd be quiet. We're both pretty shaken. But I had to tell you.

Where is Aaron now?

Don't know and don't care. It's over. He's furious. He knows about you. Don't ask me how. I want you to lock your door.

He can't get in. I'm on the first floor.

Lock your door.

Okay. Don't worry about me.

But I do. A lot. Aaron is unpredictable. And he's been drinking. Stay safe. Come to my friend's place tomorrow morning. I'll send you the address. She says she'll stay off work but I don't want that. She's a key worker. If you come and keep me company, I'll feel much better.

Of course I'll come.

Thank you. Catelyn, my friend, has given me one of her sleepers. I'm going to try to get some rest now. Thinking of you. I love you, Cam.

When I text back, there's no delivery confirmation. She's switched her phone off is my guess. I don't go back to bed. I can't. I'm on my feet pacing.

Poor Nicole. She's done this for me. For us. That bastard Aaron... It's an hour before I finally sit down on the edge of the bed and untwist the covers. But I struggle with getting my thoughts in order. If I'm honest, I've been like this since I drove to Emma's old surgery. Something's shaken up my brain, that's obvious. I crave sleep but I'm not really tired when I should be exhausted. How can that be?

Buggering up your meds, idiot.

There is that. But my mind fizzes with disjointed thoughts. The message from Nicole has only upped the white noise by fifty decibels.

Yet even through the crackle and hiss, deep down I know why I'm so restless. Nicole's hurt because of me. Just like it's my fault Emma is dead and Harriet hates me. Am I cursed? Does everything I touch get damaged?

I wrestle with these thoughts through the long hours of the night, wondering if I'll ever learn the truth. If I'll ever truly get any peace. The one slight comfort I latch on to is knowing Nicole is waiting for me come the dawn. I grasp at that soothing anticipation until it lulls me into a fitful sleep a little after 3am.

I get three-and-a-half hours before I'm wide awake again.

49

MONDAY 23 MARCH

D S Rhian Keely stares at the screen in front of her, waiting for the page she's called up to load. The server, never fast, is on the go slow and has been all morning. Another stabbing on their patch. The male victim, a teenager, seems to have been a case of mistaken identity just to make a crap situation immeasurably worse. Keely is certain it's gang-related, but she wants to make sure Dwayne Green is indeed the nice guy everyone says he is. Dwayne is out of surgery and looks like he'll live. Eyewitnesses have named his two attackers, but Keely is trying to access a local newspaper website to read an article highlighting Dwayne's athletic prowess. He's a track star, apparently. But she's learned the hard way not to trust what people say. For all she knows Dwayne may be a runner, but for the dealer in one of the estates off Jamaica Road, not on the 800 metres track in Southwark Park.

Sometimes innocent victims aren't as innocent as they're made out to be.

Finally, the page begins loading just as Messiter sticks his head around the door with an apologetic look Keely's come to recognise as a harbinger of grim news. She's told him he should never play poker.

She glances at the wall clock. 8.25am. 'It better be good,' Keely says.

Messiter's lips pull back in a rictus grin. 'It isn't. But she won't talk to me.'

'Who won't?'

'Harriet Roxburgh.'

Keely's head drops between her shoulders. This is all she needs. Already her day is two thirds down the toilet what with the stabbing and the briefing they'd had about how things would change after the new virus-related powers come in. For a start they're going to close down businesses. She knows of at least three pubs on the patch who will no doubt offer lock-ins to their favourite punters because that's what they were doing anyway. They're geared up for it. Convinced in their right to bend the law a little.

She's seen films about speakeasies but never thought she'd see the day one might appear in London. Shutting them down would not be easy. On the other hand, the power to remove people from public places to their homes is one she is looking forward to. Ever since they'd had the heads-up about it there'd been a flurry of jokers practising 'Move along there' in the corridors. No longer were stroppy feral youths effing and blinding at passers-by going to be able to say, 'You can't make me, I'm not doing anything.' Loitering with a gang of other lowlifes swearing and sipping vodka was now 'doing something'. She can't wait.

What she isn't looking forward to is dealing with arseholes who might decide it was a laugh to spit on her, or to cough in her face. She's had colleagues suffer such indignities at the hands of the mad and the bad in exactly that way. Now the arseholes will get short shrift. Even so, she is considering wearing a motorbike helmet to work.

Wordlessly, she pushes back from the desk and walks through a door Messiter holds open for her. Keely mutters as they stride the length of the corridor.

'You told her we have other cases to deal with, I hope?'

'Yes.'

'That we can't spare any more resources?'

'I did, sarge. Water off a duck's arse.'

'It's back.'

'What is?'

'Never mind.'

They reach a closed door. Keely brushes off a muffin crumb – bran and walnut mini – from her blouse, sends Messiter one last long-suffering glance, and opens the door.

Harriet Roxburgh is sitting at a desk on a steel-framed chair angled towards the door. Arms folded, legs crossed, one foot jiggling up and down maniacally as if it has lost all control. A barometer of the wild energy that seems to ripple through her like a winter storm whenever Keely sees her. She's an attractive woman, or could be, Keely thinks. If it wasn't for the sour disdain making her mouth into a thin-lipped bloodless slash of disapproval and the constant look of someone smelling a blocked drain that screws up the rest of her face.

'You've seen it, I take it?' Harriet fires off a challenge.

'Seen what?' Keely replies. For a moment she half hopes this may be some kind of anxiety over an infringement of human rights the new Coronavirus Act could be seen as. But Harriet Roxburgh has never struck Keely as an activist other than over the death of her sister. An occurrence which preoccupies her every living moment. No room for a bigger picture in Harriet's hornet's nest mind.

'Emma's fake website,' spits Harriet. 'Someone's posted more filth. And when I say someone, we both know who.'

Keely walks in to stand opposite Harriet but she doesn't sit, preferring to stand to show she's there under sufferance. 'I'm sorry to hear that. But as I explained this isn't a police matter.'

Harriet reaches for her phone and stabs and swipes at the screen before holding it out towards Keely's face.

'There. Just look at what he's written.'

Keely can't see the screen from where she's standing and does not try to take the phone. Frustrated, Harriet pulls it back and describes what's written.

'That's a photograph of my sister in a bikini. She had a nice figure. But what's written under it? DILF, that's what. Do you know what that means?'

Keely thinks she does but isn't sure. It sounds like MILF and she knows what MILF means. She glances at Messiter who shakes his head.

'Oh, come on. Take a stab in the dark. DILF. Doctors I'd Like to F... you know the rest. And under it are a dozen sick comments that leave little to the imagination.'

'Is this on Emma's site?'

'Not on her memorial site. On the other site, The Emma "Roxy" Roxburgh site.'

'And you know who put that image there?'

'The implication is it's my sister. But it isn't her because she is dead. So who do you think is doing it?'

'I don't know.'

'Cameron Todd, that's who.'

'You have proof of this?'

'No. Of course not. But we both know the man is unstable. He's accused my sister of having an illicit affair with a doctor and dabbling in drugs.'

'We've put him right on that one,' Messiter says.

The sound of his voice draws stares from both women.

'Good, delighted to hear it.' Harriet stabs at her phone again.

'But if you want proof he isn't all there, this is him down in Winchester yesterday.'

Once again, Harriet turns the screen towards Keely. This time she takes it and holds the screen closer so she can examine the image. It takes a moment to make out the details. Her eyes are drawn to the spans of a viaduct filling most of the frame, but she strokes her fingertips apart to enlarge the image and sees a figure standing on top of the parapet, arms outstretched. It isn't clear because the snap has been taken on a long lens. The light isn't great either and the big shapeless jacket the figure is wearing hides the build and blurs the features, but it still looks enough like Todd for her to sigh and snap her head up. 'How did you get this? Are you following him?'

'Really? That's the most important question to ask in this situation?' Harriet shakes her head.

'Are you?'

'No, *I* am not–'

'So what? You're paying someone to?'

Harriet is unruffled. 'This man is posting vile rubbish about my sister on Facebook. And he's standing on tall buildings like sodding Superman. Who knows what he'll do next.'

'Has he threatened you?'

'No. He doesn't need to. Anyone can see what's going on in that sick mind of his and I want you to do something about it.'

'He isn't breaking any laws, Harriet,' Keely says.

'Wonderful. Let's wait until he turns up at my parents' house with an axe, shall we? Let's wait until he breaks into my flat at midnight with an effing chainsaw singing "Saturday Night Fever".'

Messiter tries placation. 'We've already spoken to him. He didn't seem all that...'

'Go on, say it,' goads Harriet.

'Disturbed,' Messiter says.

'My sister is dead. Someone is posting on social media pretending to be her. You do not need to be a genius to see what's going on here.' She pauses, her voice dropping. 'He needs to be off the streets.'

Keely shakes her head. 'This isn't Russia or North Korea.'

Harriet stands, eyes blazing and tucks her phone away. 'I should have known this was a complete waste of bloody time. Well, don't say I didn't warn you.'

'Where are you going?' Keely asks.

'To do your job for you.'

'We've talked about this before.'

'Yes we have. And you disappoint me every time. I'd like to leave now.' Harriet glares at Messiter. He opens the door and follows her out. Keely stays in the room, wishing, for the hundredth time, that she had never heard of Cameron Todd or Emma Roxburgh.

50

I punch the address Nicole gave me into my phone. Greenwich is eight stops away on the Tube. I could drive, but it's Monday and, despite the essential journeys only warning, I'm not going to risk the traffic or overzealous police roadblocks.

Spring sunlight makes me squint as I leave the North Greenwich Tube station and head east towards the river again. The address is on Teal Street. A tall, newish building with a newsagent, coffee shop and a dentist's office sprinkled around a little courtyard at ground level. I look for names on the bell push panel but realise I don't know who Nicole's friend is. It doesn't matter as the panel is numbers only. I press number seventy-eight, something clicks, there's a static hum, and I say, 'It's Cam.'

'Come on up.' Nicole's voice, but it sounds strained. Hardly surprising under the circumstances.

The door lock buzzes, and I push it open. There's a foyer and a second door which swings open on a big green push button release. The lobby is small, with a door leading to some stairs and a lift. The foyer smells new; a chemical mix of plastic and fresh paint. I breathe it in and press the number seven. A soft female voice tells me to mind the doors closing and then I'm moving slowly upwards. Ads for a gym and the dentist sit in panels near the buttons. Above that is the maker's sign – Schindler. I know they're a big company because I've seen the name more than once. Josh says they're Swiss. He said that only he, being Jewish, could make a joke about Schindler's lifts without being offensive. I had no idea what he meant. When I asked him to explain he said it would take a teensy bit more time than travelling up three floors in an elevator would allow. He told me he'd get around to it one day. I'm still waiting.

The lift whispers to a stop on seven and I step out into another white-painted corridor. This one has light-grey carpet flooring and two abstract prints on the walls.

I look at the numbers next to the wood-panelled doors. Two, numbers three and five, have little plaques. One in opaque blue acrylic says Restoor Facial Aesthetics, one in brushed aluminium announces Astor Wireless Security. Clearly, there are businesses on this floor as well as residential properties. Number eight has a plaque too, but this one is stuck onto the door itself and says Cogni-Senses. I pause, wondering if I'm in the right place. I press the button and from within chimes tinkle in answer.

I wait in silence. But then a lock clicks, the handle turns, and the door opens.

Nicole's face peeks around the door edge.

But she looks different. Not the same Nicole I'd seen in the Snapchat image the night before. She's made-up, clipped her hair back and there is no sign of the bruises. When she steps back and opens the door fully, she smiles, and all is well with the world.

'Come in,' Nicole says.

I walk forward a few steps into a little ante room with tasteful grey walls and wait for her to close the door. When I turn to look at her, I do a double take. She looks... much better than I expected. And she's dressed in what looks almost like a uniform. Pale pink with shaped top and scrub trousers. Like a hospital nurse, but smarter and more fitted. She wears white Supergas on her feet. There's even a name badge. I glance at it. Lots of letters, too many for me to focus on, and a surname I'm sure begins with B not G, as in Grant. I glance at the first name again. Six letters. But they don't spell Nicole either.

'Are those your friend's clothes?' I ask.

'Let's go in,' she answers.

My expression must show that I sense something's off.

'Please,' she says, showing the way. She walks past me. I want to touch her, but her body language is formal. Too formal. I'm anxious now so I follow her into an unfamiliar room. This one is much bigger with a fabric sofa and two armchairs, flowers on side tables and enormous windows of the type that fold open. One of them already is and leads onto a terrace with a roof garden and a patio set on artificial grass. The sun blazes in from a cloudless sky and I squint against the sudden brightness.

Someone is standing in the open doorway looking out over the London skyline. He's dressed in olive chinos and a pale-blue shirt. Nicole walks over to him and says, 'Cameron's here.'

'Ah, good,' says a voice I'm familiar with. A jarring memory of a phone conversation stays frustratingly on the edge of recollection in my brain. He turns around and something slides deep in the pit of my stomach. A wet swooping thing that sends icy tendrils out into my arms and legs as cogs mesh in my brain. The man doesn't seem to notice and smiles like a model in a toothpaste advert.

I don't smile back. Because from my own research and from what I've learned from Harriet and the police, I'd quickly decided that if I ever met him, I'd never smile at Mathew Haldane.

51

I can hear my breathing, my heart booms in my ears. Haldane stares back with a troubled, almost pitying expression. He, too, wears a name badge pinned to his shirt.

'What is this?' I breathe out the words.

'This is nothing more than a regular follow-up, Cameron. You missed the last two, and we can talk about that, but you're here now. That's all that matters. Good to see you.' Haldane steps forward and extends his hand.

I recoil. To his left, Nicole watches impassively from behind one of the big armchairs.

I send her a desperate glance. 'Nicole?'

'Cameron,' she replies. Calmly, reassuringly. 'Why don't you take a seat.'

'Wha... what is this?'

Haldane's hand drops and he narrows his eyes. 'Tell us what you think this is.'

'A sick joke.'

'In what way?' Haldane is clean-shaven, hair styled short, the hooked nose lending him an imperious, Roman emperor air. He looks professional and very calm. It's this calmness that disturbs me the most.

'In every bloody way,' I yell. 'Nicole, tell me this is some godawful wind-up, please?'

Haldane turns to her, giving her permission, or perhaps an unspoken order. She turns her face – wearing as serious an expression as I've ever seen – towards me.

'Cameron, my name isn't Nicole. It's Selena. You know that. I'm a trained therapist and Dr Timpson's assistant.'

I glance at her badge. Focus in on the Selena and the surname that begins with a B not G. But I don't read it all. I can't because my brain refuses to. A mirthless noise that's a scathing half laugh bubbles through my lips. 'No, you're not. And his name isn't bloody Timpson. It's Haldane. Mathew Haldane.'

But the man looking at me doesn't flinch. He stays composed. 'Okay. That name must mean something to you so why don't you take a seat and tell us why you think we are... Nicola was it? And uh... Mathew Haldane?'

'Nicole,' I snap.

'Nicole. Right.'

I don't sit. I'm too angry. Too completely terrified. 'Why the hell should I explain myself when you two are the ones who are lying.'

Neither of them moves, but Nicole answers. 'Why would either of us lie, Cameron?'

'Because...' I shake my head. Suddenly I'm hot. My fingers are tingling and despite myself I get an abrupt urge to sit down.

'You're overbreathing,' Haldane says. 'Try cupping your hands over your mouth.'

I shake my head, but the tingling is worse and an orchestra of white noise tunes up in my ears, loud above the heaving of my chest as I suck in air like I've run a mile. Except I haven't run anywhere. I cup my hands over my mouth and rebreathe my exhalations, haul in carbon dioxide and slow my breathing down. After half a minute, the pins and needles in my fingers subside.

'May I speak?' Haldane asks.

I don't say yes, but I don't say no either.

'We, that is Selena and I, work with Adam Spalding. Do you remember him?'

'Of course I bloody remember him.'

'He referred you to us privately for continuing targeted cognitive therapy when you were discharged from rehab. You've been coming to us for four months.'

'No. That's not true.' I stare at Haldane through gaps in the spread-out fingers still covering my face.

'It is, Cameron. But lately, over the last month, you told us that your fugues were changing, becoming more erratic.'

I pull my hands down, more pissed off than I was before. 'This is absolute crap.' I get back up to my feet.

'Would you like some tea?' Nicole asks. 'You generally prefer camomile. We recommend it. Or I can even do coffee if you like. But only instant.'

'Tea?' I glare at her. 'Nicole, how can you do this?'

'Do what?'

'You know damn well what. Us. I'm here because of what Aaron did to you.'

'Who is Aaron?'

'Jesus Christ.' I'm shouting, but neither of them is fazed.

Haldane turns to her. 'Tea sounds like an excellent idea. Put the kettle on, Selena.'

'Her name is not Selena.' I grind out the words through clenched teeth.

Nicole ignores me and leaves the room. I'm alone with Haldane, anger burning my cheeks. 'What did you do to her?' I step forward, my index finger the accusing barrel of a loaded gun.

'What is it you think I've done?' he says and does so without flinching. Once more, I'm struck by how composed he is. How can he be so bloody sure of himself? 'Selena is–'

'Her name is not Selena. Her name is Nicole. She and I... we've shared my bed.'

Haldane's gaze is steady when he says, 'Selena and I are partners, both in business and emotionally. We have been for the last five years.'

I drop my head and laugh. It makes a hollow sound. I lift my eyes and they catch his name badge.

Dr EDWARD TIMPSON FRCPsych

I snap my eyes back up to challenge him. 'I can prove it,' I say. I reach for my phone, punch in numbers and scroll to Snapchat. The app clicks open. Empty. No messages. No photos. The Snapchat curse.

Haldane watches me fumbling. 'Last time you were here–'

'I've never been here before.'

He ignores me. 'You told us that your fugues were evolving. Becoming more... *troublesome* was the word you used. Is it possible that–'

'Don't. Don't even think about it.' I turn away, my mind spinning, a terrifying murky shadow of doubt seeping into my thoughts. I don't look at Haldane. I daren't. Instead, I half stumble to a chair and throw myself down, convincing myself that if this man wanted to attack me he would have done it by now. I sit, half turned away from him, hunched in on myself like a gargoyle, listening to the incessant chatter inside my head.

Is it possible? Could it be?

I'm still sitting like that when Nicole comes back into the

room with a tray. She puts it down on a coffee table and removes three mugs, a small jug of milk and a sugar caddy.

'One, isn't it?' she asks.

I don't answer but she spoons in the sugar anyway, adds a splash of milk and stirs the brown liquid. I watch her deft fingers and those small, exciting, adventurous hands. The ones I remember so well. Haldane sits on the sofa opposite and picks up his tea. Straight, no milk or sugar. I notice a notepad and a pen on the armrest. Haldane takes a sip, replaces the mug on the table and picks up the pad.

'Why don't you tell us about Nicole and this Haldane.'

'Jesus.' My eyes flick around at the sterile grey walls of the room. The wall art comprises seascapes and landscapes. Muted colours designed to calm the soul.

'If you feel overwhelmed, you're free to leave whenever you want. As always,' says Haldane.

Or is it Timpson?

Silence fills the space, bounces off the grey walls, flows around the seascapes like an invisible mist in which I founder.

'When I saw you last, you were about to take some driving lessons,' Timpson continues. 'A refresher course now that you got your licence back. You were looking forward.'

I realise I'm calling him Timpson in my head. That a part of my brain is already admitting defeat. I don't answer. I can't because my mind has frozen. A wild animal trapped in icy water, unable to move, desperately looking for a way out as the cold slowly snuffs out its life. He senses my distress and carries on in that smooth, controlled way he has. 'And the driving? Go well did it?'

I turn to Nicole. She's studying me intently with a mildly concerned expression. As if nothing has ever happened between us. Nothing at all.

The world tilts for me then. It tilts, and I'm sliding off the deck of a sinking ship. I reach for the camomile tea to steady my trembling hands. Somehow, the warmth of the tea and the solidity of the cup are strangely comforting. My ears are buzzing. Timpson is still talking, but I can't hear him. His voice is more white noise. The room and everything in it swims in my vision like a distant building on a heat-hazed road. I may be overbreathing again. I can't tell. But I can feel. And what I feel is a cold and blooming fear. An awareness that a terrible enemy is about to attack me. Except my enemy is not external. It's internal. Has been all along. I've been hiding from it. Running from it. Scared to turn and face it.

I clasp the mug in my hands.

Inordinately, pathetically pleased that it is real.

I lift it to my lips and, despite myself, unable to help myself, between sips of the warm liquid, I talk.

52

At first I can only stutter. I start and falter. Start again. I can't maintain eye contact with Nicole – Selena – when I regurgitate the visit to the surgery. Because that's how it is. As if I'm vomiting up bile. I tell them about how we met, went for coffee, talked of Emma's supposed infraction with an anaesthetist friend. About the photograph of us and how she told me we'd been lovers.

'And now you're going to tell me none of that happened,' I say. I throw these bitter words at Nicole. No, at Selena, because, like Timpson, I must make a call here, decide who it is I'm going to believe. But I have decided. What is the point of me pretending otherwise when the living evidence of my delusions are sitting here in front of me?

Selena speaks. 'It didn't happen, Cameron. I have never worked at Mulgrave Surgery. I did not know Emma Roxburgh.'

'And what happened after the meeting at the coffee shop?' Timpson asks.

I look away.

'Cameron.' Timpson adopts an encouraging, slightly

cajoling tone. 'We're here to help you. Whatever has happened, whatever you believe has happened, we can only unravel it if you tell us. Only then can I try to analyse your situation. See if there is anything we can do to remedy this little slip.'

'Little slip?' My reply is bitter.

'Yes,' says Timpson with the kind of earnest encouragement that dissipates my anger. Because I want to be angry. I want to rail at Timpson and Selena. But all they do is sit and wait in professional listener mode.

So I tell them the details. About my visits to the police and their reaction to my implication that Emma might have been involved with an anaesthetist who was a drug user. About contacting Stamford. About Nicole's visits to my flat, her boyfriend, her suggestion that we meet here because she'd been attacked. It sounds made-up. It sounds insane and humiliating and I keep my eyes averted. I can't look at Selena as I regurgitate it all.

'And what about Haldane?' Timpson asks.

'I looked him up. I rang him. Spoke to him. It was your face I saw online. Your voice I heard on the phone.'

Timpson shakes his head. 'You did speak to me. Or rather I spoke to you, to encourage you to come to your appointment.'

I study the tea and take another sip. I've drunk almost all of it, yet I can barely swallow what's left because it's become unpalatably cold. Like drinking muddy water.

'You understand that much of what you've told us is confabulation?' Selena says.

I study her face. Nicole's face. One that I am so sure has lain on the pillow next to me. 'No need to be embarrassed. Patients frequently channel attachments towards therapists, both positive and negative.'

Something inside me squirms.

Timpson leans forward. 'Adam has been experimenting with your medication, trying to find the right dose of quetiapine and modafinil. That's why I'm interested in what you're telling me about the fugues. How they're changing. So I can feed back.'

'They hadn't changed for months. Always the same scene. The rooftop bar. The faceless girl that I assumed was Emma,' I mutter.

'And now?'

'It's still the bar. That's the constant. Still high up. But the barman has changed. It was a play on words. His name sounds Russian, but he's Dutch. The owner of the beach bar Emma and I used to go to. And now there are others. A woman, a statue. And a man, or something in the shape of a man. But more a shadow, like smoke. These two figures appear when Emma falls. Are they the ones who push her?'

Please let it be them, not me.

'But you realise this is a hallucination,' Haldane says.

My voice is a low rumble, like a man finally confessing his sins. 'Yes, but partly memory too. Jumbled up and misinterpreted. The fugues are much more vivid. Previously, they'd take place while my body was engaged in mundane tasks that I would not remember doing. Like walking or packing a bag. But now, I'm much more active. Once to a rooftop and last time–' I pause.

'Go on, Cameron.'

'Last time I was on a viaduct.'

'A viaduct?'

'It was somewhere Emma and I liked to go. I wanted to see if it might help me remember. But I had a fugue when I was there. I ended up standing on the parapet.'

'It sounds dangerous,' Selena says.

'Perhaps. But it doesn't feel dangerous. And I didn't fall off.'

'Are you scared of heights?'

'No.'

Timpson stands. 'I'd like to try something, Cameron.' He walks over to the balcony doors and slides the other half open. A March sun is shining. Cool air wafts in, but Timpson steps out to a wooden deck. A sizeable space marked by raised concrete beds in which a few low shrubs have been planted under decorative gravel. It has a vaguely Japanese aura. One edge of the beds has wooden seating and there are wicker seats and a low table. Bordering the airy space is a hip-high wall of opaque safety glass topped by a steel barrier. It's an impressive penthouse terrace. Timpson stands with both hands on the barrier in the space between the raised beds and looks down.

'Does seeing me here bother you?'

'No,' I say.

'It doesn't make you anxious?'

Selena stands behind me in the room. I stand, too, and walk out. The faint breeze isn't at all unpleasant in the sunshine. London spreads out before us with half a dozen giant gantries adding jagged toothpick spikes to an overcrowded skyline. I look out and then down. I am not troubled by heights.

'And what you see now is London. Not the rocks of a Turkish cliff?'

Timpson's question irritates me. I stand next to him to stare out at an eerily-quiet city poleaxed by a strand of viral RNA that has made the leap into a susceptible species. London's sophisticated society has been brought to a virtual standstill.

'Of course it's London.'

'And you don't have any urge now to stand on the edge of this barrier?'

I don't but I would be lying if I said that in the moment of walking through the doorway it hadn't crossed my mind. I can recollect vividly the viaduct at Hockley. About how, if I'd been higher, I might do a better job of it. Be less of a burden. Then I'd convinced myself that people would miss me. Rachel and Vanessa and Nicole... But that was all a lie. There is no Nicole.

No Nicole.

I squeeze my eyes shut to let these thoughts traverse my consciousness. Did I imagine all that? Did I really not smell Bandit on my pillow?

I stand on the edge, still taking in the city laid out below. The sun slides behind a cloud and the chill is instant. This is not a fugue. This is reality.

Yet even as I admit my failings to myself, I sense something is different. My mind isn't as clear as it should be. There's a dullness, a fog that makes the horizon waver. The heat haze sensation again. I falter. My standing on the roof with Dr Timpson is reality... isn't it?

I glance behind. Selena has joined us. She stands with arms folded against the door frame. She's smiling, encouraging.

I catch a waft of her perfume. Light and floral. Not Bandit.

I see her lips move but there is no sound. I read what she says slowly, meaningfully.

I love you, Cameron.

My breath catches. No, no, no. Not real. This isn't real. She isn't real. I turn back to look down at the cars and the few people on the streets. The prime minister made an appeal on Friday. No one should be out unless they're exercising or walking their dogs or have an appointment.

Like me.

My eyes slide, images shift on a half-second delay. The fog in my head is worsening. And then I focus on a figure. The same figure I'd seen under the trees when I'd stood on the viaduct. The shadow man, the whistler. Big, dressed in a dark coat, but this time it's exiting a car.

Just like I seem to be exiting what I perceive as reality.

Or is this a variation of my fugue? Is that dark shape the same one that roils below the coiling smoke on Ivan's rooftop bar?

For the first time I notice that there is a chair next to me. Wood and steel, foldable. I don't look at Timpson, I can't return Selena's gaze. In my mind's eye I imagine the pressure of my foot on the seat. One step and I'd be up there. One more and I could be over. No more doubts. No more wondering if it was me who pushed Emma. From this height there would be no possibility of survival.

One step...

The noise is loud behind me. Someone knocking on a door. No, banging on a door followed by muffled words. 'Police, open up.'

I hear Timpson curse. See him shake his head and hurry past. I half turn and see Selena step forward.

'Show us, Cameron. Show us you're not scared of heights.'

I blink at her. Is it her voice? Or am I hearing it all in my head? Whatever the truth, the voice seems to fade in and out. Through the balcony doors I can see Timpson at the apartment door. The banging is loud. He seems to be protesting, but the noise persists. If anything it gets louder.

'Cam?' Selena is trying to get my attention. 'Cam?'

In the far hallway, I see the door open. Timpson looks out, hesitates for a moment before trying to quickly shut it. But he's too late as someone barges in. A woman. Wild, angry, shouting.

'Where is he? Where is he?' Her voice is distant but clearly audible.

Not the police.

For one moment I think about responding. I think about yelling that I'm here. Because it must be me she's looking for.

But I don't get the chance because Timpson grabs the woman by the arm. She swings around trying to fling him off.

That's when I see the knife.

The woman's shouts are cut off, and she convulses, bends at the hip and bows forward, mouth open in silent shock and pain as Timpson stabs Harriet Roxburgh viciously in the stomach.

53

I blurt out a shout, an incoherent bleat of protest. But as I step forward, my legs buckle, and I fall to my knees. My arms should stretch forward to break my fall in a protective reflex, but they don't. It's as if they've forgotten how to because the world has suddenly become viscous. I hit the ground and momentum tilts me forward and my head strikes the floor with a crack.

Selena kneels next to me, one arm on my shoulder. I breathe in her perfume. Her floral, not-Bandit perfume.

'Cameron, are you all right?'

I stare up at her, see double, focus, and croak, 'He stabbed Harriet.'

'No, Cameron. There's no Harriet here.'

Something skitters across the wooden decking and ends up under the chair. From where I'm lying, I can see it. A black oblong. Fuzzy in outline. Everything is fuzzy. Then something else clatters on the other side of me. Metal on wood. A bloody kitchen knife spins to a stop, the blade pointing towards me like some weird game of spin-the-bottle. My arms are heavy but I drag them forward, push up on one and reach for the knife with the other. My hand closes on a handle slick with blood. But then

Selena's foot is on my wrist. 'There's no need, Cameron. Let it go.'

I drop it and someone kicks it away. Timpson has joined us. His foot does the kicking. He stands, still calm, still unruffled, a hand extended to pick me up.

'Just a delivery,' he explains. 'Sorry about the intrusion.'

'Cameron seems to have had a bit of a turn,' Selena says.

'Oh, dear.'

I'm panting, groggy, as if I've drunk too much. But all I've had is muddy camomile tea. Timpson's arm is under my armpit. Selena on the other side. They hoist me up and turn me around so I can steady myself on the metal rail.

'Let's pick up where we left off,' Timpson says. 'You were looking out, remember? Telling us what you were seeing. London? Or is it a rooftop bar with Emma?'

I shake my head. 'It's London. Of course it's bloody London.' I pivot towards him. 'But I saw Harriet. You let her in and stabbed–'

'The term is dislocation, Cameron. You're having difficulty separating the hallucinations from reality. You're here with us at our offices. Harriet isn't here.'

'But the knife. I picked it up.'

'Only a teaspoon,' Selena says.

'No. It was the knife you used–'

'You're confused, Cameron.' Selena holds up a teaspoon. I stare at it, my head shaking from side to side.

'You've been confused for some time. Your sister worries about you. We all do. She's asking why you haven't contacted her,' Timpson says.

I glare at him. 'You know why I haven't seen her. She's isolating. One of the kids has the virus–'

'What virus?'

'What virus?' I laugh in his face. 'Coven bloody19...' I pant in irritation, speak more slowly. 'Covid-19. The lockdown. Anyone infected or in close contact has to self... self-isolate for fourteen days. The bloody apocalypse.'

Selena and Timpson exchange glances. They don't need to explain what they're thinking. But I need to know.

'What?' I ask.

'Paranoia can sometimes be a part of a deterioration. SBI patients can become manic. That and the fugues changing...'

'I'm not paranoid. It's the virus.'

'There is no virus, Cameron. No lockdown. London is as it always has been. Look.' Timpson stands next to me at the rail, Selena on the other side. I follow their gaze and see a London that I barely recognise. A tenth of the traffic. Empty streets. No sirens. No roar of jets on their flight paths above. A sudden and sickening wave of vertigo washes through me.

'What do you see, Cameron?' Selena asks.

'I see a London dished... diminished. There's hardly anyone around.'

'And yet,' Timpson says, 'we see normal traffic, bustling roads. There's even a busker.'

'I... I can't.'

'Listen, Cameron.'

I listen and hear nothing. I see the seat of the chair again. Christ, this can't go on. The damage in my head is far too great. I thought I was recovering, getting better. Instead, I'm getting worse; nothing but a burden. I can't explain any of it. I can't tell what's real anymore. Someone moans from inside the office. It sounds like someone calling my name. I turn. A bloody hand reaches up to touch the inside of the glass before falling again. It leaves a red smear.

Selena says, 'There's no one there, Cameron.'

I squeeze my eyes shut and put one foot on the seat, ready to stand. I take one last look at Selena and say, 'Nicole, I...'

But Selena only points to her name badge. There's an odd flintiness to her expression as she says, 'It's all in your head, Cameron. I am not Nicole.'

My eyes fall to the badge. Selena. Selena Burridge. It's the first time I've looked at it properly. And I notice that unlike Timpson's, there's a logo. An animal. A horse.

I stare at it and its incongruousness pierces the fog that my mind is struggling through. I recognise that logo from a well-known bank. So why would Selena the therapist be wearing this? Unless this name badge is from another life. A non-therapist life. Still it makes no sense.

Yet it makes me wonder who this Selena Burridge truly is.

An idea forms. A vague flickering ember of realisation that catches fire and instantly illuminates everything in a fresh and sickening light.

Burridge. Easy to misspell. Easy to leave out some letters, especially in translation. Burridge could become Burdge.

Become one of the names on Stamford's list of car renters.

It's a stretch.

Another moan from inside the office reaches me. And on the end of it, I hear a name. My name.

'Cameron,' in Harriet's tremulous voice.

The monstrosity of what I'm thinking comes crashing down. I may not be the person I was before I fell on that quayside in Turkey. I may be damaged physically, mentally and emotionally from all that trauma. I may have a memory like Swiss cheese. Yet despite what these two beside me want me to think, I am not going bloody mad.

'You're lying,' I say.

Timpson tenses beside me as he senses the change. I push away from the wall, kick the chair away. But then Timpson grabs me from behind, pinning my arms. I fight but my reactions are slow and the more I resist the more the world spins sickeningly. Nausea makes me close my eyes. It helps a bit but then Selena has me by the thighs. She isn't big, but she's strong. I realise that they're trying to lift me off the floor. I kick out. It loosens Selena's grip for the moment. But not for long. She comes back and I'm lifted from behind by Timpson. This time, Selena tries to grab my legs below the knees. We swivel and sway and panic surges as I realise what they're trying to do.

If I give in they'll hoist me over the edge.

I fight for my life.

I fight with all the diminished strength I can muster. Timpson is strong but I push him back against the rails and hear him grunt with pain.

I shout a curse of satisfaction. Find my voice and yell for help. I kick Selena away. 'Bastard,' she mutters.

From behind me Timpson barks out an order. 'Get a towel to stuff in his face and one to wrap around his legs.'

Selena runs to the kitchen. Hot breath close on my neck. But not Timpson's. Impossible because Timpson doesn't exist.

It's Haldane's. Has been all along.

I keep shouting, wriggling, fighting.

Selena comes back with a dishcloth. She rams it into my mouth, but I shake my head and clamp my teeth shut like a Rosie resisting her medicine. Haldane pulls my arm up from behind, torqueing my shoulder. I yelp with pain and Nicole stuffs in the cloth. I can taste soap. Smell lemons.

'We can play this game all day, Cameron. We only have to wait it out. There was enough tranq in your tea to poleaxe a horse. You're fighting a losing battle. I can hang on to you for another ten minutes and then it won't matter. Or you can let us do it quickly and easily. Put you out of your traumatised misery. What do you say?'

I try a back kick and connect with his shin. He grunts and it gives me a spurt of pleasure to think I've hurt the bastard. He adjusts his position with a wider stance.

'You little shit,' he hisses.

Selena has a long towel in her hands. I kick out at her as she approaches. But all she does is come at me from the side while Haldane holds me, and whips the towel around my thighs. She slides it down. It tightens around my knees and then my shins. I resist, kick out. No use; the towel tightens further, my legs become a single impotent unit.

'Grab his feet.'

I writhe, kick out with my tied legs, but there's little power in them bound.

'Head first,' Haldane orders. 'We can get the towel off as he dangles.'

I'm a foot below the barrier, still on the apartment side of it, Selena at one end, Haldane at the other. He has my hands gripped behind my back now. I'm sweating, fighting nausea. It would be so easy to give in. Take a breather. Fall to oblivion.

But what about Rachel?

What about Vanessa?

I fight some more.

They lift me up. My hip bangs against the metal rail. I bend forward, make Haldane twist awkwardly, weakening his grip. But I'm moments and inches away from my weight tipping me over, letting gravity do the deadly rest.

There's no noise except grunts and wheezes during this murderous dance. Everyone is intent on their purpose; Haldane and Nicole in throwing me over. Me in wriggling and writhing to stop them.

Between them they manhandle one of my shoulders on the rail. All it will take is for Nicole to heave my legs up and I am over.

From somewhere the sound of wood splintering reaches my

ears. Is it the posts for the barrier? All there is between me and death? It might be. But Nicole and Haldane ignore it. They're my executioners. They don't care about trivial damage. All they're interested in is finishing me.

We're all so preoccupied in a life or death struggle none of us see the dark-clad figure until he's almost next to us. He's a shadow in my peripheral vision. But this shape isn't made of smoke.

Haldane shouts.

'Who the fuck–'

A static buzz, a groan, and I'm falling.

But not over the edge.

My shoulders hit the floor of the balcony. Haldane isn't holding me anymore and I twist so that Nicole, who has let go of my legs, stands between me and the barrier. I see something glint in her hand. Long, sharp and wicked.

Not a bloody teaspoon.

Pure reflex makes me thrust my legs forward with all the strength I can muster. And despite them being tied, now I have the floor as leverage. It happens so quickly there's no time to think. But my feet meet with her chest in a convulsive thrust that sends her windmilling back. The knife in her hands flies up and out. Selena hits the railing with such force that her head and shoulders tip back and over.

Momentum makes her legs follow.

She doesn't scream.

The only noise is a sickening crunch five seconds later.

I don't look. I can't. I'm on my knees fighting the nausea that now returns with a vengeance. I try to get up but fall back, face down. A hand presses down on my back and I jerk away.

'Easy, pal. Easy.'

I lift my head. The world spins. I wait for it to slow. The towel is removed from my mouth and I cough and splutter.

Above me, at a strange angle, Stamford's face floats into focus. He has a taser in his hand.

'Harriet...' I croak.

'She's bleeding badly, but she's still alive.'

'Haldane?'

'Him too.' Stamford looks across to a figure lying a few feet away. He mutters, loud enough for me to hear, 'Worse bloody luck.'

54

Keely stands in the recording room adjacent to the one they're holding Haldane in at Walworth Station, gathering her thoughts. She's waiting for the signal to get things started. Has been for an hour or more. A mindless part of the job. Boxes need to be ticked. And today everyone wants to make sure that all the paperwork is complete and error free. No one wants any procedural hiccups. Especially not for this case.

The mayor of London, in his infinite wisdom, although not quite following through on his threat to close Southwark station in Borough completely, has slashed its hours. Now only open for eight hours a day and shut completely on weekends. Though still part of the same organisational area of the Central South Basic Command Unit that polices Lambeth and Southwark, Keely still considers the station at Borough High Street her home and being here, closer to Elephant and Castle than Tower Bridge, feels like she's trespassing. She's never liked Elephant and Castle because she, unlike most people she knows, has taken the trouble to find out the origin of the name. And being named after a pub popular with ivory merchants in the eighteenth century just about sums up its dubious credentials. Add to that the architectural carbuncle that is its shopping centre and a two-way roundabout that sees an accident every other day and she, for one, will not be sad to see the first bulldozer start the drastic restructuring it's about to undergo.

Was about to undergo, she muses.

Now that the virus is here, who knows when it will happen. Keely shakes her head. No point dwelling on all that. She's here in Walworth because the DCI from Major Investigation Team 12, who are now running the show, insisted. He wants her 'local knowledge'; a euphemistic reference to her knowing more than anyone in the Met about Emma Roxburgh's death and what links Cameron Todd to the man in custody. Keely is happy to oblige. Anything to get this toerag put away.

Haldane is alone in the interview room because he's refused a solicitor. If that's not a sign of the depth of his arrogance, Keely doesn't know what is. She studies him. He's calm, untroubled, despite being charged with two counts of attempted murder. It's almost six in the evening because they've taken this long to get him checked out and passed fit for interview, first by the hospital they took him to after being tasered, and then by the police medic.

The door to the anteroom opens and a man steps in. He's not tall, but wiry and fit-looking in a charcoal suit. DCI John McTeague has a kind of nervous energy and sharp smarts that has won him a lot of friends in the force and a lot of enemies amongst criminals. Keely has heard of him. Knows he runs MIT 12 with a pared back approach that elicits intense loyalty and thoroughness. The sort of leader people follow.

Even though she knows this, she's still surprised when he says, 'This is your show, Rhian. I've heard good things. So I will not do anything but listen while you and Haldane chat.'

'Okay.'

'Good. Let's do it.'

55

Keely puts her hand out and presses a button on the DIR with dual CD recorders. A red light gleams and the machine drones out a long commencement signal. She suppresses a smile. She's seen this so many times on TV as a trope. A means of stretching out the tension as the camera swings from interviewer to interviewee. Someone once measured the length as lasting up to twelve seconds. In truth it's never more than three. She knows they're also being video-taped, but there'll be no directorial instruction here. All for the record.

When the signal ends, Keely says, 'This interview is being conducted with Mathew Haldane under caution at 6.22pm on Monday March 23rd at Walworth Police Station. Present are myself, Detective Sergeant Rhian Keely, and Detective Chief Inspector John McTeague.'

McTeague sits six feet behind her, upright, quiet. They've brought in another desk to ensure an appropriate two-metre gap. Haldane, a similar distance away on the other side of the desks, is slouching a little. He's been here for a good two hours, waiting.

'For the record, Mr Haldane, you are certain you do not want any representation in the form of a solicitor.'

'Yes, I am certain. And you can call me Doctor Haldane.'

'You are no longer on the medical register,' Keely replies.

Haldane's smile is brief. 'I am not. But I still have letters after my name. They don't take away your degree, sergeant. Last time I looked there were ten after mine. That's eight more than you have, correct? Or perhaps you got none at all from night school?'

Keely ignores the posturing. 'Can you tell us what took place at flat 78, Limassol Buildings today.'

'Someone was pushed off a balcony.'

'Someone?'

'A woman. Her name was Selena Burridge. She was pushed off the balcony by a lunatic called Cameron Todd.'

'You knew Ms Burridge?'

'She was a friend of mine. Todd is unstable. He was threatening to jump off the balcony. We tried to restrain him but he pushed Ms Burridge off.'

'May I remind you that what you say now will be held against you, especially if you lie. What were you doing at the flat, Mr Haldane?'

Haldane hesitates. Keely has not agreed to his wish to address him as doctor for a reason. Her dad still does nights on call, her brother-in-law's a medic too and has slogged his guts out to become a GI surgeon and stay humble, like Viri. She respects them both. Something she most definitely does not have for this arrogant, lying dirtbag in front of her.

'Ms Burridge invited me to stay.'

'You realise that you were violating the terms of your restraining order?'

'She invited me over. We were going to self-isolate together.'

'What about Harriet Roxburgh?'

'She must have been with Todd. She demanded to see him.

Banged on the door. When she entered, he stabbed her. Is she dead?'

'Seriously injured and just out of surgery. They're trying to stabilise her.'

Haldane shakes his head. 'Like I say, Todd is a disturbed individual.'

'What was he doing in the apartment?'

'No idea. The bloke was off his head. He just turned up. Pretended he knew Selena. I don't think he had any idea where he was. He must have followed me into the building.'

'He had no connection with Ms Burridge?'

'Not that I know of.' Haldane sits up. 'After he attacked Harriet Roxburgh, he tried to jump off the balcony. When we attempted to subdue him, some lunatic broke in and the next thing I'm being tasered by some thug and Selena is dead.'

'Were you close to her?' Keely asks. She watches Haldane's expression closely, waiting for some sign of emotion.

All Haldane does is shrug. 'We were sleeping together. Does that answer your question?'

Keely doesn't think it does, but she changes tack. 'We will interview Harriet Roxburgh if and when she recovers.'

'Best of luck with that. I think she and Todd are in this together. Must have been, otherwise why should she turn up? They'll make some bullshit up to implicate me.'

'In what way?'

'Anyone's guess. But it'll be in a way that makes my life even worse than it was. The Roxburghs have it in for me.'

'And why is that?'

Haldane folds his arms. 'I wonder...'

Keely pretends to move some papers around in the file she has in front of her. 'Because you were convicted of harassing Emma Roxburgh?'

Haldane lets out a snort of derision. 'Like I said at the time, she was a willing participant. She flirted with me. I flirted back.'

'Three hundred and thirty-two texts including naked images of yourself are hardly what I'd call flirtatious.'

'No? Well, I suspect you've never sent a photo of yourself to anyone, sergeant.' Haldane leers at Keely. 'Never felt the need to spice things up, perhaps.'

She knows she will shower and use half a bottle of gel when this is over. The expensive stuff that stays on the skin for a good while.

'Whereas I,' Haldane continues, 'have no such reservations. It's the twenty-first century. Sexting is a thing. If you've got it, flaunt it.'

Keely, looking down at her notes, waits a moment before letting her gaze drift up towards Haldane who has opened his legs and spread his arms. She's met psychopathic narcissists before. Cold, empathy-free manipulators that ruin lives, including their own. But this one is a real peach.

'What can you tell us about Emma Roxburgh's death in Turkey?'

Haldane folds his hands over his crotch, feigning horrified shock. 'Is she dead? Really?'

'We interviewed you at the time.'

'Oh yeah. Now I remember.' Haldane smiles at his own little joke.

'So you will be well aware that the inquest recorded an open verdict. The Turks kept the file open. Emma fell to her death from a cliff and Cameron Todd was severely injured the same night. Do you know anything about this?'

'If he was there, why don't you ask Todd?'

'Mr Todd's injuries left him with a dense amnesia.'

'Oh, come on, we all know that's just bullshit.' He sits up. 'Can I go now?'

'Just a few more questions,' Keely says. She takes out her phone. 'When Harriet Roxburgh entered the penthouse apartment, after she was stabbed and you left her for dead, what you were not aware of was that she was in phone contact with a private investigator called John Stamford. He has software on his phone that records all incoming calls. We found a phone on the balcony. My guess is that Harriet Roxburgh threw it onto the decking so that Stamford could listen to what was being said. Amazingly clear under the circumstances. I'd like you to listen to it.'

'No thanks.' Haldane stands up.

From behind her, Keely hears McTeague speak for the first time. 'Sit down.'

Something crosses Haldane's features. A belligerent glare that evaporates on seeing McTeague's expression and hearing the command. He sits, legs out straight in front of him again like a cocky schoolboy, arms crossed, lips arced in a toothless smirk.

She slides some papers over to him. 'We've transcribed the recording. Added names to the voices. In case you get confused.'

Keely presses play. The voices they hear are muted and there is extraneous noise, but she turns up the volume and sits back.

BURRIDGE: Cameron, are you all right?

TODD: He stabbed Harriet.

BURRIDGE: No, Cameron. There's no Harriet. There's no need, Cameron. Let it go.

HALDANE: Just a delivery. Sorry about the intrusion.

BURRIDGE: Cameron seems to have had a bit of a turn.

HALDANE: Oh, dear. Let's pick up where we left off. You were looking out, remember? Telling us what you were seeing. London? Or is it a rooftop bar with Emma?

TODD: It's London. Of course it's bloody London. But I saw Harriet. You let her in and stabbed–

HALDANE: The term is dislocation, Cameron. You're having difficulty separating the hallucinations from reality. You're here with us at our offices. Harriet isn't here.

TODD: But the knife. I picked it up.

BURRIDGE: Only a teaspoon.

TODD: No. It was a knife you used–

BURRIDGE: You're confused, Cameron.

HALDANE: You've been confused for some time. Your sister is worried about you. She's asking why you haven't contacted her.

TODD: You know why I haven't seen her. She's isolating. One of the kids has the virus–

HALDANE: What virus?

TODD: What virus? Coven bloody 19... Covid-19. The lockdown. Anyone infected or in close contact has to self... self-isolate for fourteen days. The bloody apocalypse... What?

HALDANE: Paranoia can sometimes be a part of a deterioration. SBI patients can become manic. That and the fugues changing...

TODD: I'm not paranoid. It's the virus.

HALDANE: There is no virus, Cameron. No lockdown. London is as it always has been. Look.

BURRIDGE: What do you see, Cameron?

TODD: I see a London dished... diminished. There's hardly anyone around.

HALDANE: And yet, we see normal traffic, bustling roads. There's even a busker.

TODD: I... I can't.

HALDANE: Listen, Cameron.

Vague moaning.

BURRIDGE: There's no one there, Cameron.

TODD: Nicole, I...

BURRIDGE: It's all in your head, Cameron. I am not Nicole.

HARRIET: Cameron.

The recording ends. Haldane is still sitting as he was just moments before, but there is no longer a smirk. He looks up into Keely's face.

'I'm a good judge of character, sergeant. Not often am I wrong. But I didn't see you for the conniving bitch that you are. I want a solicitor.'

56

I'm in Stamford's office. Just me and him. We're sitting a good six feet apart facing a TV on his wall. There's a split screen filled by two live headshots. On one side is Rachel, on the other is Keely. They're using group software. It could be Skype or Google Hangouts, but it works whatever it is. It's Keely who does the talking.

'We confirmed with the Border Agency that Selena Burridge travelled to Greece the same week that you and Emma were in Cirali. It looks like she travelled by ferry to Antalya and hired a car there. The name on the forwarded car hire list is a simple misspelling, Burdge with a missing 'i' and one 'r' instead of two. You were right, Cameron. Human error. No one to blame for that.'

'What about the name badge?' I ask.

'Burridge was an ex-bank employee in Haldane's hometown and they became lovers.'

'Why would anyone want to be with that creep?' Rachel asks.

Keely shrugs. 'Why do men on death row get offers of marriage?'

Rachel shakes her head.

'According to Haldane, Burridge became obsessed with obtaining revenge on his behalf. She, encouraged I am certain by Haldane, blamed Emma for ruining his stellar career.'

'Stellar according to Haldane,' Rachel says with derision.

'He thinks he is the best surgeon in the country,' Keely agrees. 'Possibly the world. I kid you not. The forensic psych says it's classic aggrandisement.'

When no one speaks, she carries on. 'Since we played him the recording of what happened on that balcony, he's been more than happy to furnish details of what Burridge did and how she did it, keeping himself out of the frame, of course. According to him he pleaded with her not to do anything.'

Stamford snorts. 'This bloke is a real lizard.'

'Indeed,' Keely agrees. 'Burridge got to Cirali and observed Cameron and Emma for a few days, watched their routine. The plan was to contact Emma, maybe sneak into the hotel as a maid, falsify some connection through being related to one of Emma's GP patients, and claim that she was being held in Turkey by a man she had an affair and a child with but was desperately trying to get away from. She claimed her baby was sick, and she was terrified of taking it to a doctor or a hospital for fear of losing contact. She asked Emma for help, and not to tell anyone.'

'Emma would never say no to something like that,' Rachel says.

'Looks like that's what happened. And so Burridge arranged a meeting away from prying eyes.'

'On the beach?' Stamford fills in the unspoken detail.

'My guess is that she told Emma she'd hidden the child. Perhaps told her that night that the child was much worse. Something to make Emma react quickly.'

'And you say she was a maid?' I ask. Everyone looks at me.

'Pretending to be, yes.' Keely confirms it.

This isn't the time to bring up my fugue, so I let it hang and wait for Keely to continue.

'Haldane said that Burridge met Emma at the deserted north end of the beach to take her to the child. Once on the cliff path Emma tried to text you. That's when Burridge attacked her with a club she'd hidden. A club made out of rocks wired to a handle. Caveman style.'

'Why a club? Why not just a rock?' Rachel asks.

'Burridge wasn't big. Much more leverage and power with a club. And the blow would leave rock fragments in the wound. Be more consistent with a fall. I suspect it was Haldane's idea judging by how much he enjoyed explaining to us how she'd constructed it.'

Rachel grimaces.

'Then she pushed Emma's body off the cliff and onto the rocks below. She may or may not have been alive at that stage,' adds Keely.

Rachel's head sinks in a slow shake.

'Your arrival was a surprise,' continues Keely. 'Or so Haldane said. Burridge met you on the beach as she was returning, claimed to have seen Emma fall off the jetty. She struck you from behind as you were desperately searching, only this time lights from some boats anchored just offshore disturbed her. You fell off. Only a dozen feet or so. If you'd hit the water you'd have been fine, but you went head first into a stanchion and the rocks it was anchored to. Only then did you enter the sea where she left you to drown.'

'But I didn't.'

'No. And so, according to Haldane, Burridge became obsessed with finishing the job. Only this time it would be through your own actions. According to Haldane, she dreamed up all the gaslighting tactics. She watched you. Waited for the right moment to approach and inveigle herself into your life.

The arrival of Covid-19 was an added bonus. Isolating you from the people who might have seen the warning signals. Burridge posted the excrement through Harriet's door. Burridge set up the "Roxy" Roxburgh website. All to make it appear to someone looking in from outside that it was you.'

'What about the gasman quote?' It's bugging me.

Keely tilts her head. 'Hmm. We'll never know. But my intuition tells me it was at Haldane's suggestion even if he did not do it himself. His ego would not have been able to resist playing head games with you and the minions of the world in general. That's another quote from him by the way.'

'But surely he can't keep pretending he's innocent?' Rachel argues.

'Haldane claims he had no idea she would try to kill you in the penthouse. He says she'd arranged it all as a surprise for him, told him to play along and pretend to be a therapist.' Keely sounds almost sanguine.

'And he expects us to believe any of that?'

'His story will change as we present more evidence. He genuinely thinks he's cleverer than us. And by us, I mean the rest of the world.' She offers us a mirthless smile. 'Us minions.'

'But he stabbed Harriet.' My voice sounds shrill in Stamford's little office.

'He did. And he's claiming she had the knife, and it was self-defence. Even though the knife is part of a set from the kitchen.'

'My God,' Rachel says.

'He also claims that Burridge, masquerading as Nicole, modified your medications in your own flat. Changing dosages, etcetera.'

'I had been feeling a little odd,' I say. 'I assumed it was me forgetting my meds or doubling up occasionally.'

'Oh, Cam,' says Rachel. But she's not criticising. Just being my big sister.

Keely shrugs. 'It is difficult to comprehend how anyone in the face of all this evidence could still try to maintain his innocence, I know. But Haldane is a true psychopathic narcissist. He thinks he is Einstein and we are all cretins.' Her eyes drift away from the camera to the keyboard while she speaks. 'There is a part of the interview I wanted to show you. He spoke for hours. Lecturing us. But there is one part you ought to see.'

A small square of video appears on the screen. Keely clicks it and it expands. I see Haldane sitting in an interview room, viewed from an angle looking down from above. I recognise DS Keely in that room too. The third person, a man I don't recognise, but he looks intense and stern. Keely asks the questions.

'What was your reaction when Emma Roxburgh rejected you?'

Haldane laughs. 'She didn't reject me. It was me that rejected her. That's why she got antsy.'

'At the tribunal when you were struck-off, Emma Roxburgh's barrister had witnesses who said she had warned you off, explained that she had a boyfriend. And yet you persisted.'

'She wanted me. It was obvious. I know the signs. It's happened too often for me not to recognise a come-on. She was all for it. It was her boyfriend who stirred the pot. He couldn't take it. But Emma... she wanted a piece of the pie.' He points both index fingers towards his chest. 'This pie. I was moving up. My career was stratospheric.'

'Hardly,' Keely says. 'You'd applied but not been shortlisted for half a dozen jobs. You were a locum.'

'Temporary. I was getting experience. Until the actual job offers came in. I had to tread water because otherwise I'd be the youngest ever consultant and the establishment don't like that.' His grin is vulpine.

'Where were these job offers coming from?'

'London, Birmingham, Manchester. All the big units. I was

toying with going to the States for a year or two. Squeeze in a fellowship at Johns Hopkins.'

'The tribunal chairman said that this conviction you had that you were about to be promoted was pure fantasy.'

Haldane has his legs straight out, lounging in the chair with his arms folded. 'I know what I know.'

'Were you bitter about Emma?'

'Why should I feel bitter about a woman? She's gone. My overriding concern was that the NHS, and this country, had lost such a talented doctor.'

'You mean Emma Roxburgh.'

'No. I mean me. It's bloody tragic.'

In the video, Keely slides another page of A4 paper across the desk towards Haldane.

'These messages are taken from Selena Burridge's phone. They're text messages. Exchanges between your phone and hers. Recognise them?'

'Fake news,' says Haldane.

'No, not fake. Verifiable digital records. In September 2018, a month before Emma Roxburgh died and Cameron Todd was attacked, you wrote: *You can be my weapon of choice. They ruined me. It's time I ruined them. Emma fucking Roxburgh and everyone and everything around her. You can be my atomic bomb, Selena. One bang and the fallout does all the rest. And then we can do majestic things. I've got plans for us.'*

Keely looks up. 'Can you explain that?'

'Ask Selena,' says Haldane. And then he smiles. 'Oh, I forgot. You can't because she's jam on a pavement.'

Keely freezes the video.

Rachel has a hand over her mouth.

'Jesus,' says Stamford. He speaks for everyone.

'We're charging him with the attempted murder of Harriet

Roxburgh. She is making a good recovery and will, I am sure, make a great witness. There's also enough here for a charge of conspiracy to murder in Emma's case.' Keely finds me on the screen and looks right at me. 'And attempted murder in yours, Cameron. I'm preparing a file to the Turkish authorities as we speak.'

I hold her gaze. Nod. It's enough.

'There are several things Haldane does not, as yet, understand,' Keely continues. 'I'm telling you because I think you, of all people, deserve to know but on the clear understanding that this goes nowhere else for now. The CPS would demand my head on a silver platter if they ever found out I'd shared this evidence. But I'm a softie.'

I wait. DS Keely seems to me about as much a softie as Attila the Hun, but I don't tell her that.

'We've confiscated all Haldane's digital records. He's smart, but not half as smart as the geek squad we have working for us in the Met tech vaults. In Haldane's deleted search history is an entire day's worth of him trying to find out how much it would cost to hire a car in Antalya a month before you and Emma got there. Don't ask me how he knew you were going. But it's clear he made enquiries.'

'Oh my God,' says Rachel, emphasising each syllable. She's grinning.

'And in a toolbox in his attic, we came across a dog collar with a tag still attached. That tag has the Roxburghs' address and phone number. We think it is likely that it belongs to Peter Roxburgh's missing dog.'

'The one never found after Roxburgh hung himself?' Stamford asks.

Keely nods. 'Only now I'm wondering if throwing a rope over that tree was Peter Roxburgh's idea at all.'

No one speaks because the implications in Keely's words are

unspeakable. I glance around. Everyone is thinking what I'm thinking.

It's time I ruined them. Emma fucking Roxburgh and everyone and everything around her.

'Right.' Keely is suddenly all business. 'I'll be in touch, Cameron. God knows how long this will all take given the circumstances, but at least we have Haldane in custody, and he'll stay on remand. Meanwhile, I have to interview two thugs about a stabbing.'

There's a volley of goodbyes and thanks. 'Stay safe, everybody,' Keely says, and her face flicks off.

I turn to Stamford. 'I don't remember thanking you for getting to Haldane when you did.'

'Impeccable timing. I'm known for it.' He shakes his head. 'Harriet hadn't wanted me along at all. I couldn't stop her. No one could. She's a force of nature. This thing with Emma has screwed her up. The most she'd let me do was be her backup. She followed you into the building. Saw the lift stop at the seventh floor. She knocked on lots of doors. But at least I made her stay on the line with me all the way through. I heard everything. And the one perk of having been in the force is that one acquires some kit. I had an enforcer in the boot.'

'Enforcer?'

'A mini battering ram for forced entry.' He pauses, pins me with a look. 'It's a shame you were drugged otherwise you and I could have chucked the bastard over the edge to join his friend.'

I glance up at Rachel who is still on-screen, expecting her to be shocked. She isn't. Instead, there's an expression on her face that tells me she's thinking much the same thing.

'Did you find out what they drugged you with?' she asks.

'Flunitrazepam,' I say. 'Otherwise known as Rohypnol. I don't know what camomile tea is supposed to taste like. But I should have guessed because it was bloody awful.'

'How could you?'

It's a rhetorical question. I shrug and stand up. 'What about the office? Cogni-Senses?'

'Fake,' Stamford explains. 'Burridge had been clever. The place is an executive Airbnb. She'd booked it but used your credit card, nicked or cloned from her time in your flat. That way it looked like you'd booked the place yourself for the sole purpose of jumping off the balcony. No one would question it. Everyone who knew you suspected you were sliding off the rails by then. The penthouse balcony was not overlooked. It had a river view. No one could see the struggle.'

'What a cold-hearted bitch,' says Rachel.

No one argues. Rachel signs off and I tell her we'll chat later.

Then it's only me and Stamford in the room. Keely has searched my flat. They found flunitrazepam tucked away in a kitchen drawer. And Burridge had substituted my quetiapine with a bigger dose. If I'd fallen from the balcony with no witnesses, it would look like I had all the tools that a disturbed mind needed at my disposal. A functional delusional personality that was modifying his own drug regimen and organising his own elaborate suicide.

'I haven't shaken your hand,' I say to Stamford.

'I'm up for that. Got the ultra-strong sanitiser for that very reason.'

I walk across the room. We shake hands. Stamford slathers on the sanitiser and so do I, both of us grinning as we do so. What we haven't talked about is how Burridge fed me all that rubbish about Emma. When I told Keely about the selfie she had of her kissing me, her response was almost pitying. She said it was easy to doctor photos these days. The telling thing was that she had just the one. And, she suspected, Haldane or Burridge had forged Emma's writing on the notebook.

Liar, liar, pants on fire.

I felt stupid when she explained it. But she didn't let me wallow. She'd said simply, 'Burridge had no chance once she was in his grip. I don't expect you to forgive her but remember who it is that's the real monster here.'

All this flashes through my mind as I'm standing with Stamford in his office. He sees me zoning out and looks worried. To deflect him, I ask, 'What were you whistling when I was standing on the viaduct?'

'I was doing an impression of a police siren with four fingers in my mouth.'

'Did the job.'

'Yeah. I just love the taste of sanitiser at dusk.'

57

I speak to Rachel twice a day now. FaceTime video chats. If I don't, she threatens to drive up from Cardiff, self-isolation or no self-isolation. She'll risk arrest and argue that her journey qualifies as essential travel. Under normal circumstances she'd insist I stay with her. But these are not normal circumstances.

Easier to use the phone and keep her happy. Keep me happy too.

I've parked the car up and hung the keys behind the door. I walk everywhere. Along eerily empty locked-down London streets, keeping as fit as I can. I watch the news only occasionally. So many people are dying I'm grateful people are taking the isolation seriously. What else is there to do?

I stand two metres behind a man queuing to get into M&S Simply Food. There's someone two metres behind me. Strange, but I don't feel alone. Not anymore. I walk back to my flat along the river like I always did. Now I walk with earbuds in, listen to music. I've discovered a track that almost guarantees I can drift into a fugue. I first heard it on one of Josh's film recommendations.

'An everyday tale of split personality with Jim Carrey.' I see reflections of my own life in *Me, Myself and Irene.* But only faint ones, thank the Lord.

But the version of the Hootie and The Blowfish track 'Can't Find The Time' I prefer is the original by Orpheus from the sixties. When I listen to this, I'm transported.

If I think about it, the maid-statue and the gasman-wraith made of black smoke that haunted my fugues must have been products of my worst imaginings. Nicole had dressed as a maid to approach Emma on the night of the murder. She was still dressed like that when she saw me approaching on the beach. All part of my twisted recall played out in the fugue world. There's reason enough for her to have inveigled her way into whatever section of my damaged brain is designated casting director. After all, she did exactly that in real life.

As for the gasman, he's not so easy to rationalise. Could it be that somewhere in my head I knew about Haldane? Emma must have told me about him at some point BT. Had hearing his name woken him up like summoning a sleeping demon?

And then, when I let my imagination gallop, there's the Josh interpretation. The sci-fi, supernatural, scary movie version. That what I was hallucinating was a warning. Emma's way of telling me who was behind all this.

Who knows? Maybe he's right. Perhaps when I get the chance, I'll ask her.

On the rooftop bar Cameron chats with Ivan about zombie films. Ivan is on the Dom Perignon tonight. His two regular girlfriends are dancing to Justin Timberlake. The place is filling up, the sun is setting. It's still warm.

'What I do not understand is how in these apocalypse films the infected always want to eat non-infected. But if they do, if they chow down, how come that the now newly infected end up being zombies too? I mean, how much of them is left after a hundred zombies have buffet?'

'I get what you mean, Ivan,' Cam says. 'A zombie paradox.'

'I think people only want to see blood and gore, right?'

'Exactly.'

Cam looks up. A girl is walking towards him. Ivan grins. 'Here she is.' He turns to Cam. 'You are lucky man, Cameron.' Both men get up. Old-fashioned rules in this place.

She's about five-seven, dark hair cut short, tanned from the Turkish sun. She wears a flouncy knee-length summer dress with a bold flowery pattern.

'Hi,' she says.

Ivan responds. 'You look stunning.'

'Thank you, Ivan.' Then she turns to Cam.

'Amazing,' Cam says.

She tilts her head, pleased. 'Fancy going over to the edge of the roof to watch the sunset?'

Cam shakes his head. 'Seen it all before.'

She snorts. 'What are you after?'

'Sit with me.'

She does, shuffling around the small table so that they can both people-watch. There's a candle flickering. It throws dancing light on her face. Cam looks at her and takes in the straight nose, the generous mouth, the bright, merry eyes. All the delightful features he hasn't been able to see for so long.

'What?' she says, adding a tinkling laugh.

'Who needs a sunset when I can look at you.'

Emma looks up at Ivan, eyebrows raised. 'Any more of that champagne left? I may need two glasses.'

Ivan stands and pours the bubbly. There is no maid statue tonight. Hasn't been for weeks. Nor is there a foul smell from the drains, or a smoky shadow skulking under the tables.

'I'm glad we don't have to walk to the edge of the roof anymore,' says Emma.

'I, too, am glad that I do not have to watch you do it.' Ivan grins.

'I'm sorry for you falling all those times,' Cam says.

'Why? They had nothing to do with you.'

'So you forgive me?'

'I do. So long as you forgive yourself.' She leans across and kisses Cam on the cheek before raising her glass.

'To us,' Emma says.

On a rooftop bar with garish lights strung from poles and cocktail waitresses in catsuits, a breeze with a seaweed hint of the ocean on its breath catches her hair. She tosses it away.

Cam raises his glass, touches it to Emma's and says, in return, 'To us.'

58

L ife is very different. We're no longer in total lockdown, but local quarantines spring up sporadically and a second spike is a real threat. People adjust as much as they can. Leon's back in the gym. But it has limited entry and every day there's a fresh debate over mask-wearing. He's fully recovered and didn't need to go to hospital. But now we do a virtual workout with me at home. There's no slacking even online. Leon does some of his best sarcasm via the internet. I try to rope in Josh. One day I'll succeed.

Sometimes I wonder what things would be like if someone broke the world wide web. Then it truly would be like *28 Days Later*. People would write letters to one another. Read books. Use their own imaginations. That's why I'm glad I have the new and improved fugues. At least there I can see and talk to Emma.

The news is preoccupied by the virus. I had hoped that Selena's death and Haldane's charade in the penthouse might go unnoticed. I was wrong. The press went to town. At least with lockdown I didn't have reporters turning up at my door. They turn up in my inbox instead. And on my phone. How they get my number is a mystery.

Still, not all publicity is adverse publicity. And not everything is doom and gloom. For a start, there's Zoom.

So now, every Friday, we all go to the pub after work. Except we do it in our own living rooms. There's me, Josh and his girlfriend, and Rachel and Owen come sometimes after the kids go to bed. Stamford has even had a pint with us. But tonight is what I'm looking forward to.

Almost 6.30, so I open a beer, fill a bowl with some mixed nuts, and log on. Josh is the first up. He displays the IPA he's drinking. The elaborate decoration on the can looks like it's come straight off a wall at the Tate. Then Leon appears wearing a beanie hat and grinning.

'Peeps!' he announces.

'Hi, Leon,' chirps Josh.

'Nice hat,' I say.

A fourth panel appears on the screen, empty. All we see is an image of a door.

'Hey, Vanessa,' Leon calls out. 'You need to move your laptop so that we can see you.'

But nothing happens.

'Where is she?' Josh asks.

'She'll be along,' I say.

I watch Josh's face frown. See Leon's grin falter. What I've said sounds a bit odd. Cruel, possibly. After all, Vanessa's in a wheelchair.

On the screen, the door to Vanessa's room at the rehab centre swings inwards to reveal someone standing there, leaning forward with two sticks as support. On the outside of both of the person's legs are metallic struts and panels, jointed at the knees and hip, connected at the waist by a reinforced belt. The figure walks slowly and mechanically towards the camera that's angled up such that the face only slowly comes into shot.

Vanessa's face.

'Holy crap,' says Josh.

'Go girl,' says Leon. Or rather, shouts Leon just before he erupts in whooping laughter.

'Like it?' says Vanessa. She's grinning too. 'I've just been out for a walk. Two thousand steps.'

'Man, that's more than Josh does in a day,' Leon quips.

Vanessa presses a button on a wrist remote and the machine eases her down into a sit on a chair.

'How long has this been going on?' asks Josh. His mouth stays open and he can't stop ginning.

'Ask Cam.'

'Cam?' Josh asks.

'I spoke to the manufacturers after... you know what after. My name was all over the net. People were very generous on JustGiving. I filmed myself running a half marathon over two blocks outside my flat. This company, BioSkel is big in the States and in Germany. They want to get a foothold in the UK. I raised a shedload of cash. Enough for BioSkel to trial one of their units with Vanessa. Not easy because of Covid. There's been lots of one to one and the poor guy who's been helping her has needed to be tested every other day to make sure he's virus-free, but they've been brilliant.'

'Wow,' Leon says.

'It's called HabWalk. Backpack battery lasts a couple of hours. They're working on that,' I elaborate.

'See, almost getting murdered on a balcony has its advantages,' Josh quips.

'I can even climb stairs,' Vanessa says.

'That's *Blade Runner* shit, man.' Leon again.

That makes Josh snort into his pint. Everyone else laughs hysterically at seeing froth all over Josh's nose.

When the laughing eventually stops, Vanessa picks up a Coke Zero, holds it up to the laptop camera.

'So you know I'm not drinking and driving. But I still want to toast my friend, Cameron. Someone who has lost so much but is still there for those who need him.'

'To Cam,' echo Josh and Leon.

I lift my glass in response. I'm smiling because I must be the only man alive who can boast being toasted by the dystopian living and the wilful dead.

Later, when they've gone, I ponder for a moment what a strange world I live in. But at least I am in it. No thanks to Haldane and Burridge. And when the world gets back to normal, if it ever does, I hope that I will too.

Who knows, I may even end up on a beach in Cirali.

Not to be macabre.

Just so that Emma and I can one day say goodbye properly. Plus, I've promised Vanessa I'll take her to see the Chimaera.

'Isn't it a long trek up a stony path?' she asked.

'Of course. A kilometre at least, uphill, rocky terrain. So what's the problem?'

She liked that.

I said I'd bring the marshmallows.

THE END

AUTHOR'S NOTE

In case you're wondering, hallucinogenic fugues as experienced by Cam are a real, though highly rare, complication of brain injury. His experience is a fictional rendering of a serious condition and I hope that I've succeeded in not trivialising it in any way. Indeed, the book, in part, is an homage to those brave patients in rehabilitation units across the country. The Bermondsey that exists in Trauma, however, is a mixture of fact and fiction. Some places and roads do exist. Others do not. As the author, I get to make things up. Finally, a big thank you to Ian for being kind and constructive during Trauma's gestation. Any errors of detail, place or time are all mine.

ENJOY THE RIDE? WHY NOT HELP SPREAD THE WORD

Authors live and die by word of mouth. Honest reviews by genuine and loyal readers help bring the books to the attention of others.

Please feel free to jump right in and leave a review wherever you bought this book – it can be as short as you like on the book's Amazon/Goodreads page.

You can contact me and check out the website for forthcoming titles as well at:
www.dylanyoungauthor.com

I'm also delighted to hear from readers and will always endeavour to reply to questions or comments via:
Twitter: @dyoungwrites
FB: www.facebook.com/dyoungwrites
Email: dylanyoungauthor@gmail.com

Lightning Source UK Ltd.
Milton Keynes UK
UKHW010928281120
374240UK00004B/1397